C000137108

IMAGINE

TITAN FREY

Copyright

Imagine is a work of fiction. Any references to historical events, real people, or real locales are used fictitiously. Other names, characters, places, and incidents are products of the author's imagination, and any resemblance to actual events or locales or persons, living or dead, is entirely coincidental.

IMAGINE: A NOVEL
Copyright © 2022 by Titan Frey

All rights reserved.

Formatting & Cover Design by KP Designs
- www.kpdesignshop.com
Published by Kingston Publishing Company
- www.kingstonpublishing.com

The uploading, scanning, and distribution of this book in any form or by any means—including but not limited to electronic, mechanical, photocopying, recording, or otherwise—without the permission of the copyright holder is illegal and punishable by law. Please purchase only authorized editions of this work, and do not participate in or encourage electronic piracy of copyrighted materials. Your support of the author's rights is appreciated.

Table of Contents

Dedication

For Delilah, Wyatt, and Aiyanna.

Thank you for being my inspiration. Daddy loves you.

All we are saying is give peace a chance.
- John Lennon

Prologue

Dear Diary… heck, this is weird, I've never written a diary in my life. But I read that it can be therapeutic for people to recount a traumatic experience in their life by writing it down. So, here goes nothing...

Let's start by going back, way far back, to the incident that changed my life. When I think of my childhood, one memory stands out. This memory is from February 9, 1964. I was a hyper-six-year-old boy that couldn't sit still. In today's time, doctors would probably diagnose me with ADD or something like that. But on that winter night in 1964, one thing had me sitting still on the living room floor like a gargoyle on a church.

"Good evening, ladies and gentlemen. Tonight, live from New York… The Ed Sullivan Show!"

That's right, that's the announcer announcing The Ed Sullivan Show. I know what you're thinking. *What normal six-year-old watches The Ed Sullivan show?* I never honestly watched that show. To be honest, I only watched television on Saturday mornings to catch my new favorite cartoon, *The Magilla Gorilla Show.* But on this night, there was something I was waiting to see.

"Tonight, The Ed Sullivan Show is brought to you by *Anacin*"... The announcer continued.

He would show and talk about the sponsors of the TV show. The first one that he mentioned was some sort of headache remedy… as he put it. Also, he went on to talk about the other sponsor... *Pillsbury*. This obviously wasn't what I was watching the show for. Even if they were great products, my watching was for something far bigger.

I sat with my legs crossed and a bowl of cereal in front of me. My eyes were fixated on the TV. Slowly, I ate some cereal, not realizing half of the cereal missed my mouth and landed on the carpet.

"Hello, Joe," my father said.

Now I didn't flinch. Hell, I honestly didn't hear him. My attention was solely on the television. Could you blame me? I was six years old, home alone, waiting for something important to come on the television. Yes, that's right, I was home alone. At this point in my life, I lived alone with my father. He wasn't home while I was watching the television. In fact, he just got home from work.

"I said hello, Joe!" my father belted out.

His yelling caught my attention. I turned to see him walking in carrying his normal thermos and a plastic bag, which wasn't normal.

"Oh, hi, Daddy."

Now, before any of you readers say, *hey, why are you home alone at six years old, anyway?* This was the sixties, and kids were trusted to stay alone at very young ages. It definitely isn't like that today. Plus, my mother and father split a while back, so that's how it went.

My father laughed. "That's all I get? An oh, hi, Daddy?"

He walked into the kitchen, and I jumped up from the floor and away from the television. Some *Aero Shave* commercial was on, so I wasn't missing much at that point.

When I entered the kitchen, I saw my father put the plastic bag down on the kitchen table, and a book fell out. He walked over to the sink, and he started to rinse out his thermos. I never knew my father to be much of a reader, so seeing a book fall out of the bag intrigued me. As my father poured himself a cup of whiskey, I picked up the book.

"What's this, Daddy?"

"Oh, that's a book. I saw it at the bookstore that's down the block from my work," my father said.

My eyes fixated on the red cover, trying to figure out if the picture was a horse or not. Then, I rubbed my fingers over the title and mumbled, "*The Catcher In the Rye.*"

My father grabbed the book out of my hand. "Yeah, a guy from my work read it and said it wasn't bad, so I picked it up since the bookstore had a buy one, get one free deal."

I grabbed the book back out of his hands and stared at it some more. "Buy one, get one free? You should've got two then, Daddy."

My father laughed. "I did get two. The other book is one I read as a kid. It's one of my favorite books."

He reached into the bag and pulled out *The Time Machine* by H. G. Wells.

"Oh, wow. That's awesome," I said.

"Now yesterday and today our theater's been jammed with newspapermen and hundreds of photographers from all over the nation," Ed Sullivan said.

I heard this from the kitchen and immediately bolted back into the living room.

"Why are you running?" I heard my father call out, but I didn't answer.

"And these veterans agree with me that the city never has witnessed the excitement stirred by these youngsters from Liverpool, who call themselves *The Beatles*. Now tonight, you're going twice be entertained by them. Right now and again in the second half of our show. Ladies and gentlemen... *The Beatles!*"

The crowd screamed, it mostly was young girls, shrieking as loud as they could. Then, on the screen, the four members of *The Beatles* started playing their hit song, *All my Loving*.

A smile grew on my face as I got my first glimpse of the band I fell in love with from my daily listening to the radio. There was Paul McCartney, George Harrison, Ringo Starr, and John Lennon... damn, those boys could play the rock and roll.

"This is what you wanted to see?" my father asked.

I nodded, not looking away from the television.

"Wow, could you imagine being in front of a crowd that rowdy?" My father asked.

I nodded again. "Yes, I can imagine."

Wow, diary, the words are flowing onto the paper with ease. Hell, I haven't even started my actual story yet. Man, rather than writing a diary entry, I may as well write a memoir...

Chapter 1

Okay, so I decided now is the time to write my book on the experience that changed my life. As I sit here, my radio is on, and John Lennon's *Imagine* is beautifully flowing out.

When John says *living for today*, he's absolutely correct. We shouldn't dwell on the past, and we shouldn't worry about the future, well... in most cases. My situation went quite differently. I didn't have a chance to live for today. The past and future made their presence felt at once.

****

Before I continue my story, I suppose I should introduce myself. My name is Joe Miller, and I'm originally from a small town in Pennsylvania named Maxwell. I eventually moved to *The Big Apple* in 1975. That's right, New York, New York; the boogie down Bronx, to be exact. Ah, yes, boogie down Bronx, a term coined in the late eighties.

My story, though, starts earlier than that. Thursday, the twenty-eighth of November 1974. That's where my story starts. I was a sixteen-year-old young man in the prime of life. On that Thanksgiving morning, my father and I prepared to go on a road trip.

Bright and early, we would make a trip to New York. We still lived in Maxwell by then, but my father surprised me with tickets to the Elton John concert. I remember how excited I was, and my father loved Elton John. I liked Elton John, so I knew the concert would be fun. What I didn't know was I would be in for an amazing surprise.

My father packed a few snacks that morning, and we jumped in our *Plymouth Valiant*; my dad bought the car only a month earlier. He loved it. We drove out of Maxwell and off to our adventure. My father and I didn't say much to each other for the next three and a half hours. We blasted our radio and jammed to some music. Two Elton John songs came on, and one John Lennon song hit the station. My father and I, of course, turned the radio up to the max on those songs.

After the first three and a half hours, my father pulled the car into a small gas station in a small town named Red Lion. The service attendant pumped our gas, and my father walked into the store to use the bathroom. I jumped out of the car to stretch my legs. While stretching my legs, a loud motorcycle pulled up to the pump next to me. A *manly-looking* man stood off of the motorcycle.

"I'll get to you in a second, sir," the service attendant said.

The motorcyclist waved him off. "No need, Chuck. I'll pump myself."

"Okay. Thanks," Chuck said.

I watched as the motorcyclist pumped his gas.

He caught me staring and smiled. "Hey, young man, I've never seen you around here before. On a road trip?"

"Yeah, I'm from Maxwell, it's near Pittsburgh."

"I've heard of it," the motorcyclist said.

The service attendant finished with our gas and walked back to the store.

"Where you headed, young man?" the motorcyclist asked.

"New York."

"The Big Apple." A big smile formed on the motorcyclist's face. "Very nice."

"Thank you. This will be my first time."

The motorcyclist finished pumping his gas and hung the pump up. "So you're going to sightsee?"

"No, my dad and I are going to the Elton John concert."

The motorcyclist smirked as he joggled his head. "You like that sort of music, huh?"

"I do. It's good fun."

The motorcyclist smiled as he sat on his motorcycle. "My son likes that type of music, too. Have a good time at the concert, young man."

The motorcycle roared as it backed up to me. Now, being directly in front of me, the motorcyclist reached his hand out.

"By the way, my name is James Frey."

"Joe Miller." I shook his hand. "It's nice to meet you, James."

James smiled. "Stop by again. We are friendly here in Red Lion."

After one last smile from James, he rode off. I watched him ride down the road, and a smile formed on my face as he waved back at me.

The sound of a car door opening broke me out of my trance. "You ready, Son?"

I glanced over to see my father. He had two pops in his hands and some candy.

"Yeah, I'm ready to go." I sat down inside the car. I buckled my seatbelt and stared at the bottle of pop. "Thanks, Dad, I am thirsty."

My father handed me the pop and some candy. I sipped my drink and enjoyed the sweetness of the candy. All a while I kept thinking of James Frey. His kindness truly touched me.

To this day, I still smile when I think about our conversation. It's a memory of when times were simple, life was simple. That would surely change for me in less than a decade...

Chapter 2

We traveled for another three hours before reaching New York City. Once in New York, Dad drove us straight to *Madison Square Garden*. What a beautiful arena.

I've seen this building on the television when watching the *New York Knickerbockers* play. It looked big on the television, but it seemed a thousand times bigger in person.

My father led me to our seats, four rows from the stage. Not bad, not bad at all. The crowd roared with excitement, and so did I. My father sat with a small smile on his face. This was his first concert; he appeared to be mellow. It was my first concert as well, but I couldn't keep my composer.

I jumped up and down like a teenage girl. In fact, a teenage girl sat next to me. She jumped along with me; we gave each other high-fives... we were ready for the show.

Elton John walked out to the stage; the crowd roared even louder now. My father stood up, clapping extremely hard. I can't explain the atmosphere. It's truly one of those *you had to have been there*, situations.

Elton started the concert off by playing my father's favorite song: *Funeral for a Friend/Love Lies Bleeding*. As Elton sang his tune, I couldn't stop watching my father sing along. It brought a smile to my face as I saw my dad was truly happy.

My father, Clark Miller, worked in a factory that he hated. Every day, he'd come home in pain from the job. He worked twelve-plus hour days in a hot (during the summer) and cold (during the winter) factory.

He wanted out so badly, but being a divorced, single father (my mother left him for the neighbor man when I was five, and she gave up all her rights), he had no choice but to make money.

The factory paid well, the only good thing about it, according to Dad. To see my father being totally relaxed gave me an amazing feeling.

After Elton finished *Friend/Love Lies Bleeding*, he jumped right into *Candle in the Wind*. This song had the older folks all in their emotions. A woman sat next to my father, and she asked him to dance. My father agreed, and the two slowly danced at their seats. It touched my heart to witness true happiness in my father's eyes.

Next, Elton sang his song: *Grimsby*. During *Grimsby*, I danced with the teenage girl, no slow dancing here. We shook our hips and danced fast. It goes to show you when a slower song is being played, the older folks love to slow down, hold their partner close and be all sweet about it.

When the more upbeat song is jamming, us young kids use our energy and shake our hips. I think us *youngins* win in the dance department.

Elton performed my favorite of his songs next. *I think it's going to be a long, long time...* Ah, yes, *Rocket Man*.

Such a beautiful song. I cheerfully sang along with Elton. My father watched me. He took his fist and gently *nudged* me under my chin. We bonded at the Elton John concert more than we have at any other place or time in our lives.

Elton John performed seven more songs before the surprise of my life occurred. After finishing up his song- *You're so Static*, something amazing happened.

"Seeing its Thanksgiving, we thought we'd make tonight a little bit of a joyous occasion. Ah, by inviting someone up with us... on the stage..." Elton said.

I glanced at my father; he turned to face me. We both had no clue whom Elton would be inviting out to the stage.

Elton continued. "And, ah. I'm sure he will be no stranger to anyone in the audience..."

I rubbed my right hand through my hair. The anticipation was killing me.

Elton continued. "When I say it's our great privilege, and your great privilege, to see and hear..."

The crowd, which had been buzzing with excitement, quickly quieted down.

"MR. JOHN LENNON!" Elton said.

The crowd burst out in a glorious roar. Everyone stood up from their chairs. The atmosphere became electric. I grabbed hold of my father's arm. Hell, I couldn't help but squeeze it. I was so excited. The teenage girl who sat next to me grabbed my arm and squeezed.

Then I saw him... my idol, John Lennon, ran out onto the stage. He wore a black and red cape, black on the outside and red on the inside. He carried his guitar in his right hand as he ran up to meet Elton John. After sharing a hug and what may have been a friendly kiss (I couldn't tell for sure as Lennon's back faced me), John and Elton broke out into John's song: *Whatever Gets You Through The Night.*

John was brilliant. He seemed so unreal. I swear to this day that John Lennon appeared to have an aura around him. It was like he was Jesus. Of course, the irony about my statement is that John didn't believe in Jesus.

After performing *Whatever Gets You Through The Night,* the duo performed a classic *Beatles* song: *Lucy In The Sky With Diamonds.*

While John and Elton performed the song, my father nudged me on my shoulder.

"Hey, Son. How are you feeling?"

I turned to face my father and smiled. "This is amazing. Thank you, Daddy."

I called him *Daddy* as if I were a seven-year-old boy again. I honestly felt as if my father knew my hero, John Lennon, would be at this concert.

"You wanted to surprise me? That's why you didn't tell me John would be performing?"

My father laughed. "Son, I honestly had no clue he'd be here." He placed his arm around me and gave me one of those side hugs.

I Saw Her Standing There was the next song the duo performed, and it would also be the last song for John Lennon. While they sang, *I Saw Her Standing There,* I just so happened to glance around the crowd, and to my surprise, upfront, I saw who appeared to be Yoko Ono.

Yoko sat watching John perform with a blank expression on her face. It hit me that during this time, John and Yoko were not together. They separated a little while back. John was seeing a woman by the name of May Pang.

Funny thing about their situation, Yoko told John to date May after their marriage went through some troubles. May Pang worked as John and Yoko's personal assistant and production coordinator. Yoko believed May would treat John well and knew this separation at the time was much needed.

"Look, Dad." I pointed toward the front of the crowd. "I think that's Yoko Ono."

My father leaned closer my way; he peered up through the crowd. "Yeah, Son. I believe you might be right."

After John finished his three-song duet with Elton John, he left the stage. Elton finished up the night by performing six more songs. I found out later that this concert was the moment John and Yoko reunited. They met backstage, and not long after, John left May.

****

"Boy, was that concert good," my father said.

I hung my head out the window, peering up at the stars. "It sure was rocking. I still can't believe John Lennon performed."

My father smiled at me. I pulled my head inside the car and returned the smile. "Thank you, Dad. This was the best night of my life."

My father's smile grew larger. He tapped me on my left leg. "Me too, Son... me too."

Chapter 3

Let's skip forward in my story. You could say we will travel through time... October 26, 1980. Five days before Halloween, I was working late at my job in the candy warehouse. Oh, how I hated this job. At twenty-two years old, I realized my life had been turning out to be my father's. Working in a factory, hating every day, every moment, as my father did.

By 1979, my father and I lived in New York City. After our trip to watch the Elton John concert, my father fell in love with the city. I can't lie, I love New York, as well, and it's a blessing to live in the city. We moved into a small apartment in the Bronx. The apartment was a little small and ran down. The area also wasn't the greatest, but it was still NYC, baby.

In January 1979, my father met a woman named Rose Scott at a local dance. They fell in love, and shortly after, he moved into her Manhattan apartment. Turns out, this woman had money and a lot of it. She used to be married to a Wall Street banker. The banker supposedly cheated on her with his entire staff (well, the women on the staff). She divorced him and received a hefty settlement. So, at that dance, on a cold January night in 1979, my father's life changed. I'm really happy for him, as he's living the good life. My father quit his job at the candy warehouse (he's the reason I got my job there) and moved to Manhattan. The only downside was now he barely saw or talked to me.

Enough with the ever-dissipating relationship with my father, let's get back to 1980. Again, let's travel through time. October 26, 1980, working late in the candy factory is where you could find me. "One in the morning, and we're still here," I bellowed.

My co-worker, Rob Masterson, laughed. "Ha-ha, shit. You know Halloween is the peak time for candy. Damn, we will be lucky if we walk out of here at two in the morning."

I rolled my eyes as I grabbed a flattened box. My father got me a job as a packer, he was a supervisor. The packer position was repetitive and boring. My job requirements were as follows.

1. Grab flattened cardboard box.
2. Fold cardboard box up, tape the bottom.
3. Grab packaged candy from the conveyor belt.
4. Fill box with the required amount of candy.
5. Tape top of box.
6. Place sealed box on pallet.

There you have it, folks. That summed up my job. Now you all see why I hated it, right? I went through this mundane lifestyle five days a week, usually ten hours a day. During the Halloween season, the hours grew. I averaged around thirteen hours a day... Thirteen hours, can you believe that?

Around two in the morning, my boss yelled throughout the factory, "Okay, guys. We are done. Clean up and head the fuck out."

This was the best part of my night at work, hearing the boss say *clean up*. I went to my assigned cleanup area of the factory, and I swept up. It only took me five minutes before I placed my broom down. That was enough cleaning for me. As I left, I stuck my hand in the unpackaged candy pile and pulled a handful out. Outside, frost sat on the ground, and the sky sat crystal clear. The stars twinkled beautifully in the night.

I reached my car and stopped to admire the sky. I threw the candy in my mouth. As I chewed the tacky candy (I took a handful of fruit chews), a sharp pain shot into the back of my mouth. "Ah, damn," I mumbled as I grabbed my mouth. As I rubbed my jaw, a strange phenomenon caught my eye. Up in the starry sky, a bright orange glowing *ball* appeared. *What in the hell is that?*

"Get out of here, punk. I thought you couldn't wait to leave."

Rob stood behind me. He laughed as he lit his cigarette. "I know, I am. Hey, Rob, look at that up in the sky. You see this shit?"

Rob glanced up at the sky. He lowered his cigarette and let out a slow cloud of smoke. "Yeah, so? That's just one of those Aurora things."

I shook my head. "I doubt that. The Aurora Borealis is green, not orange."

Rob laughed and patted me on my back. "Then it's just a weird glow off of the moon. Shit, it's cold, and I'm tired. Peace out, bro."

Rob sat in his car, and I couldn't help but glance back up at the sky. What got to me wasn't the fact it was a bright orange color, the fact it looked like a giant ball scared me. Oh, and the moon wasn't present on that night.

After my stressful time working at the Candy factory, my luck finally changed. On December 1, 1980, I accepted a new job position. After searching for a long time to find a new job, I found a small floor care company that desperately needed a second-shift floor man. That morning I went to work at the Candy factory, clocking in as normal. I walked around with a smile on my face. I originally planned on working the entire night to be nice (even though I didn't want to). The entire night annoyed me. Hell, my boss annoyed me. Shit, the damn machine annoyed me. It broke down, and I had to fix it.

At lunchtime, I clocked out as normal and headed to my car. I usually sat in my car and ate my lunch, but today, I would be placing the car in drive. I hauled ass out of the parking lot and never looked back. The hell with them. I would be starting my new job tomorrow, and I should have never come in, to begin with.

My new job's office was near my place in the Bronx, but the job would send me all over the city. I ended up going to Manhattan to work on a few businesses' floors.

On December 6, my boss assigned me to work on a floor in a famous building that held high importance to me.

My boss gave me the job description that morning. "Today, Joe, you will be heading back to Manhattan to work on the floor of apartment twenty-six. This is located in the Dakota apartment building."

"What? Are you serious? The Dakota?" I screamed like a little schoolgirl. The Dakota apartment building was the home of my idol, John Lennon.

"Yes, buddy, now listen to me. They are extremely strict at the Dakota. Don't you go wandering around the halls or anything. Go straight to room twenty-six and do your job."

I knew of John Lennon living there since I moved to New York. I took a taxi by the building a few times in the past, hoping to catch a glimpse of him. Unfortunately, I never got lucky. So, you can see why the thought of me working inside excited me.

"You understand?" my boss snarled.

I shook my head twice and rubbed my hands together. "Ah, yeah. Of course, Boss."

Now, I wouldn't be working on the floor that Lennon lived on. John lived on the seventh floor. I would be working on floor number two. But I thought maybe I'd get lucky to have John pass me in the hallway or meet him on the elevator... damn, a guy could dream, right?

I drove my company van up to the Dakota building. My off-white van with the company logo peeling off must have stuck out like a sore thumb. The doorman walked up to me with a disgusted expression on his face. "May I help you, sir?"

I wound my window down, but it took me a few tries as the handle got stuck. "Ah, yes. I'm here to clean the floor of apartment twenty-six."

The doorman squinted at me. "Are you with Martin's Building and Maintenance?"

I pulled myself halfway out of the window and pointed to the side of my van. The doorman jumped back a foot as I startled him. "Yes, I am. See the name on the van?"

He glanced at my van and shook his head. "Not exactly."

Of course, the peeling of the name. My van said, *Matin's uildin An Maintenan.* "Sorry, the van is old."

He rolled his eyes. "Go ahead, sir. You can park your…" The doorman coughed sarcastically. "Van."

Jackass, I thought. I placed the van in drive, ready to pull up into the archway of the building.

"Ahem, sir. Where do you think you're going?"

My left hand reached out the window. The doorman jumped back once more. I pointed toward the beautiful archway of this enormous building. "Well, I was going to park my van right against the side there."

"No, no, no. That is not going to happen, sir."

"Well, why not?"

The doorman smirked. "We cannot have this ugly vehicle blocking our beautiful archway. You can pull around the block and park."

"But sir. I have floor machines to take in. If I have to park down the street, then I have to haul the machines all the way up here."

My desperate plea didn't seem to faze the unforgiven doorman. "Well, sir, if this is too much of a problem, then you can just leave, and I'll call your boss." I gulped at this notion. "I'll explain to your boss that you refused to do your job, and you surely will be laid out on the street."

A few obscenities flew under my breath as I put my work van in reverse. I backed out of the archway and back into the street. As I maneuvered my van around, ready to find a parking spot down the street, a limousine pulled up and parked in front of the Dakota. I watched as the driver of the limo exited the vehicle and walked over to the passenger side, facing the building. He opened the door, and out stepped John Lennon and Yoko Ono. My jaw dropped as I watched my hero stand only fifteen feet from me.

Before I could fall deeper into this world of *awe*, a loud and drawn-out *beep* brought me back down to Earth. I swung my head around to find a line of traffic sitting behind me. I glanced back, and a bit of the *awe* feeling returned. John Lennon faced me. I couldn't see his eyes since they were hidden behind his round dark glasses, but he undoubtedly stared in my direction.

The loud *beeps* rang out once more. I placed the van in drive and slowly took off down the street. *John... John looked at me,* I said over and over to myself. The job crept back into my mind, and I shook my head. After knocking off the cobwebs, I focused on finding a parking spot. An open spot shined brightly in the sun as if placed as a gift from God. The spot sat at the end of West 72nd Street (the street where the Dakota is). I parked the van and exited. As I opened the back of my work van, I couldn't help but stare down the street at the Dakota. The limo left, but a few other vehicles were pulled up in front of the building. *Damn, I hope I see John once I'm inside. I want to tell him how much he has inspired me.*

Down the street, I trotted, pushing my buffer along the cracked sidewalk. The buffer was heavy, and every crack I hit made the machine turn left or right. I nearly hit two cars that were parked on the side of the street.

"Excuse me, sir. Are you leaving this thing near the door?"

I turned back to find the doorman. He stood next to my buffer with his arms crossed. After the tough walk down the cracked street, I placed my buffer next to the door. I made sure to keep the buffer out from in front of the entrance, but apparently, having my machine sit next to the door was a problem. "Ah, yeah. I have to go back and get the rest of the stuff."

The doorman rolled his eyes. "Well, hurry up. This dirty machine brings the place down."

His statement angered me. "Well, sir, if I was able to park next to the door, I could pull all my supplies out and push them into the building right away. But no, I had to park down the street, so this is how it goes."

A chuckle shot out of the doorman's mouth. He stared at my buffer, looking all over the machine. "Ha, this machine still looks better than that old beat-up van." He connected his bright blue eyes with mine. "But you need to hurry up. If our residents see this dirty piece of equipment sitting next to the door, they might not be as forgiving as I."

This man got on my nerves. *Who does he think he is talking to me this way? Just because the rich live here doesn't mean they are better than anyone else.* Then John Lennon crossed my mind. *Okay, maybe they are better around here.* I took two more trips up and down the street before I had all the equipment, I needed to do the job. *Great, there are steps once you open the door.* I glanced at the doorman; he smiled at me. Once you enter the building, there is a small set of stairs that leads you up into the office of the building. I dragged my buffer up, luckily there were only five steps. Once inside the office of the building, I couldn't help but stare in all directions.

Wow, look at this place. The inside of the building was more beautiful than the outside. *The ceilings were huge in this building,* I thought I stood in a museum rather than an apartment building. I pushed my buffer up to the elevator. My eyes swarmed the area, hoping to catch another glimpse of John Lennon. He could be leaving and passing by. You never know, right?

"Excuse me, may I get on here?"

I turned to find a man in a suit holding a briefcase. He stood next to me in front of the elevator. "Ah, yeah, sure." The elevator opened, and the man walked on.

As I pushed my buffer onto the elevator, the man held his hands up. "Excuse me, but I'd like to ride up alone, if you don't mind."

The elevator door shut in my face. *What an asshole.* This man thought he was so high in life that riding up with a working man would be terrible. *What a prick.* Finally, the elevator returned to the first floor, and I pushed my buffer inside.

After the short ride up to the second floor, I exited the elevator to find a man in a uniform standing before me. "Oh, hello," I said.

"Good day to you, sir. Follow me, I'll take you to room twenty-six." The man led me down the hall and to a door with the number twenty-six on it. He opened the door and walked inside. "Here is the room you will be working in. As you see, our mahogany floors are damaged." I glanced at the floor and saw how scuffed they were. "As you can see, the staff here has taken the time to move everything out of the way for you. Please get to work and hurry up."

I sat my machine down and glared at the man. The staff here at the Dakota sure were assholes. Before leaving the room, I took it all in. Like the rest of the building, the ceilings were high, and fancy wallpaper covered the walls. This apartment room appeared to be a small house.

I exited the room, and the man in the uniform stood next to the opened room twenty-six door. I stepped into the elevator. It was empty, and the ride down to floor one went quickly. The door opened, and a man with round glasses stood in front of me. My stomach buckled. At first glance, this man appeared to be John Lennon.

"Are you exiting the elevator? Or are you going to block it for everyone else?" the man snarled. The man's voice sounded unpleasantly deep. It then hit me; this was not John Lennon. The man in front of me was of a husky build and, other than the glasses, held no resemblance to John Lennon. "Hello? Are you fucking dumb or something? Get out of my way!"

Quickly, I snapped back to reality. I sidestepped past the husky, round glasses-wearing man. "Ugh, sorry."

"Sorry, my ass," the man snapped back as he walked into the elevator.

Damn, these people here are nuts, I thought as I walked out of the Dakota. I took two more trips to gather all of my supplies. On my last trip, I walked into the building with my floor finish and mop. My equipment wasn't that big, but the floor finish sure was heavy. I approached the elevator to find a group of five people standing and waiting. Three men in suits stood with two women dressed in upper-class attire.

I stopped next to the group and placed my box of floor finish on the ground. The group turned to watch me. Their eyes all locked on my movements. A look of disgust formed on the two women's faces. One man wore a top hat. He took one step in my direction. "Excuse me, but what do you think you are doing?"

My eyes met each member of the group. An uncomfortable feeling overtook me. "Ah, well, I'm waiting on the elevator so I can get to floor two. I'm working in one of the rooms."

"You are, sir, but you won't be taking the elevator at this time." A voice appeared from behind me.

I turned to find my friend, the doorman, walking toward me. "Why not?" I asked with some attitude behind my voice.

The doorman smirked. "Well, because our residents are here waiting for the elevator to arrive."

I glanced back at the group. The elevator opened, and the group entered. As soon as the door closed, three more women approached. "I can let these women go on, and then I'll get on," I explained.

A group of four more people approached the elevator. The doorman took one step toward me, standing directly in front of my face. "No, sir. You may take the stairs as it's too busy for you to ride the elevator as of now."

"You know this box of lacquer is heavy," I said while glancing down at the floor finish.

The doorman smirked once more. "I don't see how that is any concern to me." My head cocked sideways. "No offense, sir," the doorman chuckled. "But the Dakota residents don't want to ride next to someone of your..." he looked me up and down. "Of your social class..."

I grabbed my box of floor finish and stormed past the doorman. Steam must have flown out of my ears; I was so hopping mad. I found the door to the stairwell and opened it, entering inside. *Wow, these stairs are made from marble.* This entire building was beautiful, but unfortunately, I couldn't say the same for the residents. I wonder if John Lennon acted like the rest of these clowns... I sure hope not.

Inside room twenty-six, I worked on the mahogany floor. The man in the uniform stood at the room's entrance the entire time I worked on the floor. After six hours of working, I finished the floor. It was now eleven at night, and I felt exhausted. I first pushed my buffer out of the room. The man in the uniform glared at the floor as I exited. He dashed down the hall as I entered the elevator. "Great job, sir. It looks fantastic."

"Thanks." I pressed the close button and watched the man disappear behind the elevator door. The elevator stopped on the first floor, and the door opened. A voice I knew all so well entered my ears.

"Let's go, Yoko. I want to wine and dine you tonight, my love." John Lennon stood at the door that led outside. He held his right hand out to his wife, Yoko

Ono. She grabbed John's hand and left out the building as the ignorant doorman I met held the door open for them.

My hands gripped hard on the handles of the buffer. I pushed my machine as fast as I could, trying hard to catch up to John and Yoko. I reached the door, ready to bust outside, until an unfriendly face blocked my path. "Excuse me, sir. You need to slow down... NOW!"

I stopped my buffer only inches from the feet of the doorman. "Oh, sorry."

"Sorry, you should be. Why are you running with that machine?"

The doorman blocked my view as I tried to look past him. I maneuvered my buffer to the left and passed the doorman. Opening the door with my butt, I darted outside. I turned to find Yoko Ono sitting down inside a limousine, followed by John Lennon. The driver of the limo shut the door, and as he did, John glanced up in my direction. John still wore those dark glasses, so I couldn't see his eyes, but I swear he locked his eyes on mine... for the second time.

The limo driver walked around the limo and up to the driver's side door. I pushed my buffer down the street as the limo pulled out. The limo slowly drove down the street, going only as fast as I walked. This excited me, I can't be certain, but maybe John was looking out of the tinted window at me just as I stared up at the limo. Before I knew it, I reached my work van, and the limo turned onto the next street.

Bye, John. I loaded my buffer into my van, and something caught my eye. *Holy shit, there it is again.* A bright orange glow from the sky took all my attention. It was the same *ball* of orange that was in the dark night sky that night at the candy factory. This freaked me out. *Please don't be some nuclear bomb the Soviets are blasting on America.*

I jogged down the street, hustling back inside the Dakota. After grabbing what I could of my supplies, I walked back out of the Dakota with the help of the doorman, opening the door for me. He gave me an evil stare as I passed. As I walked down the street, I glared up at the sky, but the orange glowing ball vanished. *Huh, where in the hell did you go?*

After one more trip up and back down the street, I had the last of my equipment and headed home for the night. Normally I'd take my work van back to the shop to drop it off, but tonight I felt tired and took the van home for the night. I knew my boss wouldn't care (well, hopefully).

I woke up the next morning to my phone ringing. "Hello?"

"Yeah, Joe. Did you take the van home with you?"

"I did. I got out of the Dakota late last night and figured it would be easier to just bring it home with me."

"That's fine, Joe." A four-second pause on the phone got me nervous. I believed something went wrong. "You know the people at the Dakota liked your work so much, Joe, that they asked if you could come back today and work on another floor."

My nervousness fell away. I couldn't believe those ignorant people actually liked my work. "Wow, okay. That sounds great, boss."

"Good. Today you will be touching up their marble stairwells. And since it's marble, that means no acidic cleaners, got that?"

"Sure do, boss."

"Good," my boss said. "You can get ready and start within the next hour."

We hung up the phone, and I rushed to get ready.

I drove to the Dakota and found the same parking spot from yesterday open. Like yesterday, I parked in the last spot on the street. Today I didn't have to bring as much equipment for the job, so one trip was enough. There was also one other thing I brought with me today, and that was my copy of John Lennon's latest album, *Double Fantasy.*

The album safely sat tucked under my shirt and into my pants. If I got lucky enough to see Lennon again and lucky enough to get close to him, I wanted to ask him if he would sign my album. Unfortunately, on this day, I wouldn't see John Lennon, not one time. The job only took me about four hours, and I left the Dakota. The doorman gave me a smug look every time I passed him, just like yesterday. Other than the doorman, I had no problems with anyone on this day.

After my short job at the Dakota, I drove back to the shop, and my boss sent me out to clean the floors in a local gas station. This job took me to about ten at night. I left the gas station and drove back to the shop. To my surprise, once back at the shop, I found my boss there.

Normally my boss leaves around five or six in the evening, but not today, though. "Hey-ya, Joe."

"Hi, boss."

"Guess where you are going tomorrow?"

"Where?" I asked.

My boss shot me a huge smile. "Back to the Dakota. Room twenty-six, once again."

"What? Why? Did I mess something up?"

My boss chuckled. "No, nothing that you did. When the staff moved back the furniture, they scratched it a bit."

"Oh, wow."

"Yeah, they just discovered the scratch today. I'll need you to head back down, okay?"

This excited me because another day at the Dakota meant another chance at seeing and hopefully meeting John Lennon. "Yes, sir, not a problem. I'll head down in the morning."

I arrived back at the Dakota bright and early the next morning. There weren't any open parking spaces on 1 W 72nd St. So, I drove down the street, and luckily for me, I found an open space at the start of Central Park West (the next street down from the Dakota). I parked my van and got out. First, I pulled my buffer out. I hoped this scratch wasn't that bad, and maybe I wouldn't need all my equipment.

Down the street, I walked, truly hoping all I needed was my buffer since I'm parked farther away from the building. As I pushed my buffer, I couldn't help but notice how beautiful a day it was. The sky looked as blue as the mighty Pacific. The sun felt warm on the back of my neck, which was a great sensation since it had been cold recently.

Something strange hovered above the Dakota. It almost looked like the sun sat above the apartment building. Yet, the sun clearly shined from behind me. I glanced back to confirm it, and yes, the bright rays blinded me in my eyes.

"Look, there he is. That's John Lennon's son." I overheard a woman talking to her friend.

My head whipped over to the Dakota, and I saw a small boy standing behind a Spanish woman. I could barely see the boy because in front of him and the Spanish woman stood a large man. He wore a green scarf over his neck and a heavy coat. The large man reached past the Spanish woman and shook the young boy's hand before they entered the building.

This struck me as odd, I'm not sure why, but this large man creeped me out. Hell, I couldn't even see his face, but something about him didn't feel right. I continued to push my buffer up to the Dakota. The large man didn't move; he stood facing the Dakota building with his hands in his coat pockets. I passed him and felt tempted to take a gander at his face but decided against it.

As I reached the door, a different doorman greeted me. "Hello, good day to you, sir."

This doorman seemed friendly. His attitude made me feel good. I smiled at the doorman and pushed the buffer inside. The doorman even helped me lift my buffer up the first set of stairs. "Thank you, Mr. Doorman."

"No need to call me that. The name is Jose. It's nice to meet you."

Jose extended his hand, and I shook it. "It's nice to meet you as well." I pushed my buffer to the elevator and got lucky. No one stood waiting for the elevator. I rode up to the second floor and met the same man in the uniform. "Hello, again."

"Good day, sir. Follow me." The man in the uniform led me to room twenty-six once again. Inside the room, I noticed the dining room table moved out from where a table would sit. I walked up and saw the scratch on the floor. "Sorry, sir, when the staff moved the furniture back, they didn't realize they scratched the floor."

"No worries, it happens." Walking up to the scratch, I sat my buffer down.

I bent down to observe the scratch; it looked deep. "Damn. Okay, I must grab the rest of my equipment."

It took two more trips for me to get the rest of my equipment, and on both trips, I caught the same large man standing near the building. Both times that I passed by, I couldn't see the large man's face. First, he stood talking to a woman, and the next trip, the large man bent down to tie his shoes.

Up in room twenty-six, I forgot about the large man. I worked feverishly on the floor and finished the job around four in the evening. *Looks wonderful*. I pushed my buffer out into the hall, and the man in the uniform stepped in front of me. "Excuse me, sir."

"Ah, yeah?"

The man in the uniform smirked. "I have a favor to ask you, and we will happily pay your company for your services."

I wasn't sure where this was headed, but I certainly felt intrigued. "Okay, what is it that you need?"

"Well, there is a small scratch in the dining room of room forty-six. Could you possibly fix it?" I rubbed my right hand under my chin, unsure if I wanted to stay and work here any longer. "I'll call your boss to let him know," the man in the uniform said.

My stomach growled, and I rubbed it. "Okay, you call my boss, and if he says it is okay, then I'll stay. But first, I want to run out to grab a bite to eat."

"Sure," the man in the uniform said as he smiled.

I walked outside of the Dakota and glanced around to see if I could find the large man lurking around the building once more. The man had vanished. He was nowhere to be found. Even though I don't know this man and have never even seen his face, I felt a sense of relief not seeing him standing around the building. So down the street I went, rubbing my oh-so-hungry tummy.

I drove to a local fast-food joint and grabbed myself a burger, and it tasted so good. Lettuce, tomato, pickle, and lots of mayo packed my burger... so delicious. I drove back to the Dakota with a full stomach. I didn't even attempt to park in front of the building; I drove right to the same parking spot I had on Central Park West.

After I unloaded my buffer, I glanced at my watch. *Ugh, it's about five. I hope I can get this done and be out by ten.* Down the street, I pushed my buffer, inching closer to the Dakota. As I approached the building, I noticed a small crowd of people and heard some commotion. *Ah, shit, it's John.* From a distance, I saw John Lennon and Yoko Ono walking out of the Dakota. I quickly touched around my waistband, going for my *Double Fantasy* album. *Damn, I don't have my album, it must have fallen out of my pants.*

Something I saw next made my stomach turn, and I don't exactly know why. This large man walked out to greet John. I knew this must have been the same *large* man I saw earlier. The man wore the same heavy overcoat, with a green scarf over his neck as the one I noticed earlier. On this occasion, I saw the man's face. He wore these large glasses and had a strange expression on his face. As the large man stopped in front of John, he held out what appeared to be an album.

I took a few steps closer, and I heard the voice of this large man. "John, would you sign my album?"

Yoko walked past the man and entered the limousine. John looked the man in the eyes and replied, "Sure."

I stood frozen in a trance-like state. My idol stood near me, and I couldn't get over the fear of meeting him. I watched John sign the large man's album; it looked to be a copy of *Double Fantasy*. This upset me to a degree because if I had my copy still with me, maybe John would sign it. Of course, if I still acted too scared to approach John, it wouldn't matter, anyway.

"Is that all?" John asked. The large man joggled his head *yes,* and John walked past to join Yoko in the limousine. Once John disappeared behind the tinted window of the limo, I snapped back to reality and pushed my buffer up toward the Dakota.

The large man stood staring at the limo as it drove off. He had a weird expression on his face. This large man's gaze made the hair stand up on my arms. I cannot explain his expression, but it seemed evil.

The nice doorman on this evening opened the door for me and said, "Good day, sir."

Inside the Dakota, I found it to be empty and quiet. I pushed my buffer to the elevator and pressed the button. I rode up to the fourth floor and found the man in the uniform waiting for me. "Hello, again, sir."

"Hello." I followed him down the hall and to room forty-six.

The uniform man opened the door and gestured for me to follow him in. "Here, over by where the dining room table sits, is where the scratch is."

The other room had all the furniture moved out before I entered the room, but not room forty-six. "Ah, does this mean I will have to move the furniture myself?"

"Well, you only should have to move the table and chairs... right?" The man in the uniform asked.

I scratched my head as I looked around the room. "Yeah, that should be it."

"Okay, I'll summon for someone to move it for you."

"Thanks," I said. "I have to run out to get the rest of my equipment."

"Someone will move the furniture once you get back."

"Sounds good," I said. I walked past him and, for some unknown reason, I took the stairs down. Four flights down took my breath slightly, but at least I wasn't walking up them. I admired the marble stairs. They truly were beautiful to look at.

Out of the stairwell, I walked toward the door, and it opened. "Good day, sir," the doorman said as he opened the door.

I liked this doorman. He seemed polite, and he always wore a big smile. The doorman's smile was contagious. I walked outside on this pleasantly warm

December evening. My smile didn't last too long, though. Two things I saw wiped the smile straight off of my face. A bright and familiar orange glow shone up in the dark sky. My eyes shot to the glow, and a sense of fear struck. But it gets worse... my eyes lowered from the sky, and underneath the orange glow stood the large man. He stood with a blank expression on his face. Behind those large glasses, I noticed his eyes staring in my direction. His gaze was cold. Evil seemed to be behind those eyes.

A shiver shot down my spine, and I turned my head away from the large man. I picked up my speed and power-walked down to my van. On this trip to my van, I wanted to grab all my equipment so badly, just so I didn't have to walk past the large man anymore. Something didn't seem right with this man. Unfortunately, I couldn't grab everything, so I would need another trip.

I approached the Dakota, and I didn't see the large man. A sense of relief hit me, but it wouldn't last. As I inched closer to the Dakota, the large man appeared. He sat just inside the archway, on the curb. His head lowered to the ground. I turned around to glance back up at the sky. The orange glow vanished, and when I turned back around, the large man's eyes locked onto me.

My head turned away, and I picked up my speed. As I passed the large man, I heard a soft voice say, "Hello."

I slowly turned to face him. The large man stared at me with a strange smile on his face. "Ah, hi," I replied in a jittery tone.

The doorman opened the door for me. "Hello, again, sir."

"Hello..." I waved the doorman inside. He walked up, and I leaned toward his ear. "Do you see that large man?"

The doorman glanced back toward the large man, who now stared out toward the street. "Yes, sir."

"He's a little weird," I said. "I think you should keep your eye on him."

A small chuckle shot out of the doorman. "Oh, mister. He's just a fan of Lennon, I heard him talking to some other fans earlier. We get them a lot around here. Trying to catch a glimpse or get an autograph."

"Oh, okay." I walked away from the doorman and thought, *but this man already met John and he received an autograph. Yet, he's still here.*

I took the elevator up to the room and dropped off my equipment. Once again, I took the steps down, and out the door, I went. The large man sat in the same spot, staring toward the street. I glanced away from him and focused my eyes down the street.

I retrieved the remaining equipment and headed back to the Dakota. On this trip back, I kept my head turned in the opposite direction of where the large man sat. My eyes squinted, and my left pointer finger did its job and pointed at some imaginary object. I wanted to act like I was focused on something, hoping not to hear the large man's voice, and it worked.

The job in room forty-six took over five hours to finish. I glanced at my watch: 10:33 p.m. *Ugh, I'm ready to go.* By now, I felt beat, beyond tired from my hard work. First, I pushed my buffer down and out to my van. When I left the building, I found the large man standing and talking to the doorman. I couldn't believe this man was still here. After loading my buffer into the van, I noticed the orange ball in the night sky again. It seemed to hover above the Dakota. My speed picked up again, and I rushed past the large man and the doorman. I was in and out of the building in a flash.

After placing my equipment in my van, I walked back up the street to get my remaining equipment. The orange ball in the sky appeared to grow two times in size. It also seemed to shake, almost vibrating. *Jesus.* I hurried back to the Dakota. This time I found the large man standing off to the side, reading a book. I glanced up into the sky and shook my head.

The doorman let me inside, and I ran to the elevator. I grabbed the rest of my equipment, and the man in the uniform wished me a good night as he shut the door to room forty-six. *Jeez, I hope we all make it through tonight;* I thought as the glowing orange ball in the sky replayed in my mind. Once more, I took the stairs as I only had a few small things in my hands. Once in the main lobby, I stopped to tie my shoe. After tying my shoe, I took a gander at my watch: 10:46 P.M. *Damn, I'm ready for bed.*

I hope that orange ball is gone; I pray that nothing bad happens to me… hell, to anyone.

This time, I had to open the door myself. The doorman stood near the sidewalk. The large man, once again, sat on the curb of the archway, reading his book. As I passed, I took notice of the book he was reading: *The Catcher in the Rye*. I scratched my head. *Huh, I never got around to reading that book.*

I passed by the doorman and gently patted him on his right shoulder. "Goodnight."

"All done?" he asked. I nodded. "All right, have a great night, señor."

I took three steps, and the orange ball re-entered my mind. I turned to find that the orange ball still hung in the sky, but it appeared to be much smaller by now. As I glanced at the sky, I couldn't help but notice the large man. He stood up and lowered *The Catcher in the Rye*.

The sound of an approaching vehicle caught my attention. I swung around and discovered a limousine pulling up to the Dakota. The limo stopped, and the backdoor opened. Out stood Yoko Ono. I froze, knowing John would appear next. A few seconds after Yoko, John appeared. John seemed to be holding a tape recorder and a few cassettes. A smile formed on my face as I realized that this may be the last time I'll be working in this building, and this may be the last time I get to see John Lennon in person. Well, unless I stand around the building all day, like the large man…

John's head turned toward the large man. They appeared to glance at each other. I didn't see John's face, but the large man had a stone-cold demeanor on his. John passed the man and continued on toward the building. The large man jumped out behind John. He appeared to jump into a combat stance.

"Mr. Lennon," the large man softly said.

At that moment, the orange ball changed to a bright red color. It also grew larger as it hung directly above the Dakota. Five loud *bangs* rang out; they sounded like firecrackers. The scream of a woman sounded next. The doorman rushed toward the large man. John staggered toward the door, blood poured out from his body. A flash of orange light occurred behind where I was, then it disappeared.

This man has a gun! I turned and ran fast down the street toward my van. Fear struck me; my body shook. I reached my van and jumped inside. I threw my equipment down and laid my head against the steering wheel. *John's been shot, John's been shot.*

Loud police sirens quickly filled the night air. I peered out my window, swarms of people covered the archway of the Dakota. A bunch of police vehicles pulled up to the building, and in a minute or so, one police vehicle rushed by my van. I shook uncontrollably; I knew something horrible had happened. I knew my idol, John Lennon, had been shot.... and he might not make it…

Chapter 4

I sped all the way back to the shop, passing a bunch of cop cars on the way; none of them cared to stop me. Approaching my company workshop, I saw the lights were out, so my boss wouldn't be here tonight. I pressed the garage door button (my boss clipped it on the sun visor), and the garage door slowly opened. My hands squeezed the steering wheel as my arms shook like I suffered from Parkinson's disease.

Inside the garage, I turned the van off, but yet, I didn't exit the vehicle. Sitting in silence, watching my arms tremble, my night replayed in my mind. From the orange glowing ball in the sky to hearing those loud *bangs*, to seeing the blood pour from John Lennon's body, to the stone-cold expression on the large man's face... Tears flooded my lap as I broke down into complete hysteria. Every emotion in the book hit me. From sadness to anger to fear, I couldn't help myself. I sat in my work van for five hours before I got out and left for home.

My apartment sat only two blocks from work, but this walk home felt like it took an eternity. The orange ball hung in the night sky, seemingly watching me as I walked home. Once home, I couldn't sleep. I lay in bed till noon before I got up to make myself some eggs. After finishing my eggs, I decided today wasn't a good day to work, so I called my boss and told him I wouldn't be coming in. He didn't say much, he just muttered,

Lennon, and I said, "Yeah." He told me no worries and to show up the next day. I agreed and hung up the phone.

Next, I turned my small colored television on, and what I feared to be true was confirmed. The news anchor talked about John Lennon. He talked about his music, his life, and his untimely death. He also talked about the shooter, John Lennon's killer. They said his name, but I refused to say it. This monster wanted fame, and I'm not going to give it to him... yes, *monster* is a good name for him. They showed his mugshot on the television, and that stupid expression on his face angered me. He had the same stone-cold expression he had last night when I saw him in person.

This angered me to my core. I picked up my coffee cup and threw it as hard as I could. The cup smacked the wall and busted into a million pieces. Down on my knees, I fell, weeping all over again. That's how my day went, the most emotional day in my life. Later on in the evening, I lay in my darkroom since I didn't turn the light on. I had no care to see anything around. All I did was place John Lennon's first solo album on my record player. I played the first song: *Mother*, over and over.

Hearing John's voice, his raw emotion, touched me dearly. This legendary man, an idol not only to me but to millions around the world, was dead... I stood near the crime; I saw the killer. We met face to face, and the son of a bitch spoke to me. Shit, I spoke back to him. I could have... I should have stopped him...

Sitting alone in my apartment became too depressing. I left out and headed straight for the local bar. As I walked down the street, people screamed out: *give peace a chance*. Radio's in passing cars blared John Lennon and *Beatles* songs. Walking inside the bar, a man stood near the back, singing karaoke. Of course, the man sang John Lennon songs.

The event replayed in my mind as I sat down. "What will you have, partner?" the bartender asked. My eyes filled with tears. "Lennon fan?" I nodded. "Yeah, I am too. This tragedy has shaken the entire city." Words left me, I couldn't speak about John Lennon, so I just nodded again. "Well, what will you have?"

"*Coke* and rum. Please."

"Coming right up." The bartender said. He poured my drink and placed my cup in front of me. I chugged my drink down in a matter of seconds. "Whoa, slow down, buddy."

The drink burned going down. I squinted as I held my pointer finger up. "Please," I finally caught my breath. "Another... please."

"All right, but take this one slow, will you, buddy?" The bartender asked, and I nodded in agreement. He placed my second drink in front of me, and I took his advice and sipped this one. I spun around on my barstool, turning to watch the karaoke. Two women now stood up, singing *Come Together* while holding onto each other's hips. A pretty blonde and a pretty brunette sang in harmony.

The two women finished their duet and the entire bar clapped and roared. "Would anyone else like to come up and honor John Lennon?" the blonde asked.

A shot of confidence ran through me. Sliding off my barstool (after drinking the rest of my second cup of *Coke* and rum), I darted up to the microphone. "I would like to honor John."

The two women smiled, and the blonde handed me the mic. "Go get them, slugger."

Something overtook me as I grabbed the mic… I also grabbed the blonde. Then I planted a big kiss on her lips. She jumped back, looking stunned at first, then she shot me a smile. The brunette surprised me by grabbing and pulling me into her. She kissed me, and the two women giggled to each other as they sat down.

"Thank you, ladies," I said with a slur. As I scanned the room, I found an array of different races and ethnic people, all sitting together in harmony. This is what John Lennon wanted, everyone to come together and have love for one another.

A wide mix of emotions was present on the faces of the patrons. Some people looked sad, tears were in their eyes. A few had a look of anger, and a bunch seemed to be laughing and trying to enjoy life. "Everyone, I'd like to sing a song, that is truly special to me and I think to the world... especially now. I'd like to sing John Lennon's song: *Imagine*."

I broke down as I sang, *Imagine*. Tears fell, my voice cracked throughout the entire lyrics. My heart and soul poured through my performance, my tribute to the now late-great John Lennon. After I finished the song, the bar sat quietly. Lowering the mic, I huffed and puffed. The thought crossed my mind that maybe my performance sucked. Just as doubt entered my mind, the bar erupted louder than anything I ever heard before.

Three guys ran up and hoisted me up on their shoulders. The bar all chanted, *LENNON, LENNON, LENNON*. This made me feel better, for a little while at least. I stayed at the bar till two in the morning, closing time. The blonde and brunette women asked me if I wanted to ride along with them in the cab they called, but I turned them down. The walk home wasn't long, and I wanted to take the late-night walk home alone to reflect some more.

A light cool breeze hit the back of my neck; gooseflesh formed on my skin. A bright glow in the night sky caught my attention. I didn't feel scared at all, I had become used to seeing the orange glow by now, and this time around, it angered me.

"This is your fault, isn't it?" I shook my fist at the sky. "You're the reason John Lennon got killed! What in the hell are you?" I stopped by a light post, and I grabbed a hold of the pole. After pulling myself up, I screamed, "Are you the devil? Some evil presence that is trying to kill me?" My hands lost grip on the light post, and I fell from the light, landing on my feet. "Kill me, why don't you? Kill me now, you son of a bitch!"

Naturally, I received no answer from the mysterious orange glowing ball in the sky. *Ugh, come old flat-top, stop fucking with me... please.* A single tear fell from my right eye. Once back at home, I flopped down on my bed. I couldn't help it, but anger filled my blood. The most intense feeling of anger I've ever felt.

My bedroom window sat cracked, I jumped out of bed and rushed over to the window. That large, glowing, mysterious ball hovered in the sky. The bartender let me sneak out a bottle of rum. I took a mouthful, opened the window full-way, and spit it out up in the night sky. Lowering my head on the window seal, I cried.

That monster who killed my idol would have to pay, and I don't mean by serving time. No, if Lennon can't live another day, then why should the monster be able to stay alive? Eating food, breathing... no, I wanted to end his pathetic life because that's what he was… no, is. He is a pathetic man. My head lifted, and to my surprise, the orange glowing ball vanished. *The time to act is now. This bird has flown.*

Six months have passed since that horrible night. I became obsessed with killing the monster who killed my boyhood idol. This became everything to me. Hell, it was the only thing I thought about. I cut out and kept every article about the killing and everything about the killer himself. Shit, I even went out and purchased a copy of the book that asshole had on the night of the killing.

To be honest, I read *The Catcher in the Rye* and didn't see anything that would possess me to become crazy. This monster didn't get any help from a book. No, he became a nut job all by himself. But at the same time, I'm sure that the monster inspired others to perform heinous acts. Like back in March, some wacko shot President Regan. I have no knowledge of the monster being the inspiration for the shooting. But let's get real, two shootings of famous people, less than four months apart, I think there was a chance.

All I could think about was a trial, the trial of the monster who killed Lennon. I couldn't wait for it, I planned on heading down to the trial and doing something to the monster, finding an opening, and killing him. June 21, 1981, I hovered down at the courtroom. The news said today would be the day the monster would make his plea; I hoped to get a front-row seat. Unfortunately, I found it to be a closed proceeding. This angered me, but I didn't leave, I wanted this man to walk outside.

Inside my pants pocket, I held onto a *Charter Arms .38-caliber pistol.* This was the same model gun the monster used to shoot Lennon. *Instant Karma's gonna get you*, I thought over and over, pacing around out front of the courthouse.

"Excuse me, sir. May I help you?"

I turned around to find a heavy-set police officer. He had a concerned look on his face. But I needed to play it cool, so I put a smile on my face. "Oh, hello, officer. Yes, everything is good. I'm just enjoying this beautiful sunny day we are having."

"Oh, okay. Well, I hate to be the bearer of bad news, but this is a no-loitering zone." My eyes made their way over to the entrance of the courthouse. "I need to ask you to move along," the officer said.

"No problem, I'll leave now." I walked across the street, and as I stopped to let a car pass, I saw the *second sun* again. This was the first time I'd seen the orange glowing ball since the night after the murder. *What are you?* The car passed and I jogged onto the sidewalk.

For the rest of the evening I remained on the sidewalk, waiting around just like the monster waited for Lennon in front of the Dakota. The officer stood across the street in front of the courthouse, watching me the entire time. There wasn't much I could do, yet the same went for him. I could loiter all day on this side of the street. To my disgust, the monster never exited the courthouse. Well, not out the front door at least.

My walk home felt lonely. I kept my head down for most of the way, till an orange glow entered into my preferable vision. The orange ball appeared for a few minutes earlier in the day, but it quickly dissipated. Now it returned, in all its glory. This phenomenon truly seemed to be stalking me and I wasn't sure why.

"What do you want?" I screamed toward the sky. I stood across the street from my apartment building, but I didn't want to go inside. "Why don't you just kill me?" The thought of Lennon's killer reentered my mind. "I haven't seen you since the night after the killing, now, with me going to the courthouse, ready to kill that monster, you reappear..."

The gun re-emerged in my mind. *This orange glowing ball is something evil, and it wants me.* My eyes met the orange ball, it appeared to grow brighter. "You aren't going to take me, I won't let you!"

My right hand gripped around the gun in my pocket; I pulled it out. Holding the gun against my temple, my tears flowed like a running river. *This must be the only way out of this mess, the only way to not let this thing take me.* A deafening *buzzing* noise echoed in the night.

"Ah, shit," I cried as I fell to my knees. The orange glowing ball expanded in size and turned a red color. I suddenly felt my finger slowly pulling the trigger, yet, I didn't think I was pulling it. The light quickly changed back to orange and my finger eased off the trigger, just as the *buzzing* became more intense. A bright light shot out, blinding me. The gun fell out of my hand; it hit the sidewalk. I screamed but I couldn't even hear myself. *This is it, the orange ball has taken me, this must be death... can you Imagine?*

Chapter 5

My eyes slowly blinked open. My head hurt and my mind felt fuzzy. It took me a few minutes before I realized that I was in a bed. Two people stood over me, a man in a white overcoat and a woman in scrubs. The man in the white coat smiled at me. "Hello, how are you feeling?"

"Huh?"

"Do you know your name?" I didn't respond because I actually couldn't think of my name. The man in the white coat looked over at the woman in scrubs. He whispered something to her and turned back to me. He pulled out a small flashlight and shined them into my eyes as he held open my eyelids.

The woman in scrubs bent down to me, gently grabbing my hand. "Hello, sir, would you like a drink or some food?"

I licked my lips and remembered my favorite snack. "Can I get some *M&M's*, please?"

The woman in scrubs smiled. "Sure."

As she walked away, the rest of my memory came back.

"Are you a doctor?" I asked.

The man in the white coat, who had been looking over some papers, glanced up at me. "Why, yes, I am. You are in a hospital. People found you lying on the side of a street."

"Lennon..." I mumbled under my breath.

The doctor adjusted his glasses and stepped over to the side of my bed. "What was that? Is your name Lennon?"

"Ah, no, I do remember my name. I'm Joe Miller."

"Well, Joe Miller, do you remember what happened to you?"

Footsteps caught my attention. I glanced behind the doctor to see the woman in scrubs returning. "Here you go, sir." She handed me a pack of M&M's. "Here's the candy you requested." She also handed me a foam cup. "I also grabbed you a cup of water."

"Thank you so much." I took a sip of the water; it tasted pure and cold. I ripped open the bag of M&M's.

"So Joe," the doctor leaned closer to me. "What do you last remember?"

I dumped a handful of M&M's out and something I saw disturbed me. "Hey, miss, you gave me an old bag of M&M's. I can't eat this, I could get sick."

The woman in scrubs tilted her head to her right side; she looked dumbfounded. "Ah, I assure you they won't make you sick and they shouldn't be old."

I grabbed a hold of one red M&M, holding it up. "See, this is old. The red ones are banned because of the red dye causing cancer."

The woman in scrubs shrugged, looking at the doctor. He gestured with his hand to let her know he would take care of this. Pushing his glasses back on his face, the doctor stepped closer. "Eh, Joe. The red dye ban lasted from 1976 to 1987. That's all."

"Huh?"

"What I mean is the red *M&M's* are safe to eat. They've been back for a long time."

I threw the bag of *M&M's;* it smacked against the wall, candy pieces splattered in every direction. "I don't know what the fuck you are talking about!" I screamed, grabbing a handful of my hair. "It's only 1981, Doc. What in the hell do you mean they brought the red ones back in 1987? You don't make any sense!"

The doctor whispered in the woman's ear. She ran out of the room and the doctor approached me once more. "Joe, you think the year is 1981?"

Scratching my head, I replied, "It is 1981. It has been for the last six months."

The doctor sighed and walked over to the wall. Bending down, he grabbed the bag of *M&M's.* "Here, Joe. Take a look at this." He brought the bag toward my face, his finger pointed to something printed on the package. "This is the best by date for this candy package."

The doctor dropped the wrapper into my hands. I twisted the bag around, searching for the date. *Best By December 2023*. "Who knew *M&M's* could last this long," I said, glancing up at the doctor.

"No, Joe. The year now is 2023, it's May 2023."

I laughed, while throwing a handful of the M&M's in my mouth (I purposely made sure not to eat any of the red ones). "What is this? An episode of the *Twilight*

Zone? It's June 1981, not May 2099 or whatever year you said."

"2023, Joe. It's the year 2023. I'm not kidding you."

These people are playing a joke on me. Or this is some wild dream. The woman walked over to the window and she opened the blinds. The warm rays of the sun shone bright on my face. My eyes squinted out the window to the sun. The bright light hurt my eyes, but I didn't look away, I focused on the sun, on that orange glowing ball...

"Are you okay?"

I glanced up to see the woman walking over to my bed, reaching her hand out to touch my shoulder. "Ugh, yeah, lady. I think I might need some more water."

The woman smirked. "Well, sir, you can call me Nurse, Nurse Williams. No need for the lady stuff."

"Sorry, Nurse Williams."

Nurse Williams smiled. "No problem. I'll go get you another water."

The nurse left and my mind immediately went to the mysterious orange glowing ball that I kept seeing. *Did the orange ball kill me? Is this the afterlife? Are these people the products of this thing?*

"Joe, you must remember something, don't you? It will help us a lot... and yourself if you can tell me what you remember last."

"Ah, well, I remember the orange glowing ball in the sky."

The doctor adjusted his glasses as he shot me a confused look. "Are you talking about the sun?" He turned and pointed out the window.

"No, this orange glowing ball would be out at night, as well," I said. "There was some sort of evil energy coming off it, especially when it turned red. The evil seemed especially strong the night Lennon died-"

"How old are you, Joe?"

"I'm twenty-three, just had a birthday in May."

The doctor adjusted his glasses. "Well, Joe. That would mean you were born in 2000."

"2000?" I asked.

"What day is your birthday, Joe?"

My head hurt from this conversation, something truly wasn't right. "It's May 14, that's my birthday."

The doctor pointed over to my wall, I glanced over to see a whiteboard. "Well, then, you haven't quite turned twenty-three yet. Today's date is the ninth of May." My mouth felt dry, I let out an irritating cough. Sure enough, the whiteboard said May 9.

It can't be May 9, it's June, it must be… right?

"Joe, are you on any type of drug? It's okay if you are, I just need you to be honest with me."

I jumped out of my bed, startling the doctor. "I don't know what the hell is going on!" The doctor stepped toward me, I grabbed a bedpan that lay next to my bed. "Stay away from me, you mind controller!" I threw the bedpan, but the doctor blocked it beautifully. "It's 1981, red *M&M's* are fucking banned. John Lennon was recently killed by a fat fuck who stalked him." Nurse Williams and a few other nurses ran into the room. "I was at the Dakota, I saw Lennon get killed, then after the monster's court date, I wanted to end my life, but the orange fucking glow stopped me!"

Two men in security guard uniforms entered the room. I backed up to the far corner of the room. Glancing around at all the nervous, yet strange faces, I felt like a zebra being surrounded by a pack of lions.

"Please, Joe, I need you to lie back down," the doctor said. He reached his hand back and Nurse Williams placed a needle in his hand. *These people are going to drug me and knock me out. I can't let this happen.* This was what I thought, and it scared the shit out of me.

"Joe." The doctor inched closer, "You need to get back into your bed."

"This isn't my bed!" I shouted. "My bed is in the Bronx, back in 1981!"

The doctor nodded at the two security guards. They rushed me, knocking me back into the wall. The hit took my breath away. I must admit, they got me good. Nurse Williams grabbed ahold of my left arm, twisting it over. She rubbed what smelled like rubbing alcohol on my arm, directly over a vein.

"You sons a bitches, get off of me, now!"

My pleas didn't work. The doctor brought the long needle to my arm. "This won't hurt, Joe. Just relax, this is for your own good."

"Lier! You're probably a communist!" The next thing I knew, I felt a sharp pinch on my arm. The doctor certainly lied, and you know what? It hurt like hell. "Ah, shit!" Everything became hazy for a split second, and then blackness...

"How are you feeling, Joe?"

"Ugh," my eyes slowly blinked open. In front of me stood the doctor and the nurse, a true case of Deja Vu. "You drugged me, you son of a-"

"I had to sedate you, you were acting psychotic," the doctor snapped. "Are you feeling better?"

I went to sit up and felt a tug at my right wrist. "Huh?" My eyes discovered my wrist was handcuffed to the bed. "Now, what in God's name is this?"

"This is for yours and our protection, Joe," Nurse Williams said as she walked over toward me. I noticed she held a cup in her hand. The cup had a long straw shoved in it. "Here's some water. Please, take a drink."

"I'm not drinking anything from you people, nothing at all!"

"Well, then, Joe." The doctor stood above me, "Then I suppose we will have to stick you with another needle to administer the IV so you don't dehydrate."

The idea of these people sticking me with another needle shot a shiver down my spine. "Here, I'll drink it." Nurse Williams handed me the cup and I drank the entire cup in less than a minute. The water tasted great, and the ice made the water deliciously cold.

"Now, Joe, I need you to talk to this gentleman here." The doctor pointed to the corner of the room. Leaning against the wall stood a man in a nice fitted suit. A toothpick wiggled in the man's mouth, I didn't even realize he stood there when I woke back up. "This gentleman is a detective, he'd like to hear your story."

"A detective? Why in the hell do I have to talk to Dick Tracy over here?"

The detective chuckled as he pushed himself off of the walk. "The names actually Detective Wallace. It's nice to meet you, Joe Miller."

"Well, it's not nice to meet you. I want to get out of this bed, and I want this handcuff off of my wrist."

Detective Wallace nodded at the doctor, and he and Nurse Williams left the room. The door shut and Detective Wallace turned to face me once more. "Look here, Joe. I need to sort through this situation that you found yourself in. Why were you lying in the middle of the street? What type of drug did you take?"

These questions pissed me off. "No, I didn't take any drugs and I already told the doctor what I remember."

"Joe, they found you with no pulse. The doctor ran a bunch of tests, and you are as healthy as a horse. You remarkably wake back up with slight memory loss but no other symptoms." Detective Wallace leaned forward, causing the wrinkles on his forehead to shoot out at me. "What did you take? We need to know to make sure there won't be any side effects later on for you."

I sipped through my straw, hoping to get another drop of water, but received none. "Can you call my nurse to get me more water? I'm extremely thirsty."

"Is this a side effect to the drug you took, you think?" Detective Wallace asked.

This far-out cop doesn't get it, he really doesn't get it. "Please, Detective... ugh-"

"Wallace, Detective Wallace."

"Ah, yeah. Detective Wallace. I swear I haven't taken any drugs. It's the orange glowing ball in the sky... and John Lennon..."

"John Lennon?"

"Yeah!" I screamed. "John Lennon, his murder made the orange ball in the sky go crazy! It must have taken me and shot me out in your time."

"What do you mean, my time?"

I let out a big sigh. "I'm from the year 1981, but the doctor told me that it's the year 2023. Unless he lied to me."

The detective's face cringed. He glanced back toward the shut room door and back to me. "Wait, so you truly believe you're from the year 1981?"

"I don't believe it, I know it."

Detective Wallace suddenly gave me a weird smile. "Okay, Joe. I hope you have a wonderful day." He promptly turned and walked out of my room. I scratched my head with my free hand, wondering why he would smile and leave like that.

The detective opened the door and walked outside my room. He only shut the door halfway, and I heard his conversation with the doctor. "He's not on any drug, he's just got a screw loose upstairs. Give him some dope and send him off to the looney bin."

I shook my head in disgust. The detective pushed me hard to find out what *drug* I was on to help *save* my life. Yet, when he thought I was crazy, he wanted to put me on a drug. The doctor answered back, but he spoke too softly for me to hear. Footsteps led away from my room and the doctor opened my door. "Look, Joe, I have to send you for some tests."

"Tests?"

"Yeah, I have to find out if there is some sort of trauma to your brain that we can fix. Or, just see if there is some underlying problem because it is 2023, not 1981. If you are not playing a joke and truly believe you're from the past, then they will lock you up in the funny house," the doctor snapped.

I couldn't do anything, so I accepted all the tests the doctor gave me. These tests were weird, man. They made me lie down on this table and it moved, sliding me inside of this large machine. Inside they took photos of my brain, I guess. They also took a bunch of blood to run tests and even my pee. As I felt worn down from what I believed to be a loss of blood, they took me to a small room and told me to *lie down on the couch.* That's exactly what I did. In walked another doctor, but this time a psychiatrist.

"Hello, Joe, are you comfortable?"

As I placed my left arm behind my head. The psychiatrist sat down in a chair that sat across from the couch. "Ah, yeah, I guess I am pretty comfortable."

"Good." The psychiatrist held a big yellow pad. He seemingly jotted something down on that big yellow pad. "Joe, can you tell me about your childhood?"

"My childhood?"

"Yes," the psychiatrist replied. "Did you have a pleasant childhood? Or was it painful? For example, did your father drink and beat you? Did an older brother pick on you and beat you up every day?"

The psychiatrist's questions baffled me. I busted out in a sarcastic laugh. The psychiatrist didn't even look up from his big yellow pad. He just kept writing. "No, first off, I am an only child. And second, my father wasn't an alcoholic."

"And your mother?"

This question touched home. I never liked to talk about my mother. "Don't know her and don't care." I sat up on the couch, my face felt hot by now, it must have been redder than all hell by this point.

The psychiatrist never looked up from his big yellow pad; he continued to write. "Tell me, why don't you care to know your mother?"

My head involuntarily turned away from the psychiatrist... I truly don't like to talk about my mother. "Because she ran out on my father and me when I was only five. She didn't give two shits about her only child." I sat up on my knees, glaring at the psychiatrist. He still kept his eyes stuck on that big yellow pad. "Tell me, Doc, why should I care about her?"

"Um-hmm."

"Um-hmm?" I belted. "What in the hell is that supposed to mean?"

The psychiatrist's eyes focused on his big yellow pad. "What I mean is, maybe the reason you fainted and woke up confused is because of the stress your mother brought to you when she left your father and yourself."

This crazy doctor may be right... The psychiatrist knew how to get into my head. This dick twisted my feelings around and got me thinking my mother fucked me up in life. You know what? She most certainly did. But in this case, he's so fucking wrong. "Okay, Doc, shut up!" I jumped off the couch, slamming hard just before his chair.

The psychiatrist finally lowered the big yellow pad and locked his eyes onto mine. "Well, Joe. I finally found what made you lose consciousness. And the reason you had memory problems when you first woke up. It's because of your ill relationship with your mother."

"My ill relationship with my mother?" I said. "That's the stupidest shit I ever heard. I told you, I don't know that bitch because she left when I was five."

"That's why you hurt... your own mother left and abandoned you when you were only five. That isn't an easy thing to overcome. It has clearly affected your way of thinking..."

I sprang up off the couch, pointing my finger directly into his beady bright green eyes. "You have no idea what in the hell you are talking about! This has nothing to do with my mom. This has to do with..." My voice changed from loud and fierce to soft and gentle. "John Lennon... the orange glowing ball..."

"Excuse me?" the psychiatrist asked as he sat up. "Did you say John Lennon?"

"Ah-"

"Orange glowing ball?" The psychiatrist mumbled to himself.

"Ah, no. Not John Lennon, Ron Lemon, just like the fruit, you see?" I lied through my stupid grin.

This entire experience wore me out I didn't want to participate anymore. Someway, somehow that bright glowing orange ball sucked me in and shot me out into the future. These people would never believe me, this was certain. My best-case scenario with these *doctors* would end up putting me in a padded cell. Nah, I would have to change my gameplay, gather myself, and lie.

"Ron Lemon? Who is this?" The psychiatrist asked.

I stood only a couple of feet from the psychiatrist as of now, twiddling my thumbs. "Ah, he's an old childhood friend of mine."

"Oh, and has something happened between you two?"

I had to think of something fast. The first thing that entered my mind was an episode of the TV show, *The Brady Bunch*. "Yes, something happened. I liked this girl and wanted to go out with her. I even broke up with another girl I'd been seeing for a short amount of time. Well, days before my date, Ron threw a football and it smacked me in the face, breaking my nose."

"Oh, my," the psychiatrist gasped.

"Yeah, and the worst part was that after the girl saw my nose, she didn't want to go out with me anymore and Ron started to date my crush. So yeah, that's about it."

Now, the psychiatrist's eyes locked on me. I wasn't sure if he bought my story or not. Let's hope he wasn't a *Brady Bunch* fan (Marsha, Marsha, Marsha).

"Okay, Joe. Tell me, after this incident, what happened? Did you stop talking to Ron? Did this incident turn you to drugs?"

I sat back down on the couch, and a bead of sweat dripped from my head. "Yeah, you got me, I smoked a lot of *Mary Jane* after that fight and it led me to my blackout. But I'm good now, everything is groovy."

"Groovy, Joe?"

"Yeah, I'm fine. I promise to stay off the *Mary Jane* from now on."

The psychiatrist jotted fiercely on his big yellow pad. "Um-hm." A sudden stoppage in writing made me sit up straight on the couch. "Tell me, Joe. What is this orange glowing ball? Also, tell me the impact that John Lennon has had on your life?"

Slouching back down onto the couch, I rubbed my eyes. *This needs to end, I want to go to bed.* "There isn't no orange ball... I kept staring at the sun when I was high, that's all." I pushed myself back up, sitting upright once more. "And John Lennon is a great musician. I love his songs and love *The Beatles*... that's all."

"Um-hmm," the psychiatrist mumbled as he flipped a page in his big yellow pad to write on another.

"I'm really tired. I'd like to go back to my room and lie down, can I?"

"Sure, Joe." The psychiatrist stood up and walked over to the door. He opened it and called for a guy named *Bud*. A large stocky fellow entered the room; he wore a security uniform. "Joe, you can follow Bud, he will take you to your room."

Bud led me to my room. As we walked down the hallway, it seemed as if every nurse stopped to watch me. This made me feel awkward and eager to leave.

Chapter 6

The doctor came into my room about half an hour after Bud led me back. He wanted to check my vitals, and everything looked good. A few different nurses stopped in to give me a snack or a pop. I felt tired, but I didn't sleep; my mind raced. *Come on, Joe. This is a dream; you have to wake up!* I stood at the window, opening a section of the blinds with my fingers. Peering outside, I took in the view.

It was hard to see much because of it being dark, but with some light coming off the buildings across the street I recognized that I, in fact, was in a big city. Now I had to figure out which city these people took me to. It could be New York but I didn't recognize a few of the other buildings outside my window.

I flopped down on my bed and looked all around. *Wow, is that a TV?* Up on the wall hung what appeared to be a flat rectangular TV. This wowed me, I've only seen large box television sets. I walked over to the wall; the TV hung too far up on the wall that I couldn't reach it. *How in the hell do I turn this thing on?*

My door creaked open from behind me and a young nurse walked in. "Hello, Joe. May I assist you with anything?"

I turned to see the nurse, she had flowing blonde hair and the brightest blue eyes I'd ever seen. My face instantly became hot, I lowered my hand from reaching up toward the TV. "Ah, yeah. I wanted to turn this, ah, television on."

The young nurse giggled. "Here, silly." The young nurse walked over to my bed. On the left side rail hung a device, she pulled it off the rail and it appeared to be attached by a cord. "Your remote is here, just click the power button."

Wow, I had a buddy whose family had a television remote, but my family has never been so lucky. I slowly walked over to the nurse, still blushing. "Okay, thank you, ma'am."

The young nurse giggled again. "Oh, please, Joe. Call me Nurse Brown."

"Okay, Nurse Brown it is." My smile felt like it stretched from ear to ear. Now Nurse Brown blushed. I decided to end the brief, awkward silence by asking more about this bedside remote. "How does this thing truly work?"

A dumbfounded look formed on her face. "Well, Joe, it's like any other remote, really." She pointed to the buttons. My eyes reluctantly left her beautiful blue eyes and followed to the remote. "This is your power button. These here are your volume, and these are your channel buttons."

I saw a button toward the top that read *DVD*. "What's this button do?"

Nurse Brown chuckled. "It's the *DVD* button, silly."

I scratched my head, not sure what in the hell a *DVD* was. "Ah, and what does it do?"

She lowered the remote and that dumbfounded expression returned to her face. "Joe, really?" I nodded and she continued. "It gives you the option to play a *DVD* movie if you brought any. We, unfortunately, don't have any *DVD's* on hand here at the hospital."

"Oh, okay, groovy," I said, acting like I understood. I certainly did not.

She giggled once more. "Groovy? You're funny, Joe." Nurse Brown aimed the remote at the TV, turning it on. She flipped through the channels. "What would you like to watch? I'll turn it on for you."

Scratching my head, I didn't answer, just made some *groaning* noises as I stared at the TV.

"Um, how about *ESPN*?" Nurse Brown asked.

I snapped out of my little trance. "Yeah, *ESPN* works."

The TV stopped on *ESPN* and a *Ford* truck commercial blared from the flat rectangular TV. "Financing options are available, get your new *2024 Ford F150* today!"

The voice from the commercial startled me. "A 2024 *Ford*? It really can't be the future," I whispered.

Nurse Brown leaned closer. "What did you say, Joe?"

"Ah, nothing. Just remarking on the 2024 truck in, ah, 2023."

"Yeah, they always come out with next year's model when it's still the previous year," Nurse Brown said. "Joe, I originally came in to check your vitals. May I?"

I nodded and jumped into my bed. The sweet nurse took my vitals (perfect) and she left the room (not before giving me a big smile). Now, back in my room alone, I focused on the TV. The television program returned, and I saw a familiar face, yet something seemed off.

"Welcome back to *Outside the Lines* with yours truly, *Bob Ley.*"

Shit, that is Bob Ley, yet he's old looking. Damn, I really must be in the future. I needed to leave this hospital and find the orange glowing ball in the sky. That mysterious ball of light led me to the future, and that meant there must be a way to get back... I hoped.

My mind raced, thinking of the orange glowing ball, to John Lennon, to the fat monster reading *The Catcher in the Rye,* to the beautiful Nurse Brown, to my father... *shit, I need to find my dad, I must find him. But how? How will I find my pops?* As I pondered this question, I finally fell asleep.

I woke up refreshed as the sun shined through the bent blinds (they became bent when I peeked out the window last night). The beautiful and warm sun had just enough space to shine in on my face; the warming rays comforted me. On my flat rectangular TV, I now watched the game show *Jeopardy.* But this wasn't the *Art Fleming* show that I remembered. In 1975, *Jeopardy* got canceled. In 1978 they brought it back with the name-*All-New Jeopardy!* (That version was canceled the following year in 1979). The version I watched now had a gentleman named *Alex Trebek* hosting. I can't lie, this man blew *Art Fleming* away as a host.

College kids played on the show this week as the program claimed this to be college week. These kids told the host they would be graduating next year: the year 2010. This blew my mind. Here I am, from the year 1981, which, a part of me still didn't believe it wasn't 1981, and I'm watching a show from 2010, a re-run, a show from my current past, yet, my distant future... trippy, man. I still felt like this must be some wild dream. I kept waiting to wake up, but the dream never seemed to end.

"Good morning, Joe."

Two knocks at the door messed up my *Jeopardy* watching. In walked my doctor. "Hey, Doc. Say, what is your name anyway?"

The doctor smiled. "I thought I told you, but maybe I didn't. I'm Doctor Foster."

"Okay, Doctor Foster. When can I leave this place?"

Doctor Foster walked over to me, pulling at his stethoscope. "Should be soon, just need to perform a few more tests." He held the stethoscope up in front of my face. "Can you lift your shirt, Joe? I want to listen to your heart and breathing."

"Sure, Doc." I did what he asked and pulled my shirt up.

He placed the cold stethoscope against my chest and again on my back. "Everything sounds good, Joe. I'll see you later on today."

As Doctor Foster stepped out of my room, I yelled for him to come back. "Hey, Doc! Seriously, when will I be able to leave? I'm tired of being here."

He adjusted his glasses, observing me. "I will be honest with you, Joe." Doctor Foster shut the door behind him. "You're in perfect health, and if it was up to me, I'd release you right now."

"Well, who is it up to?" I asked as I sat up in my bed.

Doctor Foster sighed. "It's up to the authorities."

"Those punk cops are the reason why I can't leave?" I asked.

"No, not them specifically, and not the cops in general."

I sat on the edge of my bed, with a dumbfounded expression on my face. "Then, please, Doc. Who are these *authorities* that won't let me leave?"

Doctor Foster approached my bed, he kneeled down to become face-to-face with me. "It's the FBI, Joe. They are trying to figure out who you are."

I turned to glance out the window. It baffled me that I would be linked to the FBI.

Doctor Foster whispered, "No one truly knows who you are, Joe. People found you, yet, your fingerprints are matching someone who should be sixty-five years old."

"Jesus."

"I was told," Doctor Foster continued his whisper. "The feds ran a background check on the supposed sixty-five-year-old man your fingerprints are matching, and the guy vanished back in 1981." Doctor Foster stood up, stretching his back. "The missing person is Joe Miller, the same person who you are acting like. You stole his identity, and they won't let you leave till you confess who you truly are..." Doctor Foster turned and glared out the window. "Well, they might let you leave here, to take you to prison."

"Prison?" I bellowed. "I didn't steal no one's identity! I am Joe Miller and I time-traveled to this date. I've already told you that!"

"No one believes your damn story! All the tests came back normal. You are not crazy, you are not sick. This shit is serious, and if you don't come clean about who you are, then you probably will spend the rest of your life in a federal prison!"

I rolled over in my bed, facing away from the doctor. *This is crazy! Not only have I somehow traveled to the future, but now in the future, they might throw me in jail.* This thought ran over and over in my head. "Doc, why do you even care what happens to me?"

"Because, you're my patient, and as a patient of mine, I want what's best for you."

I didn't say another word, just stared hopelessly at the wall. After a minute, Doctor Foster left my room. Right after Doctor Foster left, I jumped out of bed and ran over to my door, closing it shut. I wanted to be alone, and good thing I closed the door. Standing outside my room were two men in black suits. These men must have been from the FBI...

Later that night, around eleven, I lay in my bed watching the TV. I searched through the channels, and I must say, this TV had so many more channels than I ever remembered. My TV back home, and apparently back in 1981, had ten channels. Four major channels and the remaining six were all local channels. This TV here in the hospital had over two hundred channels...

unbelievable. While clicking through most of the channels, I found one that I particularly liked. The channel's name was *TV Land*. It played all the shows I remembered watching, yet it claims that these shows are all *oldies* and *classics*.

"Ha-ha," I laughed while sipping my ginger ale and watching one of my favorite TV shows: *Three's Company.* Two knocks rang out my door, I jumped as the knocks startled me.

To my surprise, I saw the beautiful Nurse Brown standing at my entrance. "Hello, Joe. I'm so sorry, I didn't mean to frighten you."

"Oh, no, you didn't scare me, not at all," I lied through my teeth. "So let me guess, you need to take my vitals?"

Nurse Brown waved her hands. "Oh, no. I just started my shift and wanted to pop in and say hi." She smiled brightly at me. "So hi, Joe."

I smiled back. "Hi, Nurse Brown. Thank you for stopping in."

She walked closer to me. As Nurse Brown reached my bed, she grabbed my hand and held it tight. "Joe." She leaned to my ear, speaking in a soft tone. "I wanted to warn you that two cops are on constant watch of your room... you're not alone..."

The hair on my neck stood up. On the TV, a commercial came on and it showed a few cartoon characters talking about diabetes and the medicine to help it. In the commercial, a bright orange glowing ball bounced around the cartoon characters... I turned to Nurse Brown, I felt her warm breath on my face. "I know..."

The next morning, I woke up to a bunch of commotion and action. The two cops in suits that stood outside my room busted into my room. "Time to get up, Joe. You've been here long enough. You need to come with us now."

The two men grabbed me, lifting me up from my bed. "Hey, who in the fuck are you guys? Where are you taking me?"

"We work with the FBI." Both men held out their badges; Special Agent Jones and Special Agent Carter.

"Shit, can I take a piss before we leave?" I snarled. Sure enough, the agents let me take that piss, but after, they placed me into a black van and told me to relax.

The FBI agents drove me down to Washington, D.C., to the FBI headquarters. They took me into a cold cell; the air conditioner appeared to be on high. They left me alone with a foam cup of water, yet, inside the cup, little black pieces of dirt floated around. The light that hung above my head flickered on and off. This clearly was their way of breaking me down.

"We aren't fucking with you!" Special Agent Jones slammed his fist on the table, knocking over my dirty cup of water.

The water splashed out, I watched as it ran down and off the table. *Like you, water, I must find a way to escape...*

"Are you with us? Or are you just plain stupid?" Special Agent Carter snapped his fingers in front of my head, snapping me out of my trance.

I held my hands up in a *defensive* manner. "Please, guys, let me go. I haven't done shit wrong."

Special Agent Carter grabbed my left wrist, twisting it. He pushed my face into the table. I saw a flash of bright light from the impact of my head crashing into the table. Everything became hazy, the bright flash of light returned, but it appeared to be off in the distance, blackness surrounded the light. The light grew, and it turned into an orange color. A loud *buzz* pierced my ears... something moved...

A figure stood in the light; it started to walk toward me. "Hello? Who are you?" I screamed but received no answer. As the figure slowly ambled my way, the distinct sound of footsteps gave me gooseflesh. "Please, answer me! Who are you? Where am I?" The loud buzz grew even louder, as did the footsteps. The figure stepped up to me. Still, the figure appeared black, as if this person stood in the shadows. "Ah, please, I don't want to die..."

The buzzing sound suddenly ceased. An eerie, familiar voice spoke to me. "I won't hurt you. Here, can you sign my album?"

John Lennon's *Double Fantasy* album appeared in the light directly in front of me. Written on the album, over the photo of Yoko Ono, was the signature of John Lennon and a date that read: 1980.

I glanced up from the album and a face shot out from the shadows. The face belonged to the fat monster. A devilish smile was plastered on his face... "Ah!" I screamed.

"Do you hear me, you piece of scum!" The face of the monster quickly changed into Special Agent Carter's face. I observed my surroundings and realized I sat in the cold cell with the flickering light. My head lay on the table and pressure grew on my back and neck. *These bastards slammed my head against that table, I must have blacked out and imagined the orange light and the monster.*

"Your little faggot ass is going to spend the rest of your life in a federal prison if you don't tell us the truth," Special Agent Jones yelled. "You want that? Huh, bitch?"

Special Agent Jones pulled my face off the table and a numbness overtook the right side of my face. "I-I'm not lying. I promise to you, I didn't steal anyone's identity."

"Can you believe this faggot?" Special Agent Carter laughed. "This puny little bitch won't last a day in prison."

"Yeah, you're right," Special Agent Jones chimed in. "They will eat him alive, make him their girlfriend." Both agents laughed; my bottom lip trembled. "If you don't tell us where you put the body of the real Joe Miller, that's exactly what's going to happen to you."

"I told both of you, I didn't steal any identity, or kill anyone. Now let me leave!"

Special Agent Carter grabbed my arm. As he twisted my arm, I moved my body up and off the chair. With my right hand, I grabbed Special Agent Carter's shoulder, pushing him into the table. His head bounced off the table and his hair popped off. "Ha-ha." I laughed at the sight of this man's toupee falling off. My laughter didn't last long as a strong sensation of pain entered my once numb right side of my face.

My knees buckled and I fell over Special Agent Carter's unconscious body. On my way to the ground, in a haze, I saw the extended arm of Special Agent Jones. Before I knew anything else, everything went black...

Chapter 7

"Ugh." I woke up on a hard metal cot. No mattress lay beneath me. My head ached, and my jaw burned. I touched the right side of my face, the pain quickly intensified as I realized my jaw must have swollen two sizes.

"Rise and shine, roomie." A voice appeared from below me, and I didn't respond. "I hear you mumbling up there. Why don't you come down and introduce yourself?"

It then hit me that those agents placed me in a jail cell. I found the door to the room, a tiny window graced the top, and thick steel made up the remainder of the door. I swung my legs to the edge of the cot; they dangled off like two vines swaying in the wind. A vibration from underneath my ass startled me as I pulled my legs back up on the cot. A bald head appeared, coming up from the edge of my cot. "Who are you? What do you want?"

The bald head lifted up, and a grizzly-looking face met mine. The man's face sported a large scar from his temple down to his beard. "Why are you acting like such a pussy? I'm your new roomie, and I won't hurt you if you follow these simple rules..." This man's face and voice struck a nerve in me. He gave me the same feeling as the monster I met outside of the Dakota. "Rule number one, this is my room and whatever I say goes. If you're on the toilet taking a shit and I have to shit, you need to get up and move. Oh, and don't shit on my floor, you hold it in till I'm finished."

I sat back in the cot, hitting the wall behind me, trying not to make eye contact with this grizzly man.

"Rule number two, at breakfast, lunch, and dinner, you will sit with me. If I want something off your tray, you will give it to me."

My hands rubbed through my hair. *This man is crazy, I can't live with him.*

The grizzly man pushed himself up farther on my cot, exposing his large and cut muscles. "Rule number three, any commissary you receive will become mine, everything you own will become mine. Do we have an understanding, roomie?"

My head slowly nodded, seemingly on its own. "Yes."

"Good boy. Now lie the fuck back down and keep quiet. I'm going to take a nap."

I listened to the grizzly man and flopped back down on the hard and cold cot. Rolling on my right side, I faced the cement wall and cried. My entire life changed in a flash of light... an orange, glowing light. I wanted out of this cell, out of this future existence and back to my time, back in my bed.

"Hey! You better stop crying, or I'll come up there and beat the pulp out of you!" the grizzly man's voice roared. "I told you I'm trying to sleep!"

"Ah, sorry," I whispered. My crying didn't cease, but I held it in, trying to be as quiet as a mouse.

Titan Frey

After what seemed to be hours, I finally fell asleep. Just as my mind shut down, a loud scream woke me up. "All right, you maggots, it's roll call. Get up, put your pants on and approach your doors!"

I rolled over on my uncomfortable cot and found an intercom speaker up in the back corner of the cell. My cot shook as the grizzly man jumped out of his bed. *Damn, these bunk beds don't seem too safe.*

"Hey, you little bitch, you better get down here. If you aren't at the door when the guard comes, they will put our cell on lockdown." The grizzly man's eyes narrowed. "If we get put on lockdown, I'll choke you in your sleep."

Of course, I didn't argue, I jumped down off of my cot. The grizzly man's bare back faced me, he had muscles on top of muscles in his back. I inched toward the door, stopping a couple of steps behind my new *roomie.* A loud snap echoed in our room. It sounded like a bolt being unlocked. The door slowly opened and a pack of four guards stood outside our room.

The guard up front held a baton in his hand, the guard in the far back held up a gun. "Alright, Casey, turn around and put your fist together."

The grizzly man turned around and his evil eyes met mine.

"You turn around too, newbie."

I glanced up to see one of the other guards yelling at me. Before I could turn myself around, the guard

90

grabbed and twisted me. He locked some cuffs on my wrist, they were tight as hell, but I didn't complain.

The guards dragged me, and my grizzly roomie named Casey out of our cell. They marched us down this eerie hallway. The lights above flickered in the same manner as the light in the FBI interrogation room. In the tiny windows of every cell door, eyes peered out, meeting me. Finally, the small hallway opened, and I saw the cafeteria to my right. We didn't go to the cafeteria, though (I could've used something to eat, to be honest), we kept walking, going in and out two doors.

After walking through the second door, I came face to face with another door. The guard opened the door and sunlight shone near my feet. The beautiful and bright orange light gave me a sense of happiness, yet sorrow as well. I really don't like any bright orange light.

"Stay out of trouble, you two. We will come back and get you when we're done," the guard said, slamming the door in my face.

As I stood underneath the rays of the sun, I could sense my roomie's eyes on the back of my neck. I turned to find him staring me down. "Ah, what did he mean, when they are done?" I politely asked.

"Ugh," Casey grunted. "Those fucks always do a cell check once a new inmate enters the cell. I guess they want to check and make sure I don't have any shanks to use on you."

The idea of the guards searching our cell gave me a sense of relief after hearing that statement. "Oh." I cleared my throat, watching Casey, my grizzly companion. "So, your name is Casey? My name is Joe, it's nice-"

"I don't give a fuck if your name is Barack Obama, don't talk to me unless I talk to you first!"

Barack Obama?

I stood alone now, which was quite alright with me. Looking around, I observed the area. A basketball court sat toward the south of the yard. Across from the basketball court were a bunch of old dumbbells and weight benches. An old concrete set of bleachers resided directly behind me. I walked over to the benches and sat down. Casey and I were the only two in the yard. He went straight to the weights, something I wasn't willing to do. I didn't want to show him how weak I was.

Why me? Why did the orange glowing ball pick me? This thought replayed in my mind. I sat on the concrete bleachers for another hour before three guards walked out into the yard. They screamed and told me to get inside. The guards pushed me into my cell, and I found Casey's mattress had been flipped and thrown in the middle of the cell. The guards also scattered all of Casey's possessions around the tiny cell.

As I stood looking around at the mess, one guard pushed me in the back. I flew across the cell, tripping over the overturned mattress. "Hey," I belted.

"Okay, newbie," a husky, bald guard said as he approached me. The guard held up something long and sharp in his right hand. "I'm going to ask you one time, and one time only." The guard's eyes narrowed. "If I have to repeat myself, I'll beat the piss out of you. Then, I'll send you to the hole for a couple months." I shook my head and the guard pointed at the object in his hand. "Is this shank yours? Or is it Casey's?"

"Ah, it's not mine-"

"Speak the fuck up! I swear I'll stab you myself!"

"It's not mine! I just got here at this jail, it isn't mine at all."

The guard smiled, a gold tooth in the front of his smile twinkled in the light. "Good boy. That bastard Casey will rot in the hole. Now, clean this mess up, newbie."

Pushing myself off the ground, I dusted my pants off. The guard grabbed the door and just before the door shut, the guard turned his head back to me. "Oh, and newbie, you better watch your back. When Casey gets out, he'll kill you."

The door slammed shut, I ran to the door, slamming my fists into it. "Hey! What do you mean Casey will kill me?"

A loud bang rattled the door. "Because asshole." The guard's voice echoed from behind the door. "Casey will think you ratted him out and seek revenge."

"But I didn't!"

The guard's laughter struck a nerve in me. "Sure, newbie. I guess you don't remember telling me the shank was his. Now, clean up that fucking mess, or I'll put you in the same hole as Casey."

One last loud bang rumbled through the door. I turned to face the mess in the cell. I quickly fell to my knees, weeping uncontrollably. The light in my cell flickered, I glared up at the light. The flickering stopped, and the bright light shined down on me. In that instance, the yellowish light turned orange...

Three weeks passed and my prison life didn't get much easier. Every day I had to sit in the *white* section of the prison or risk getting the shit kicked out of me. Even though I personally never had ill feelings against another race, in prison, you MUST stick with your own *kind*. I found this out the hard way. On my third day here in prison, I sat down in an empty chair at a table where nothing but Hispanics sat. As my ass hit the chair, four of these huge Hispanics towered above me. They gave me the option to stay and get beat up or the option to run and leave my tray; that day, I went hungry.

I would lay in my cot, reading *The Catcher in the Rye*. My legs hung off the cot, resting peacefully on the floor. Ever since the guards removed Casey, I moved myself to the bottom cot, and after a week, I even received a pillow and a blanket. Things weren't too bad when I stayed in my cell. All this alone time gave me a chance to think about my situation. My alone time wouldn't last much longer.

The loud unlocking of the door's bolt interrupted my reading. I lowered my book to find the bald guard with the gold tooth; he entered my cell with a smile on his face.

"Good to see you again, bitch." His comment pissed me off, but I couldn't respond. "You're getting a new cellmate today and you two better not fight or cause problems."

My mind raced, I prayed that Casey wouldn't walk into the cell. Luckily for me, it wasn't Casey. A tall and skinny man with long greasy black hair entered my cell. "Hey man, the names Joe. Nice to meet you." I stood up and offered my hand; the tall skinny man accepted my offer.

"Lenny's the name. It's nice to meet you." Lenny and I shook hands.

As my new cellmate and I got acquainted, a bunch of giggles from the door caught our attention. "Bunch of faggots!" The guard laughed as he slammed the door.

"Ugh, I need to get out of here," I mumbled as I jumped back into my cot.

"Shit, I won't be leaving here anytime soon, I know that," Lenny said, throwing his pillow and blanket on the top cot.

Shit, Lenny already has a pillow and blanket? I sure as hell didn't. I placed the book back up to my face. "Oh, yeah? Why? What did you do?"

"Eh, man. I stole from a few Federal banks here in New York."

"Oh, shit."

"Ha, yeah. Funny, I steal from Federal banks and now I get thrown in the Federal Bureau of Prisons."

"Yeah, I guess instant karma got you, huh?" I placed the book down. "So, you say the prison I'm in right now is the Federal Bureau of Prisons?"

"Right."

"And this is in D.C.?"

Lenny scratched his head. "D.C.? Nah, dawg, we are in Brooklyn."

"Brooklyn?" I asked.

Lenny nodded as he climbed up to the top bunk. *I'm back in New York, close to my home…* I picked back up my prison-rented copy of *The Catcher in the Rye*. My hands clenched the book. *I need to get out of this jail, I need to be free. What if the orange glowing ball comes back, and I'm inside?*

Lenny's head popped down from the top, cot. "Doesn't this remind you of your childhood? Bunking up with ya brother?"

I held the book up and covered my face. "No, I am an only child. Never had bunk beds."

"Oh, well, try to look at the bright side of things, Joe."

Yeah, that's my problem. I looked at the bright, orange glowing things in life, and now look at me… I tried to focus on reading the book, not really in a talkative mood. "Yeah, I'll look at the bright things, sure."

"Say, you're reading *The Catcher in the Rye*?"

I pulled the book away from my face, turning it over to look at the cover. "Ah, yeah, I suppose I am." I turned the book back over to read, held it up against my face and chuckled. *What an idiot.*

"That's cool, dawg. The last prison I was at, I met a prisoner who also read this book and got famous from it."

I lowered the book. "He got famous from it?" My nerves jumped, an eerie sensation shot up my spine.

"Yeah, you've probably heard of him. I mean, I know you look young but I think everyone knows about this man."

"Is it..." I couldn't bring myself to say his full name out loud. And for the sake of writing this memoir, as I stated before, I would not write his name. NOT EVEN ONCE. The fat monster of a man deserves no more recognition. Lenny stated the full name of the large man I met on that unseasonably warm December night. I cringed to the mere sound of his name.

"So, you say you were cellmates with him?"

Lenny pulled himself back up to his cot. "Nah, dawg." He jumped from his cot, landing hard on the cement floor. "I think he had his own cell, for safety reasons. But they would let him out in the general pop."

"Damn..." the thought of going to the jail where the monster lived and killing him intrigued me. *He has to be the reason the orange glowing ball took me. If I kill that fat monster, maybe I can go back to my time...*

"Yeah, I even talked to him once, I asked him why he killed Lennon."

"What he say?" I screamed.

"Whoa, relax dawg." Lenny quickly jumped back up onto his cot.

Anger flew through my veins, my face felt hot. "Don't tell me to relax, I want to fucking know what that fat bastard said."

Lenny held his hands up defensively. "Whoa, dawg, chill."

"Sorry, man," I said, jumping down off the cot. "I'm really intrigued by the whole killing of Lennon. Please, tell me what he said."

Lenny scooted over to the edge of his cot, he dangled his string bean legs off the edge. "I asked him why he killed Lennon, and he said, as reported, he wanted to be famous."

Anger hit me once more, I knew there had to be more of a reason than that to kill a man. "Nothing else?"

"Well, he did say Lennon angered him by not being a fan of Jesus and some other little shit like that. Lennon was a phony, he told me, so that played a part in it too, I guess."

I sat on the floor in the middle of the cell. Lenny jumped down, inches from my legs. "Man, you seem really bummed out about this. You some hardcore *Beatles* fan or something?"

My head hurt, helplessness overtook me. "Yeah, you could say that..."

Another month passed by, and I can't lie, Lenny's not a bad cellmate to have. He's a pretty deep thinking guy. Many nights we'd stay up talking about the meaning of life and death. I even asked him once if he truly believed everyone on Earth had a purpose, and he said yes. He told me his purpose in life was to take care of his mother.

Lenny's mother was involved in a bad car crash a few years ago and is stuck in a wheelchair. The family didn't have insurance and couldn't afford the proper care. This led to Lenny's stealing of the Federal banks. I felt bad for him. Yeah, stealing is wrong, but if it's helping his mother, could you blame him?

Lenny asked me what my purpose in life was, or at least what I thought it could be. "To change the world," I said. This made Lenny laugh, but I didn't laugh. I started to realize that this orange glowing light picked me to change the world; I just didn't know how yet...

On a beautiful sunny July day, I sat outside on the bleachers, rereading *The Catcher in the Rye*. I finished the book and felt unimpressed. The book pissed me off, to be honest. I decided to read it again, hoping to find some reason of why it helped the monster want to kill Lennon. As I immersed myself into the book, I heard my name being screamed.

"Joe! Yo, Joe!"

"Yeah, man?" I lowered my book to see Lenny running up to me. He stopped and bent over, huffing and puffing. "What's wrong with you?"

"Y-you n-need to r-un."

I laughed. "Run? Now why in the hell would I need to run?"

"Because, the word is they let Casey out of the hole and he's coming for you."

"Oh, shit," I bellowed. "Where's he at now?"

"I heard he's coming from the workout area."

I stood up on the bleachers, and sure enough, big ass Casey headed my way. Two my right, near the door to go inside, two guards stood talking to each other. "Hey! Guards!" I screamed as I jumped off the bleachers.

"Pussy! You pussy!" The unpleasant voice of Casey rang in my ears.

Lenny grabbed my arm. "Shit, is that Casey?"

I nodded.

"Yeah, the rumors that he'd break you in half weren't a lie. You better get the fuck outta here, Joe."

I ran fast toward the guards, waving my arms around like a crazy person. "Hey, guards! I need your help!"

One of the guards stepped toward me, he pulled out his baton. I noticed this and tried to stop, but the guard met me by shoving the club directly into my stomach. The worst pain I've ever felt followed next. My knees buckled and I dropped to the ground. While kneeling on the ground, I quickly discovered the new *worst* pain I've ever experienced. The guard slammed his club on the back of my neck.

I blacked out from the hit and awoke sometime later. My neck and back ached as I lay on my hard cot; someone took my mattress and pillow. I sat up and a sharp pain shot through the back of my neck. *Ugh, my damn neck is spasming.* I reached back and rubbed my neck. As I worked to get the spasm out of my neck, the loud, distinct opening of the door caught my attention.

"Get the fuck up, inmate Miller!"

"Huh?" To my disgust, old bald-headed bitch of a guard stood at my cell door.

"You heard me, you scum. Get up, now!" I stood up slowly. As I walked, rubbing my neck, the guard reached out and grabbed hold of my arm, pushing me out the door. "You're so lucky, I swear," the guard mumbled as he pushed me along.

I wondered what he meant by *you're so lucky*, but before I could think, he pushed on my neck, causing the spasm to return. My neck hurt like hell, but I manned up and tried not to show any weakness. The guard led me to a small room, which was near the front of the prison.

Old baldy slammed me down into a metal chair. "Sit and keep your mouth shut till spoken too." Baldly left the room and the bolt on the door locked.

They kept me waiting in the room for over two hours. *At least this room isn't as bad as the room the FBI agents left me in*, I thought. The door swung open and in walked Special Agent Jones and Special Agent Carter. *Speak of the devils.*

Agent Carter walked in front of me as Agent Jones stood behind me. "I hope you know that you're one lucky son of a bitch," Agent Carter said.

"Ah, I am?" I scratched my head.

Agent Jones' head crept alongside me. "That's right, Joe." I leaned away. Agent Jones grabbed the back of my chair. "Looks like we will be releasing you today."

"Wha- what? You're releasing me?"

"Clean your fucking ears out, didn't you hear Agent Jones? Yes, you're getting out today," Agent Carter snarled.

My legs jumped, my toes curled, happiness overtook me. "That's awesome!"

Agent Carter's face changed to a bright red. "Damn, you're so lucky. I don't like your punk ass. So lucky..."

I jumped out of my chair and Agent Jones stepped up to me. "Slow your roll. I have to pat you down."

He motioned for me to turn around, so I did. As Agent Jones patted me down, my curiosity took over. "So, what happened? You guys finally found out I am who I say I am?"

"We don't fucking know who you really are, boy." To my left, Agent Carter power-walked up to me. He dangled his dirty finger in my face. "We have to let you out because we don't have enough evidence to hold you. We've reached our limit to keep you here."

"Oh," I mumbled.

"Don't get too happy." Agent Carter grabbed hold of my left shoulder. "We'll be watching you."

The two dumbass FBI agents walked me out of the room. They led me to a counter where a woman sat behind what appeared to be bulletproof glass. The woman gave me a bunch of papers to sign, and I signed them with my name: *Joe Miller.* Agent Carter stood behind me, he glanced over my shoulder and gasped, "Joe Miller my ass," as I signed my name. Shit, I didn't care, I just wanted out of this godforsaken prison.

After the paperwork, the woman slid me a tray of the possessions I had when I came into the prison. The only thing I had was the clothes on my back (the same outfit I wore in 1981). Lucky for me, I didn't have on my hospital gown when those FBI clowns dragged me to prison. I grabbed my clothes, and the FBI agents led me to a small bathroom. My bright orange prison uniform hit the floor quicker than the eruption of *Mount St. Helens.* Something about bright orange didn't sit well with me...

Back into my *regular* clothes, I exited the bathroom and Agent Jones held the door open for me. I walked outside and the bright orange sun hit my face. Turning around, I saw the entrance of the prison, and it felt amazing being on this side of the building.

I walked down the narrow sidewalk and glanced to my left; there sat two fences. The first fence blocked the public. About ten feet back from the first fence sat the second fence. This fence kept the prisoners inside, and I myself had leaned against that fence many times dreaming of escaping.

A bunch of the prisoners were outside, enjoying *rec* time. As I walked, I noticed my cellmate and friend, Lenny.

"Hey! Lenny!"

Lenny turned around and saw me. He waved his hands in the air as he ran up to the fence. "Yo! Joe! What in the hell are you doing on that side of the fence?"

"They let me out!" I clenched the fence, smiling. "It's been nice having you as a cellmate, Lenny!"

"Huh? It's hard to hear you, Joe!"

I cleared my throat, preparing myself to scream louder. "I said it was nice meeting you!"

"Oh, yeah! The same with you, dawg! Good luck out in the real world!"

My smile changed to a serious demeanor. "Hey, Lenny! Can you do me a solid?"

"A solid?"

"What I mean is, can you do me a favor?"

Lenny scratched his head. "Eh, sure! What's the favor, dawg?"

I cleared my throat once more. "You said you went to prison with the guy who killed John Lennon. What prison was that at?"

"Wende Correctional Facility, that's it!" Lenny screamed.

Another scream hit my ear, but this time the voice belonged to Agent Carter. "You motherfucker! Get away from that fence and leave the property! Unless you want to go back in and live there, you son of a bitch!"

My hands let go of the fence, and I took off down the sidewalk. During my entire run to get off the prison property, I never turned around...

Chapter 8

Life sometimes throws you into a predicament. Your goal is to overcome that particular predicament. In my case, life threw me a bundle of predicaments. The first predicament life threw at me was being trapped in the future. Can I adapt to this time? Will I be able to survive here? Is there a way I can get back to my time?

This seemed like a lot, and that's because it was. But unfortunately for me, that was just the start. My second predicament was staying out of prison. The first glimpse of *future* life for me was living in a prison cell. This wasn't a good example of life in an advanced time. The bozos that called themselves FBI agents said they would watch me, so I didn't believe for once that I would be a free man for good.

These are problems that could fill an entire lifetime, but again, unfortunately for me, there was more. The third predicament on the list was how to handle the *monster* who killed my idol... John Lennon. The orange glowing ball of light hand-selected me; I believe this now. It picked me to perform a task. This wasn't luck, it had to be fate. On the night of December 8, 1980, I just so happened to be working on the floors at the Dakota apartment building. Even though I finished the original job, the staff at the apartment asked me to fix another floor, to stay around an extra day.

See where I'm heading with this? That day I so happened to come face-to-face with a large man who lingered in front of the apartment. It just so happened that this large man, who showed himself to be a monster, spoke to me. When he spoke, terror shot through my body, I knew something wasn't right. When I walked back outside, this monster of a man stood underneath the glowing bright orange light, which at the time shined brighter than I ever saw it... and it turned blood red. No, this wasn't a coincidence, not one bit.

My last predicament was a simple one. Do I want to do anything? Should I forget about the monster? Forget about trying to find a way back to 1981? Maybe I should live my life as normal in this new time, and go on as a normal person. Of course, I had no control over the actions of the FBI agents. I wish they'd stop dipping in my *Kool-Aid*, but again, I doubt they're finished with me.

I left New York City the day after being released from prison. There's no way I wanted to stay around the city, not at that time at least. I looked to find a taxi, but when I asked a fellow at a bar I stopped into, he told me to just call an *Uber*. This baffled me, I had no idea what the hell an *Uber* was.

"You don't know what *Uber* is? It's like a taxi service, but regular people use their cars to get you. It's simpler, trust."

"Oh," I replied as I finished off my delicious blood orange beer. I never heard of this flavor of beer back in 1981. "Do I find the *Uber* number in the yellow pages?"

"Yellow pages?" The bar patron asked while raising his left eyebrow. "No, just go on your smartphone and download the app."

Now my left eyebrow raised. "Huh? Smartphone? App?"

The bar patron's mouth dropped open.

"Do you mean I have to write out an application to get one of these Ubers?" I asked.

"Have you been living under a rock, my friend?" The bar patron asked. He chugged down the rest of his beer and motioned for the bartender to pour him another. "No, these apps are applications that run on your smartphone."

"Smartphone?"

"Yes, your smartphone. Damn, buddy, you are strange."

I spun around on my barstool. My mind tried to wrap around what exactly a smartphone was. "Let me get this straight." My spinning stopped and I focused on my fellow bar patron. "You have a telephone that is smart? What, can you tell it who you want to call and the phone itself calls the person?"

The bar patron laughed. "Well, buddy, that is one function it can do." He reached into his pocket and pulled out something in a cameo design. "Here, buddy, this is my phone."

I reached out toward this *phone*.

The bar patron pulled it back to his body. "Whoa, buddy. You're not trying to steal it, are you?"

"No, no," I laughed. "I'm just marveled over the fact this phone is camouflaged."

The bar patron chuckled. "This isn't the phone, it's the phone case, buddy."

He flipped the phone all around, showing me the design. After clicking a button on the side of the phone, a bright screen lit up. "You really are a strange dude, buddy," the bar patron said. "Here, let me show you how to use one of these."

For the next half an hour, the nice bar patron, David, as I found his name to be, gave me step-by-step instructions on how to work the smartphone. David explained how to make calls, he even showed me this crazy new way to communicate called texting.

This phone blew my mind, I had nothing even close to this back in my time. David went over the apps and showed me a bunch. From writing apps, to games, to something he called *Facebook*. This smartphone of his appeared to do it all. David also showed me the *Uber* app and set me up with one.

I left the bar feeling amazed... and a little drunk too. I stood outside, looking for this *Uber* driver. David waited outside with me till the driver showed up. He even paid for my ride, which was truly generous. This was especially true since I checked my wallet and only had forty-three dollars. My money from 1981.

David told me about a hotel that wasn't too far from the bar. He said a room should cost forty-two dollars. That would only leave me with a dollar, enough to get a

Coke out of a vendor machine. There was no way I could pay for the driver and the room. So again, I'm truly grateful.

My *Uber* driver, a man in his late forties, stopped me in front of the Bubba D's Hotel. The sign's light flickered on and off. It also shined in a bright orange color. This shot a cold shiver down my spine. I thought about turning around, getting back into the car and asking my driver to find me another hotel. But I never did as I heard the squealing of my driver's tires burning some rubber.

My hand grabbed the glass door of the hotel. I pulled but yet; the door didn't budge. *Hmm, I'm pretty sure the sign says open twenty-four hours.* Sure enough, hanging in the window, next to the door was that open *twenty-four hours* sign. My right hand gripped the door tighter; I pulled harder... the door wouldn't budge. *Oh, come on, I need to get a room.* I balled up both my fists and banged on the glass door. "Hey! Anyone inside? I need to get a room!"

A husky man walked into my view. He had a bald head with three strings of hair combed over from left to right. The husky man wore sunglasses, yet they sat up on his forehead. He pointed at the door and screamed toward me. I couldn't make out what he said, but as I pulled again, the door still didn't open.

The husky man shook his head in disgust as he reached the door. "You don't pull, you push!" the husky man screamed through the glass door. He grabbed the door handle and pulled the door in his direction; it opened.

"Damn, I can't believe I didn't try to push it open," I said, blushing in shame.

The husky man laughed. "Yeah, you did look pathetic pulling at the door."

He turned to walk back behind the front desk. My fist balled up again, this time in anger. "Yeah, guess I must have." I rested my elbows on the front desk. "Do you have an open room?"

The husky man smirked. "Yes, as a matter of fact, we do. How many nights are you looking for?"

"Just one, for tonight."

"That'll be forty-two dollars." The husky man coughed into his shoulder.

I reached into my wallet and pulled out the money.

"Oh, you're paying with cash?" the husky man asked.

I nodded.

"Well, you can pay in cash, but I'll need your checking account information as well."

My wallet fell from my hands, slamming on the desk. "Are you kidding me? I only have cash and I have no car to get anywhere."

The husky man rolled his eyes. He glanced past me, looking outside. "Shit, just gives me the cash and I'll let you stay." He grabbed the cash out of my hand. "And this is only good for one night. If you decide to stay longer, you must give me your account information or a credit card. You got that?"

"Yeah, no problem," I said. "It will only be one night, I promise."

The husky man smirked and walked over to the wall in the far corner behind the desk. Many hooks hung on the wall. Keys dangled off about half of those hooks. The husky man reached up and grabbed the key. The wall behind the hooks were numbered. I glanced past the husky man, who walked toward me, and found he grabbed the key marked twenty-six.

The husky man slapped the key down on the desk. "Here you are. Room twenty-six."

I grabbed at my head, a pain shot through my brain. The first apartment I worked on at the Dakota, back in 1980, was apartment twenty-six...

The husky man cleared his throat. "Do you want this or not?"

"Ah, yeah," I said, while shaking out the cobwebs. "Thank you."

"Go out the door." The husky man pointed out the front door. "Turn right and walk about ten feet. You'll find an entranceway and a set of steps."

I turned to face the door, looking outside, trying to follow his finger and directions. There, on the wall, next to the door, hung a newspaper that showed the World Trade Center, with an airplane flying toward it. The caption read: *Never Forget 9/11.*

"Go up the stairs and go to the door marked *second floor*. Turn right once inside the door and walk down to the end of the first short halfway. Then, turn left and it will be the second door on your left. You got that?" the husky man said.

Once again, I nodded and I grabbed the key. "Hey man, what's nine-eleven?" I pointed at the newspaper on the wall.

The husky man gave me a dumbfounded look. "You don't know about the terrorists who flew planes into the Twin Towers back on September 11, 2001?"

"I, ah-"

"You been living under a rock, buddy?" the husky man asked.

The husky man proceeded to tell me about the events that occurred on September 11, 2001. I wasn't positive of course, but I believe this terrible event might have occurred because John Lennon was killed. Maybe, just maybe...

After hearing this story, I decided it was time to go and I ran out of the office and up to my room door. My eyes fixed on the 26 that was etched into the key. I made the *right* turn and walked the ten feet. An entranceway stood before me. I walked into the entranceway and found the set of steps; I climbed them. At the top I came face-to-face with the door that read *second floor*; I opened it. Inside I made the *right* turn and down the short hallway I went. At the end of the hallway, right before my left turn, a soda machine sat against the wall.

Damn, I could use a Coke. And I still have that dollar. Hopefully, they give change at the front desk. As I turned to head back to the front desk, something on the soda machine caught my eye. *$1.25?* My right fist slammed into the wall. *When did a can of pop get this expensive?* My mind still had a hard time adjusting to the idea of living in the future. I kicked the soda machine out of frustration and walked to the end of the hallway.

My eyes couldn't help but stare at the wallpaper. It was a bright orange color with faint circles. A disgusted taste entered my mouth as I turned the corner. After making the left turn, I quickly found room twenty-six. Dazed and confused, these emotions clouded my mind as I stared at the 26 on the door. *Why is this the same room number as the room I first worked on at the Dakota? Why is this ugly ass wallpaper orange with circles?*

I let out a deep breath, gathered myself and placed the key inside the keyhole. Opening the door, I found this room to be slightly small. But hell, it beat living out on the street. This hotel room was where I started writing my memoir. After everything that I've been through, I felt like talking to someone about it. Of course, I couldn't tell anyone. So I decided to write it down. In a dresser drawer next to the bed, I found a paper notebook and a single number two pencil.

For the remainder of the night, I wrote intensely. I knocked out thirty pages of writing before I finally called it quits and went to sleep. The last thing I remember before falling asleep was the time on the clock that sat on the nightstand; 5:18 A.M.

Loud knocks at my door woke me. My eyes blinked open and found the time on the clock; 7:36 A.M. My head ached. I stroked my forehead, just above my nose. The knocks at my door continued. As I sat up in bed, the door swung open.

"Hello?" I asked.

"Oh, hi. I didn't know if anyone still occupied this room." A woman, most likely in her sixties, stood at the entrance of my room.

I rubbed my forehead harder. "Yeah, it is occupied. Say, what time do I have to be out?"

The elderly woman grabbed the door handle. "Not till eleven this morning. Sorry for waking you. I'll come back." She closed the door and I flopped back down into bed.

I lay in bed for three hours, tired but awake. I finally got up around 10:30 A.M. Sitting in bed, I contemplated my next move. *What do I do? Where do I go? How can I get another Uber?* I opened the door to find the sun to be bright and warm.

I stood for a few minutes, staring in each direction, still contemplating my next move. "Good morning again, sir."

My head turned to the left and found the same elderly woman who woke me up early in the morning. "Oh, hi. Good morning, ma'am."

"Sorry again for waking you up."

I waved the elderly woman off. "No worries, it's okay."

The elderly woman smiled, and I returned a smile as well. She entered my former room, and I took off down the street.

After a solid twenty minutes of walking, I came across a diner. *Bob's Diner.* I read the sign and entered the diner. Inside the diner older folks ruled, it didn't seem like anyone under fifty ate here. I approached the counter and sat down on a bar stool.

A woman in her fifties, sporting a headband covering part of her blondish-gray hair, approached me. "Whadda have?"

I sat still, thinking about the single bill in my wallet. "Ah, how much is a cup of coffee?"

"One dollar."

"Is it exactly one dollar? Or is there some tax to be added on too?" I asked.

The woman smirked. "Yes, dear. Just one plain old dollar."

I pulled my dollar bill out of my wallet and placed it on the counter. The woman grabbed and pulled the bill in; she smirked again. The woman walked over and grabbed a cup. She poured the coffee into the cup, the steam beautifully rose up into the air. I licked my lips, watching her bring the cup over.

She slid the cup to me and smirked. "Enjoy."

"Thanks," I said. "I believe I will."

I sipped the coffee, it burned my mouth slightly, but I didn't care, it tasted good. After finishing my coffee, I leaned back on my stool and stretched.

The woman approached me holding the coffee pot. "You want a refill?"

"Ah, I can't. I have no more money."

The woman laughed. "Refills are free, dear."

A smile formed on my face.

"Well..." I glanced at the woman and found a name tag pinned on her shirt; *Jane*. "Then, Jane. I'll take another cup."

Jane smirked and poured me the second cup. The steam flew up into my nose. A sense of relaxation hit me.

As I sipped my second cup of coffee, I pondered about being in the future and what I believed to be my mission; kill the monster who killed John Lennon. "Say, Jane."

She turned around from talking to another customer and locked eyes with me. "Yeah?"

"Is the library still on fifth avenue?"

Jane smirked. "Yeah, same place it's always been."

I blushed, feeling stupid by my question. But hell, I'm from the past and you never know what may still be around. "Okay, thank you, Jane."

I thanked Jane and left the diner. During my coffee break, I realized I needed to find out all the information I could on the monster who killed John Lennon. What's the best place to do research? That's right, the library.

The orange glowing ball hand-selected me to kill the monster, I must avenge the death of John, I thought as I walked down the street. *This has to be the only way I can get back to my time. Yes, I will kill this monster. He killed such an important person who could have done so much good in this hateful world.* Glancing up in the sky, I squinted at the sun. *Damn, imagine me as a killer.... It's the only way.*

I walked for around an hour, sweat dripped from my forehead. My mouth felt dry, but with no money, there wasn't anything I could do. Finally, I reached the enormous Manhattan Bridge. *Damn, the drive up here would have only been about eight minutes or so. Ugh, I'm tired.*

With my head lowered, I felt like giving up. But my father entered my mind. *Could Dad still be alive? Does he still live in Manhattan? The library could probably give me that information.* My head raised up and my eyes caught the sun again. *Where's that other bright orange glowing ball? Ugh, I have to kill the monster, I must... I need to get to the library.*

Bending down, I retied my shoelaces. The walk had already been long, but it would be another hour or longer till I reached the library; I wanted to be ready. At the Manhattan Bridge, I turned left to get onto the pedestrian path. *I'll have to check the microfilm at the library. They must have a lot of information on the day the monster went into court,* I pondered. *Maybe they have something on the mysterious orange glowing ball...*

Chapter 9

I walked another hour till I reached the public library. Bent over, I huffed and puffed; I never wanted to walk anywhere ever again. After regaining my breath, I walked up to the door. My hand reached to grab the door and the door swung open. "Oh, sorry," I belted.

"Oh, no. I'm the one who is sorry," the sweet voice of a woman said.

My eyes went up and down, to back up again on the woman. At that moment, I realized I knew the beautiful woman who stood before me. "Hey, I know you."

In front of me stood Nurse Brown. "Oh, my God. Joe, right?"

"Yeah." My face blushed bright red, *she remembered my name.*

"How are you doing? It's great to see you up and out of the hospital bed."

I laughed, placing my hands into my pockets, trying to hide the shaking of my nerves. "Yeah, I can't lie, I'm glad not to be in the hospital."

"So are you feeling good? No symptoms of anything?" Nurse Brown asked.

After glancing up and down at myself, I met the eyes of the beautiful Nurse Brown. "Ah, no. Nothing at all, I feel amazing."

An awkward silence hit for about ten seconds, then Nurse Brown surprised me. "Say, Joe. Could I maybe get your *Instagram,* so we can keep in touch?"

"Ah..."

"You know, if you want to get a drink or something," Nurse Brown said.

A nervous bead of sweat dripped down my forehead; my left hand swiped the sweat away. "Ah, well, I don't have an *Instagram*."

"Oh," Nurse Brown yelped. "Well, you can give me your *Snapchat* or *Facebook*..." She paused, a sad expression formed on her face. "Unless you don't want to go out for a drink. I understand... I'm sorry."

I rubbed my hands through my hair. "Ah, I don't have them either. I don't really know what they are."

"Oh."

"Hell, I don't even have one of those smartiephones."

"Smartiephones?" Nurse Brown took a step backward. "Well, how about this? I can give you my address and tomorrow around... let's say eight, you come by and pick me up. Sound good?"

A nervous laugh exited my mouth, I felt like such a loser. "Ah, I don't have a car either..."

An elderly woman walked out of the library, Nurse Brown and I stepped aside to let her pass. She smiled at us as she passed. Once the elderly woman walked by, I turned back to see Nurse Brown now standing only inches from me. Her hand was touching my hand, and she held it there for a few seconds before moving it away. "Sorry, Joe."

My red-blushed face returned. "Ah, it's okay." I took a deep breath. "I really would like to take you out for that drink." My eyes glanced past Nurse Brown, staring at the enormous building that sat behind us. "Say, how about this? Tomorrow, around eight, you come by the library and get me. How's that sound?"

Nurse Brown smiled. "Sounds like a date..." Her face suddenly turned a bright red, she took a step back once more. "I-I mean, it sounds good, yeah, good."

We both shared a laugh and she gingerly walked by me. I opened the door of the library and turned to get one last glimpse of Nurse Brown. She turned around the same time I did and shot me the most beautiful smile I've ever seen.

Now inside the library, I tried to shift my focus off the beautiful nurse and onto what I've deemed my *mission* in life. The library looked different inside than I last remembered, but hell, I skipped over forty-one years.

Behind a large desk sat a woman with gray tied-up hair. She wore those glasses with chains that wrap around your ears. The librarian's attention was deep into a book she was reading. As I approached, she glanced up and greeted me with a smile.

"Hello, sir. How may I assist you?"

I returned the smile. "Hi, yes, I'd like to use your microfilm. Need to do a bit of research."

"Ah, sweetie, the library has stopped using the microfilm for a little while now." She pointed toward her left, my right. "If you need to do some research, you may use the computers."

Scratching my head, I thought about the computers from my time.

"You know how to use a computer, right?" the librarian asked.

My head shook slightly. "Well, I've seen them and I did play around on one that a buddy of mine had."

"Oh."

"And, I looked one time at a *Commodore VIC-20* model, but it cost $299. That was too much for me to spend," I explained.

"*Commodore VIC-20?*" Her left eyebrow raised. "You never used a newer model?"

Newer model? Hell, the Commodore VIC-20 was pretty hip tech to me, I thought. "Ah, no." I shot her a smile. "I'm not really a tech person."

The librarian's eyes slowly moved up and down. "Oh, okay."

"You think you may be able to show me how to use these computers in your time?" *Shit, not your time, don't say that Joe!*

"Wait, what do you mean about my time?" the librarian asked. She adjusted her chained glasses.

My head glanced around the entire library, nervous, trying to figure out what to say. "Ah..."

The librarian shook her head and waved her hands. "No matter, sir. Here, follow me to the computers."

At that moment, I knew I was truly lucky. I dodged a bullet with my dumb-ass comment. I'm fortunate it didn't come back to nip me in the bud.

We walked down the library and turned left, there sat a bunch of tables with thin rectangular machines. These looked similar to the TV I had in the hospital, just smaller. The librarian pulled a chair out. "Please, sit down."

I nodded and sat down.

"Okay, let me show you how this computer works."

The librarian graciously gave me a fifteen-minute crash course on this new-age computer. These computers here in 2023 are so much more advanced than anything we ever had back in 1981. She showed me something that seemed similar to microfilm, as it gave out information. This *thing* the librarian called *Google* could find information on anything you wanted. All you have to do is type it in what she called a *search bar* and click search.

This technology blew my mind. The librarian said you could do so much on what she called *the internet*. Hell, the guy who sat next to me was playing some high-tech games with sweet graphics. The guy told me he downloaded some emulator thing to play a video game system, it truly was the highest quality of video gaming I've ever seen. Back in my time, I had an *APF Imagination Machine*, but it doesn't hold a candle to the incredible gaming system he called *The Super Nintendo*.

After the guy left from playing his game, I sat all alone in the first row of computers. The helpful librarian walked back to her desk, and I stared helplessly at the bright computer screen. I can't lie, I felt nervous, this technology was above me, but I had to find out the information that I came here for.

My fingers hit the keys, but nothing happened. No words appeared on the screen. The search bar remained empty; I scratched my head. *Well, jeez, this seemed easy when the librarian did it.* I turned around in my chair and snapped my fingers; people stared. *Come on, Joe, don't do that.* I felt like an idiot. Sliding my chair back, I stood up and walked back to the front desk. I asked the kind librarian to show me how to search for information once more; she rolled her eyes.

Even though I interrupted the librarian from her reading, she got up and followed me back to the computers. The librarian showed me where I went wrong. Apparently, you need to use the mouse cursor to move the little arrow on the screen over top of the search bar. Once the arrow is over top of the search bar, you click on the mouse cursor, the right button, and then you can begin your typing.

The librarian stayed around to watch me. She wanted to make sure I knew what the hell I was doing, so she wouldn't have to come back over. She wanted me to type something in. So, I typed *Lake Placid Winter Olympics*. A bunch of search results popped up, including *The Miracle on Ice* hockey game. Damn, that game was amazing. The mighty Soviets, the four-time defending Gold medal-winning Soviets going up against the youngest team in the Olympics, the United States.

The American team wasn't supposed to do anything in those Olympics, especially since they had a bunch of amateurs playing. But they pulled off the unthinkable and defeated those communist bastards by a score of 4–3. The game meant a lot to me, not just for home country pride, but that was the last time I saw my father. Yes, the night of the hockey match was one of the very few times (since that cold January night in 1979) that my father and I spent time together.

My father came over to my small apartment to watch the game, he surprised me, actually. The past few weeks before the hockey game, my father and I were supposed to get together to grab a bite to eat or to get a couple of beers, but he'd canceled every time. So when a few knocks rang at my door, and I opened it to find my father, I figured it must be a dream. Thankfully, it wasn't, and we enjoyed watching that amazing upset win of a game together...

Dad, I miss you and must find you. This, I thought as I stared at the computer screen, reminiscing of our time together watching the hockey game. Then John Lennon entered my mind. I replayed the Elton John concert my father and I saw together. My mind replayed the image of my father, excited as all hell to see Elton perform. It also replayed the exact moment when John Lennon came out onto the stage.

My mind didn't stop, I now saw John, but this time, he was in front of the Dakota apartment building.

"Watch out, John," I mumbled under my breath.

A woman walked by and heard me. She shot me a confused look and continued on her way. My vision went back into my memory, back to the Dakota. There, standing off the side... the large man... the monster, standing with a blank expression on his face. He held his *Catcher in the Rye* book up to me...

"Hi-ya, Joe. Or should I call you Holden Caulfield... I know you've read the book."

My vision stayed locked on the monster. I tried to look away, tried to move, yet I couldn't. A haze of fog lifted from the ground that covered the area. The monster shook the book around in his hand.

"Holden, it's your mission in life... you depressed son of a bitch..."

The fog intensified, and the monster disappeared. My mind thought, *what is my mission in life according to him?*

The monster's prissy voice echoed out through the fog. "Your mission is to kill me, restore the universe, you must kill me, Holden..."

Two bright orange glowing circles appeared in the fog. These were like the bright orange glowing ball in the sky, yet smaller.

"I will kill you, I swear on my life, I'll kill you to avenge John Lennon," I screamed.

The two orange glowing bright lights flashed, blinding my eyes for a split second. The lights ceased, the fog remained thick...

"Argh!"

Out of the fog, the monster rushed toward me. His eyes shined bright red, and the skin on his face appeared to be melting off. A hole in the side of his left cheek exposed his teeth. His dingy hands reached for me, I turned, cowering in fright... something squeezed my right shoulder, the monster got me...

"Get away from me, you monster fuck!" I screamed, jumping at my computer.

The librarian stood above me and jumped back from my outburst. Every single person in the library stood up, mouths hung open as they stared at me.

The librarian fiddled with her glasses. "Are you okay? You fell asleep at your computer and you were making some grunting noises."

A dream, it was only a dream, I thought. A severe shot of pain entered my head, I rubbed just above my nose, in between my eyes. *No, it wasn't a dream; it was a nightmare...*

"Are you going to be okay?" The librarian asked. "Would you like a cup of water or anything?"

"Yeah, a cup of water would be great. Thank you so much."

Titan Frey

The librarian walked about ten feet away to a water cooler. She grabbed a paper cup and filled it with some water. The librarian walked back to me and handed me the water, I thanked her and chugged it down; boy, did it taste good.

After my little incident calmed down and everyone took their eyes off of me, I went back to my research. After clicking on the right button of the mouse, I found the delete button and repeatedly clicked it. The words *Lake Placid Winter Olympics* vanished. Placing my hands together, I pushed against my fingers, cracking them. I took a deep breath and typed in the monster's name.

The search results popped up on the computer screen. Seeing this monster's name pissed me off. There were articles that talked about the killing, newspaper articles from 1980. Also, I found an article about the monster from 2022, it was about him coming up for parole.

The article read: *John Lennon's Killer, Mark David Chapman, Denied Parole for the 12th Time.* I clicked on the article and inside, a written statement caught my attention. It read: *The panel has determined that your release would be incompatible with the welfare and safety of society, parole board tells.*

Again, I will not mention the monster's name, but you get the gist. I read more into the article and found out more about this bastard. After finishing the article, I clicked on a few more articles, old and new, and read up as much as I could on the entire situation.

Anger boiled my blood. This monster of a man truly killed a living legend just to be famous. I read over the name of the prison where they kept this monster; Wende Correctional Facility. *This needs to happen, I must pay the monster a visit.*

I clicked the back button and returned to the first *Google* page. After deleting the search bar, I typed in *Wende Correctional Facility.* Pictures of the building came up on the screen. The first line of the search said, notable prisoners. Next to notable prisoners was the name of the monster.

Toward the top of the screen, I saw a link saying get directions; I clicked it. Exactly what the link said happened. Directions from the library to the prison showed up. *I must get these directions.* I stood up and made my way back to the librarian's desk.

As I approached, the librarian lowered her book; she sighed.

"How may I help you now?"

"May I borrow a piece of paper and a pencil?"

"Well, here." The librarian picked up a notebook and ripped a page of the paper out. She slid it over to me and pulled open her desk drawer. "Will a pen work for you?"

"Ah, yeah, a pen is good."

"Here." The librarian handed me the pen. "Obviously, you can keep the paper, but if you don't mind, can you bring the pen back?"

"Sure, not a problem," I said with a smile.

I walked back to my computer and wrote down the address of the monster's prison. After sliding the paper into my pocket, I returned the pen.

After returning the pen, I left the library. I had enough of dealing with these computers and having people stare at me, I needed some air. Standing outside of the library, I took a deep breath while staring at the setting sun. It looked beautiful, yet being an orange glowing ball, it looked frightening as well. *You're not the orange glowing ball I need...*

"Excuse me."

A young teenager walked past me, he donned huge headphones over his ears. I nodded nervously and stepped out from in front of the door. The teenager went inside the library, and I walked out to the sidewalk.

Glancing back up at the setting sun, a train wreck of emotions ran through my mind. Finally, I thought of my father. *Damn, I fell asleep and forgot to look my father up. Shit, if alive still, my father would be in his eighties.* At that moment, standing alone with no money, no car, and no home, I decided I needed to walk to my father's home... or what used to be his home, at least.

I headed toward Manhattan, to the last place my father lived. *Could Dad really still live there? What sort of condition is he in, if he's even alive?* These thoughts replayed in my head during the long walk to Manhattan.

It took me slightly less than an hour to reach Manhattan. Once in Manhattan, I walked another fifteen minutes till I reached the apartment building where my father lived at. My nerves got the best of me, I walked up to the door and turned back around. *Come on, Joe, just knock on the door.* By now, darkness arrived, I stood under a street lamp. Glancing up, my eyes locked onto the orange glowing light.

A strange cold wind suddenly blew, causing goose flesh on the back of my neck. *Do it, Joe.* I listened to myself and ran back into the apartment building. My right fist balled up, and I slammed it against the door four times. After waiting a few seconds, I pounded on the door four more times.

After my last pound on the door, I heard footsteps. I stepped back three feet, taking a deep breath; the door swung open. Sadness immediately hit in the now open doorway as I watched a young man with blond hair stand in the home of my father. The blond haired man couldn't have been older than twenty-one, he stood with no shirt on and an evil glare in his eyes.

"What in the fuck do you want?" the blond haired man screamed. "And you better have a good ass reason for banging on my door that loud."

"Ah," I mumbled while stumbling backward.

"Well? Why you banging on my door?"

I tried looking past the blond hair man, wanting to get a glimpse inside, but he successfully blocked my view.

"I'm so sorry to disturb you, I am looking for a guy named Clark Miller who used to live here. Apparently, he does not anymore."

The blond haired man rubbed his eyes. "Well, no one by the name of Clark Miller lives here now."

My left hand raised up to the back of my neck, massaging it. "Ah, may I ask one question?"

"Make it quick," the blond haired man said.

"How long have you lived here?" The blond haired man sighed and rolled his eyes.

"Why does that matter, man?"

"Because the guy I'm looking for is old and may be dead. I need to know so maybe I can figure out his situation... please."

The blond haired man sighed again.

"I've been living here for a little over a year now. Okay? Good, now bye."

Before I could let out a sound, he slammed the door in my face.

Damn, now what do I do? I left the apartment building alone and scared. My eyes met the orange glowing street light once more. *I need to find a place to sleep.* Down the street, I walked, the strange cold wind for this time of the year blew again. Panic hit me. Tonight I had no money for a hotel room, my father didn't live in the fancy apartment anymore. *What can I do?*

Darkness to the orange glowing light, back to darkness. The orange glow returned for a split second, then back to darkness. This is what I saw during my long walk. With no place to go, I wandered the streets. Around five in the morning (according to a street clock), I came across a small bridge. This was a good thing, too, since rain started to fall from the sky.

Just as I walked underneath the bridge, the rain fell harder. For a few minutes, I stood staring at the pouring rain, listening to the giant drops of water hitting the ground. I walked to the middle of the bridge and lay myself down. *I guess this is goodnight...*

Chapter 10

My eyes slowly blinked open, a bright orange glow blinded me. At first, I thought *my* orange glowing ball finally returned, but no, it was just the sun again. It must have been early in the morning since the sun sat low enough in the sky to shine under the bridge.

The next thing I knew, two sets of legs approached me. Both sets wore ripped-up jeans, and one wore dirty brown work boots. The other set of legs dawned some old black tennis shoes with the right front of the shoe hanging halfway off.

"What in the hell are you doing in my bed?" A screechy voice asked.

"Huh?" I replied, trying to sit up.

The foot that wore the black, falling-off tennis shoe raised up and kicked me down.

"Yeah, you heard my friend, asshole!"

I fell onto my side, scraping my elbow in the process. Finally, raising my head up, I found two homeless men standing before me.

"Ah, I'm sorry if I slept on your bed," I said, glancing down at the hard cement ground. "But it won't happen again."

"It better not!" Work Boots shouted.

"Yeah, you're not from around here, as I've never seen you before. We don't like newcomers in our area," Black Tennis Shoes snarled.

I stood up and dusted my pants off. These men didn't want me here, and to be honest, I didn't want to be under the bridge any longer, either. After tying my left shoe, I shot a small wave and headed out from underneath the bridge. Just as I almost cleared the bridge, I heard the screechy voice once more.

"I'm glad he's leaving, I think he came from the orange ball of magic..."

I stopped dead in my tracks, every hair on my body stood up. *Could this man mean the orange glowing ball that has brought me to this time?* Slowly, I turned around. The two homeless men backed up defensively. My feet moved slowly at first, then the speed picked up.

"Stay away from us, newcomer, I told you we don't want you here!" Black Tennis Shoes screamed.

The two homeless men grabbed hold of each other. They crouched down to the ground.

"Please, stay away from us!" Work Boots bellowed.

I ran up to the two crouched men, waving my hands around, trying to get them to calm down.

"Hey, guys!" I yelled. "I'm not here to hurt you, I promise. But you said I'm from the orange ball of magic." Standing above the two men, I watched as they trembled in fear. "Please, guys. Tell me what you know, I won't hurt you."

Work Boots held up his hand. "Please, we just want to be left alone, we don't want any trouble."

Anger crept into me, I wanted to know what the fuck this man meant by saying orange ball of magic.

"Listen up, I'm going to ask you guys again and I want an answer." I leered at both men. "One way or another, I'll get the answer out of you two. So tell me!"

The two homeless men stared at each other, then their eyes locked onto mine. They pulled each other up onto their feet, still with their eyes locked onto mine.

"Fine," Work Boots bellowed. "Follow us."

The two homeless men walked to the other end of the bridge. Work Boots held up his pointer finger and disappeared behind the lower cement wall of the bridge. Black Tennis Shoes shot me an eerie smile as we waited. The fear in his eyes that was there a minute ago disappeared.

A minute passed by, but it seemed like an hour. Then, Work Boots returned. I stepped toward the two men and something shining in the sun stopped me in my tracks.

"Whoa," I bellowed. "Put the knife down, man."

Work Boots pointed his sharp pocket knife in my direction. Black Tennis Shoes kept his eerie smile on.

"You won't get us, we won't betray it, " Work Boots said.

"Betray what?" I cried. "Please tell me."

Work Boots lunged the knife directly into the neck of Black Tennis Shoes. Blood splattered everywhere; the image of the blood pouring out of John Lennon flashed in my mind.

"Why did you do that?" I asked, taking a few steps back. "Why did you kill your friend?"

Work Boots frowned. "Because it's the only way..."

The arm of Work Boots raised up, I took another few steps backward.

"Please, stop. Let me help you."

"You can't help me, " Work Boots' frown grew larger. "This is the only way."

Work Boots placed the knife against his throat and sliced from left to right. Blood sprayed out like a sprinkler. His body fell to the ground next to his dead friend.

I ran as fast as I could out from underneath the bridge, and I didn't stop running for twenty minutes. After bolting down the street for twenty minutes, I stopped to rest against a streetlight. Leaning against the pole, I struggled to catch my breath. While fighting through a coughing spell, I glanced up at the unlit light. Just as my eyes locked onto the bulb, the orange glowing light popped on. *Huh? These lights aren't supposed to come on during the daytime.* As I fixated on the streetlight, the distinct sound of a car coming to a gentle stop behind me caught my attention.

"Well, look who it is, our old buddy, Joe Miller."

"Good to see you, Joey, ol' boy."

Fear struck, the two voices belonged to my FBI buddies... "Ah," I mumbled as I slowly turned around.

Special Agent Jones sat in the passenger side of the car, leaning halfway out, smiling. "How are you, Joe?"

Special Agent Carter firmly gripped the steering wheel, grinning at me. "We've missed you, old buddy."

I took one step away from the agent's car, smacking my right shoulder into the streetlight pole. Just as I hit the pole, the orange glowing light faded off.

"What's wrong, Joe?" Agent Jones asked. "You seem a little jumpy this morning."

Agent Carter leaned closer from the driver's side. "Where are you going this early in the morning, buddy?"

I glanced around, hoping to find someone else on the street with us; unfortunately, we were alone. "Ah, I'm heading to the library."

These FBI agents made me nervous, I wanted to get away from them badly.

"Oh," Agent Jones said. He glanced down the street and back at me. "Here, Joe, hop on in. We will give you a ride, won't we, Special Agent Carter?"

Agent Carter smiled. "Sure, anything for our buddy, Joe."

The door swung open and Agent Carter stepped out. He wore the finest suit on the market, an American flag pin on his lapel. "Please, let us give you a ride." Agent Carter opened the back door of the car.

I stepped away, tripping over the streetlight pole. Luckily, I placed my hand on the sidewalk and pushed myself back up.

The car door slammed shut, Agent Jones walked around the driver's side of the car. "What's a matter, Joe? You seem nervous."

"You're right, Agent Jones." Agent Carter took two steps toward me. "Are you really going to the library?"

I glanced around, still no one in sight. "Ah, yeah, I am. I want to do some research."

"Research?" Agent Carter laughed. "What sort of bullshit research are you doing?"

My lower lip trembled, I needed to get away from these men and fast. "Ah, it's personal, I don't feel like discussing it."

Agent Jones stepped up on the sidewalk, I took two more steps backward. "Tell me, Joe, where are you coming from?"

"Yeah, you weren't up to no good, were you, Joe?" Agent Carter sneered.

"No, ah, of course not," I mumbled. My mind replayed the incident of the homeless man killing his friend and himself. I wanted to be rid of these fools. Just when I thought they were a distant memory, they crept back in like a bad dream.

"Well, where were you coming from then?" Agent Carter asked.

My nerves ran wild. "I slept under-" I almost slipped up and said *I slept under the bridge...* that would have been bad. In no way did I want these clowns poking around under the bridge, finding the lifeless bodies of the two homeless men. "Ah, I slept under the stars last night. I have no money, so no way I can get a room."

Agent Carter smirked. "Where at, under the stars, did you sleep last night?"

My mind bounced around, trying to think of somewhere far away from the bridge. As I tried to think of an answer, a strange *jingle* saved me. Agent Jones whipped out a phone, he answered it, turning his back to me. After a few seconds, he turned back to face Agent Carter.

"Agent Carter, we have to go. The NYPD has a *10-10*. They are requesting some assistance."

Agent Jones locked eyes with me. A ghostly grin on his face quickly erupted into a smile. "Well, Joe, I'll have to find you again sometime soon. Then, we can finish our little chat."

"Bye, Joe," Agent Carter chimed in.

Agent Jones shot me a wink. They sped off, nearly hitting me. A sense of relief struck me as I darted down the street, building as much distance as I could between myself and the bridge.

My run didn't cease till I reached the library. The back of my throat felt dry and irritated, I honestly thought my calves were going to burst out of my legs. The bright orange sun beat down on my face, I needed to get inside and get some water. So that's exactly what I did, you can believe that. Inside the library, I trotted, making my way back to the bathrooms to hit up the water fountain.

In between the men's and women's bathrooms hung the water fountain. My hands slammed into the water fountain button so hard that the water flew out, smacking me square in the face. The surprise of the water hitting my face jumped me back a foot, but I couldn't help but laugh. The water felt great, nice, and cold. I pressed the button again, this time in a much gentler way.

The flow came out much smoother now, I lowered my lips to the water. The cold water quenched my thirst, *ah*. Now, feeling better after my run, I decided to do more of my research. After going through the motions with the librarian, I found myself sitting back in front of the computer.

Before I did anything else, I needed to find out where my father was. On the search engine, I typed my father's name. An entire page of results popped up. After scrolling through and clicking on every link, I found that none of these *Clark Miller* links were about my father. So I revamped my search by typing in *Clark Miller of Maxwell, Pennsylvania*. Maxwell, of course, being where we are from. If this didn't work, I'd type in *Clark Miller of New York* since the last place he lived was the Big Apple (well, as far as I know).

I didn't have to bother with typing in *New York*. An article popped up saying *Clark Miller, 69, formerly from Maxwell, passed away from a heart attack.* I noticed the date of the article was September 26, 2005. My breathing became heavy, and my chest hurt. Seeing this nearly made me pass out. But I remained strong and clicked on the link. There, I read the entire article.

Clark Miller, 69, formerly from Maxwell, passes away from a heart attack. He lived in New York City with his wife of twenty years, Rose Scott. Clark had one child, Joe Miller, who disappeared in 1981, he was never found.

I sat in my chair, holding my hand over my mouth, trying to control my breathing. I reread the article about ten more times. It still didn't seem real. *Wife? He married that woman?* I thought as I read through the article. *Damn, it even says my name and how they never found me. Shit, I wonder if my disappearance even affected my father?*

After reading about my father and seeing how I missed being there for him, I thought about what else I might have missed. Next, I decided to do some general research from 1981 to 2023. *Damn, forty-two years passed by without me. So much could've happened, and I just skipped it all.* This made me sad because who knows what wonderful things would've happened to me if that God-forsaken glowing ball didn't suck me up and spit me out in 2023.

I typed in the year *1981* and began reading up through the history. I found that President Regan would rebound from his shooting and go on to serve two full terms. After President Regan, his Vice President, George H. W. Bush, would win the 1988 election, defeating Michael Dukakis of Massachusetts. President Bush would serve only one term, and under his leadership, America would enter into a war named the Gulf War. This would involve America, England, France, and a few other countries. They went to war against the Republic of Kuwait and Iraq.

Huh, interesting. I scrolled through and read everything. What I read next was in 1992, a young and upcoming candidate from Arkansas named Bill Clinton ran for president. Clinton would end up defeating Bush, and many claimed Bill Clinton's appearance on *MTV* helped get him that win. *What the hell is a MTV?*

I continued on with my reading. What I found next was President Clinton did very well with the economy but ran into a scandal with a few women. This led him to be impeached. President Clinton wasn't removed from office since the Senate failed to convict him. What I read next brought me some sadness. The article stated: *July 16, 1999, tragedy strikes the Kennedy family again.* After clicking the link, I found the article. I read how JFK JR. flew his small plane on July 16, 1999, and how that plane crashed, killing him. *Damn, that family has no good luck at all.* As a kid, the visual of President Kennedy's head exploding gave me nightmares.

I moved on to learn about the new millennium (I know technically the new millennium started on January 1, 2001, but like most people, I say January 1, 2000). In the year 2000, George H. W. Bush's son, George W. Bush ran against President Clinton's Vice President, Al Gore. This election would be one of the closest elections ever, coming down to a recount in Florida. After some controversy, George W. Bush was declared the winner.

Damn, two George Bush's as president. That's odd. Just as I was about to look up more history, an ad popped up on my screen. This wasn't just any ad, either. The ad showed an orange glowing ball, and every three seconds, it would change to a bright red. On top of the ball that changed colors, it read: *Solar Eclipse Night Club*. Underneath the ball, it read: *Open now in NYC*.

This ad hit me like a ton of bricks. *Is this a sign?* This, I would never know. But after seeing the ad, I shifted my focus on the orange ball. On the search bar I typed, *glowing orange ball.* A bunch of searches popped up. The dates on these articles were not too far from the current time that I found myself living in.

The first article that popped up on the search bar read *Glowing balls spotted near Charlotte as scientists look for aliens - Charlotte Observer Jan 10, 2018.* This article told the story of an elderly man and his grandson, who were outside and saw a single ball hovering silently above them. Less than a minute later, a group of three balls appeared. *Three balls?* I thought, scratching my head. *I've only seen one orange ball.*

The article stated that scientists could not come up with a distinct reason for the sightings and even wouldn't rule out the idea of aliens, as quoted in the article: *slight possibility of extraterrestrial explanations for some recent observations.* I clicked out of the article, scrolled my mouse cursor down to the next article: *Mysterious Balls of Light Aren't UFOs, Says Science National Geographic.*

This sounded promising to me, hoping to read some solid evidence on the orange ball. *A "flying object" was seen over Russia last night,* the article stated. *Intercontinental ballistic missile tests are to blame for a series of mysterious orange orbs flying in the skies.*

I shook my head in disgust. *No, this isn't my answer.* The orange glowing ball I witnessed hovering in the sky certainly wasn't from a ballistic missile test. No way did I believe that, and certainly not from Russia. I dismissed this October 27, 2017 article.

The next search result on the orange glowing ball wasn't an article but a link to a website to buy a tee shirt. The shirt, a black tee, sported a picture of an orange glowing ball in the center. Below the orange ball, captions read- *Breathe In. Breathe out.* A meditation yoga tee shirt, simple, yet, effective. The caption was right, maybe. The orange glowing ball that sucked me in and spat me out into this foreign time may be the definition of life. Breathe in, kill the monster who killed the influential John Lennon. Breathe out, be rewarded for completing my destiny, and get the chance to travel back to my time to live a prosperous life. This idea wasn't new to me (as you know), but it had to be the reason.

After looking over the tee shirt, I proceeded to click and read the other articles on sightings of orange glowing balls in the sky; there were pages full of articles. So much information, yet not much that seemed useful. Most of what I read seemed to be people thinking they saw alien spaceships. In many cases, these people saw three orange glowing lights at one time. Plus, these orange glowing lights all seemed, by how the people in the articles described them, to be small orange glowing balls. The orange glowing ball that I witnessed certainly wasn't small.

My mind stayed warped into the computer, focusing on the articles, trying to figure out how I came to this time. I scratched the back of my head, irritated by the fact I couldn't find any definite information on my situation. Then, on page twenty-six of the search results, something caught my eye. An article titled: *The Outer Space Conspiracy Society.* Now the title itself didn't necessarily catch my eye, even though it did say Outer Space and Conspiracy Society. These clowns may know about my orange bright glowing ball, but maybe not. The real reason this article caught my attention was the owner of the Outer Space Conspiracy Society. His name was Barry Frey from Red Lion, Pennsylvania.

Whoa, I thought. *Could Barry Frey of Red Lion be related to that wonderful man I met back in 1974?* It took me a few seconds to try to think of the man's name. A loud, rumbling motorcycle blasted past the library. *Motorcycle? Yes, the man on the motorcycle...* "James Frey!" I screamed, the entire library patrons and staff glanced at me. A few *hush* calls echoed from all around me.

I blushed and leaned closer to the computer screen. As I stared at the screen, a sudden sensation of pressure overtook my right shoulder; I squirmed around in my chair.

"Huh?"

"Joe, I thought that was you." The beautiful Nurse Brown stood behind my chair. "I'm sorry, I didn't mean to scare you."

"Ah, you didn't scare me, not at all," I said, lying through my teeth.

Nurse Brown giggled. "Sure, I didn't." She shot me a wink.

"You ended up coming to the library early?" I asked.

A confused look formed on Nurse Brown's face.

"Do you want to go out on our date now? Or would you rather wait till eight?" I politely asked.

Nurse Brown laughed again. "Silly, it is eight." She pointed over to her right, my left. I glanced over to see a clock on the wall. Sure enough, the small hand on the clock pointed to the eight. "I'm ready if you are..." Nurse Brown paused, glancing around the room. "Unless you don't want to, I'd understand completely."

Once again, this beautiful, seductive woman appeared to be self-conscious and I didn't understand why.

"Of course, I want to take you out. I just didn't realize it was eight already." Standing up, I shot Nurse Brown a smile. "Time really flew by on me today." I raised my arm up to her. She smiled and grabbed ahold of it. "Let's go and get out of here."

We walked out of the library, and everyone, including the librarian, stared at us. I took notice of

Titan Frey

Nurse Brown blushing; this baffled me. *Why does she seem embarrassed?*

I grabbed the door and opened it. "After you," I said, holding my arm out.

"Why, thank you, Joe."

Nurse Brown walked out the door, I stopped to take her all in. She wore a blue blouse up top and tight black pants down below. Right at that moment, I knew this woman would be mine...

Chapter 11

After much debating, Nurse Brown and I decided to go to a Japanese Restaurant. Nurse Brown really picked the restaurant, not me, but I didn't mind. She drove us up to the joint... Wow, truly stunning. There were two giant dragon statues sitting outside. Walking up, I noticed a pond filled with koi.

"This place is pretty rad," I said.

Nurse Brown grabbed her mouth, giggling the entire time. "Rad? That's funny."

"Huh? What's so funny?"

Nurse Brown grabbed the door, I quickly jumped in front of her and held the door. After gesturing for her to enter, she did.

"Thank you. And I laughed because I haven't heard anyone say *rad* since, I think the *Teenage Mutant Ninja Turtles.*"

Teenage Mutant Ninja Turtles? I thought. That didn't ring a bell. It must have been something I missed... a side effect of time travel.

"Oh, yeah. Ha-ha, that's where I got it from," I laughed nervously.

Inside the restaurant, Nurse Brown ordered sushi. For me, I ordered the chicken hibachi. To be perfectly frank, I don't think I could eat raw fish. But apparently, it was *Lit,* as Nurse Brown put it... whatever that meant.

First, the waitress brought the sushi out. Nurse Brown attempted to feed me a piece, but I declined. She

149

laughed, looking extremely adorable as she did. A minute later, the cook walked out, pushing a cart. On the cart, the cook had my raw food and his supplies. He asked me if my order was correct and I told him it was. Then the show began. The Hibachi cook put on a glorious show. From fire volcanoes made from onions, to his amazing spatula flips, this guy rocked. The only thing I dug more than the cook's performance was his food... delicious.

Nurse Brown and I ate and laughed. We were getting to know each other and to be honest, I'm glad I traveled through time. The feelings this woman gave me was something I've never felt before. Would I have met someone back in my time that made me feel this way? Possibly, but what are the chances I travel through time and instantly fall for someone? Not high, I'll tell you that much.

After an hour, Nurse Brown and I finished our meals. Just as we got ready to leave, a large crowd of people walked into the restaurant.

"What's going on?" Nurse Brown asked.

I shook my head, "I honestly don't know."

In the middle of the crowd, I saw an Asian woman walking. She looked familiar, yet I couldn't place her. Next to the woman walked a younger man, maybe in his forties. This man reminded me of someone...

"Oh, my God. Look, Joe, it's Yoko Ono and her son, Sean."

"No fucking way, that's Yoko... and little Sean, look how big he got," I shouted.

"How big he got? What do you mean?" Nurse Brown asked.

I felt like an idiot, speaking out loud about the growth of a child that has been grown probably ever since Nurse Brown discovered him.

"Ah, nothing." My face blushed as I rubbed the back of my head.

The group passed us by. They headed toward a back room that had a *do not enter* sign. Yoko and Sean were only a few feet away from me when they walked by. All I wanted to do was run up and hug them both, tell them how I plan on saving John. But I couldn't. I'd look like a crazy person, and shit, maybe I was crazy. Plus, with that crowd of people, I wouldn't make it to them, anyway.

Nurse Brown grabbed my hand and we walked out of the restaurant. Like a star-struck child, I kept turning back around, trying to catch one last glimpse of John's family.

Outside, the moon lit up the sky, big and full. "Wow, look at the moon, Nurse Brown, it's so beautiful... and it's not orange."

Nurse Brown tugged on my hand. "Please, Joe, don't call me Nurse Brown. It makes me feel weird since I'm not at work. Just call me by my name, Alexis."

My eyes danced around Nurse Brown... sorry, Alexis. I stared up at the moon, then back at Alexis. "Ah, yeah, sorry about that."

She rubbed her fingers over my knuckles. "No worries, Joe." A confused expression formed on her face. "Say, what did you mean when you said it's *not orange?*"

Shit! I screamed in my head. *I got to stop slipping up.*

"Do you mean a blood moon?" Alexis asked. "I've seen that before and I thought it looked beautiful."

I smiled. "Ah, yeah, that's what I meant." Now I had to change the subject... and fast. "Do you work tomorrow?"

Alexis shook her head. "Nah, I'm off actually. Thank God, that place drives me nuts sometimes." I opened the car door for Alexis; she sat down in the driver's seat. "Why, thank you, Joe."

A smile formed on my face. I shut her door and walked to the passenger side. Now inside of her car, I kept the conversation going. "So you don't like your job?"

Alexis turned the key, her car's engine roared. "It's not that I don't like it, but the hospital can get crazy at times. Those days are very stressful."

"Oh, yeah, I can imagine..." Instantly John Lennon's beautiful song, *Imagine,* entered my mind. A small tear fell from my eye.

Alexis took notice to the tear, she placed the car back in park, even though she just put the gear in drive. "Is everything okay, Joe?"

Her eyes focused on the tear, I quickly wiped it away. "Yeah, I'm okay, just my allergies acting up." Once again, I needed to change the subject. "Say, this is a nice car, what kind is it?"

"It's a *2010 Hyundai Genesis Coupe.*"

"Nice," I said, rubbing the back of my hand on the seat. "I really like the bright red color of the car too."

Alexis laughed. "Yeah, it's pretty, but you know the saying, *arrest me red.*"

"Huh? Arrest me red? I've never heard of that saying."

Again, Alexis laughed. "You never heard of that saying? It basically means that because of my bright red color, cops will notice my car more and stop me more."

"Oh."

"Yeah, but I haven't been pulled over yet." Alexis placed the gear back in drive. "But if I do, then it's whatever. *YOLO*, am I right?"

These terminologies really had me scratching my head... literally. "YOLO?"

Alexis took her eyes off the road to glance at me. Her left eyebrow raised up. "Let me guess, Joe. You haven't heard of the saying, YOLO before, right?"

I shrugged my shoulders.

"Darn, Joe, where have you been in the past few decades? Living under a rock?"

Laughter exited my mouth. *If you only knew, my dear.* I rubbed my forehead. "I have a strict father, he kept me away from other kids." Jeez, I hated to lie to this woman. It didn't feel right.

"Oh, I'm so sorry, Joe." We pulled up to a red light. "Well, YOLO is an acronym of *you only live once.* You know how us texting users like to shorten words and terms."

I laughed some more. "Ah, yeah, you're right."

The light turned green. Alexis hit the gas and down the street we went. "Anyway, what's your address?"

"My address?"

"Yeah, so I know where to drop you off at, silly."

I glanced out the window and saw the library across the street. "Just drop me off at the library."

"Eh, Joe. The library is closed now, you won't be able to get in."

Shit, now what do I say? I can't tell her I sleep under bridges. I saw the library get farther away as Alexis kept on driving. "No, it's okay. I can wait till they reopen."

"Reopen?" Alexis said with a chuckle. "They don't open till ten in the morning." We hit another red light. She turned to face me. "If you don't want me to know where you live, that's fine. Take me somewhere close to your place and I'll drop you off. Then, you can walk to your home."

I let out a deep breath. "No, it's not that at all, Alexis." My head shifted to the window, I glared outside. "I don't have a home, I've been living on the streets."

Alexis suddenly whipped the car to the right, cutting off a white truck, barely missing it. She pulled the car into a vacant parking lot. "*OMG*, you're homeless?"

"OMG? Now, what in the hell is that?"

Alexis slammed her fist on the steering wheel. "Never mind that. You're homeless? Why didn't you tell me this?"

I tapped on my knee. "I guess I didn't want you to know. It's embarrassing, you know?"

Alexis sighed. "Okay, Joe. Well, you will come back to my house."

I swung my hands around. "No, no, no. You do not need to do this, Alexis."

"Yes, I do. I will not let you sleep on the street. You realize it's dangerous out there, right?"

My mind replayed the incident with Work Boots and Black Tennis Shoes. A shiver shot down my spine. "Yeah, I suppose it is dangerous out there."

Alexis pulled the car out of the vacant parking lot and continued down the road. "Yes, it is. So it's settled, you're staying at my place."

After about a twenty-minute drive, just outside of the city, we pulled up to a pretty nice looking house. The house was made from stone, a truly beautiful sight to see. "Wow, this is your home?"

Alexis nodded. "Yup."

We got out and I followed her up the driveway. "What suburb is this? I can't say that I've ever been out here before."

As Alexis opened her front door, she glanced back at me. "This suburb is Kensington. Supposedly one of the best suburbs outside of the city."

"Oh, nice."

Once inside, I found that the house looked even better. There was a beautiful fireplace, a spiral staircase, and a bunch of paintings on the wall. Plus, Alexis appeared to be a neat freak, not a single ounce of dust around.

"Jesus, your home is beautiful."

Alexis walked over to her white couch. She fluffed a few pillows. "Thanks, Joe."

Her couch had pillows all over it... seven, to be exact. I glanced back at her walls. Like I mentioned earlier, she had a bunch of paintings hanging up. "Are you an art collector?"

Alexis turned to face the wall. She walked over and grabbed one of the paintings. A smile formed on her face. "Do you like these paintings?"

I approached Alexis, looking at the painting. "Yeah, it's beautifully done."

She smirked. "Turn it over and read the name."

I flipped the painting around and saw the name: Alexis Brown. "No way, you painted this?"

Alexis laughed and clapped her hands. "Why, yes, I did." She pointed to the other paintings on the wall. "I've painted each and everyone one of them."

This woman truly blew my mind. She's beautiful, caring (working as a nurse means she has to care for people, right?), and now artistic? Jeez, this woman had me falling for her.

"Wow, that is far out, Alexis."

The left eyebrow of Alexis raised once again. "Far out? What are you saying?"

I turned to look at the paintings on the wall. "You know, far out, it means cool."

Alexis shook her head. "Man, Joe. You with these phrases and not knowing anything I say." Alexis laughed, "Are you some sort of time traveler?"

The hair stood up on the back of my neck. "Ha-ha, very funny." I turned and looked at the front door. "Alexis, I don't want to be a bother, I should go. I'll be okay."

Just as I started to walk toward the front door, Alexis grabbed my arm. She waved her finger in my face. "You aren't going anywhere, mister." She slapped the couch. "Here, you can sleep on the couch. I'll go get you a blanket."

Alexis removed all but one of the pillows. She ran up the spiral staircase, just to return shortly after with an orange blanket. *It has to be orange,* I thought as I watched her walk down the stairs.

"Here you go, Joe."

I smiled and took the blanket. "Aw, thank you. You're too kind."

Alexis handed me the remote to her large TV. She told me that she had a wonderful time and we said our good night's. I lay on the white couch, watching Alexis walk up the spiral steps. *Damn, she's great.*

I lay on Alexis's neat white couch for a few hours. While switching through the television channels, I came across a show where they showed a bunch of clips from the internet and a comedian cracked jokes on each one. I cannot lie, this show had me laughing. After watching three episodes of the show, I fell asleep...

Thick, dark clouds filled the sky. One minute that bright orange ball was there, the next minute it was gone. Flashes of light seemingly danced through the dark clouds. Drops of rain started to land on my head, then my arms.

I glanced up, the rain intensified, I turned to run back inside... "What the?" Behind me, there was nothing, nothing but a field. No house, and no Big Apple. "Where am I?" I asked.

Not surprisingly, I received no answer. As I walked around in this deserted grass field, the lighting appeared to pick up. The sky was flashing every two seconds or so. The wind blew hard.

Through the blowing wind, an eerie soft voice spoke to me. "Joe Miller, you will not succeed..."

The voice undoubtedly belonged to the monster.

"Where are you? Where am I?" I asked.

The wind blew again, this time harder. "You can't stop what's already happened."

Lightning flashes filled the sky again. In the middle of the sky, the dark clouds moved away just enough to create a round hole. There, crystal clear blue sky could be seen.

"Fuck you, monster!" I screamed. "I will stop you and save John's life!"

A glowing ball filled the blue sky, yet it wasn't the orange glowing ball of light. This time, the red glowing ball appeared. A sense of hate poured into me, making my blood boil.

The wind blew once more. "You're pathetic, Joe. You weren't there when your own father died and you didn't save Lennon when you had the chance."

"Fuck you!" I screamed at the top of my lungs.

The largest lightning bolt I've ever seen struck down just feet in front of me. A loud bang pierced my ears...

"Good morning, Joe."

The loud bang woke me up. Now awake, I discovered the bang came from Alexis placing a tray of food on the coffee table. I sat up, rubbing my eyes. "Oh, hey, good morning."

"I hope you don't mind me waking you up. I made breakfast and I didn't feel like eating it alone."

"Ah, no, I don't mind, it smells really good," I said as I rubbed the back of my head.

Alexis smiled. "It's scrambled eggs, hash browns, and I even made a bunch of those little sausage links."

"Yummy, it all sounds so good." I tried my best to get that nightmare out of my mind. Alexis certainly did help. Her smile brought me back to a sense of peace.

"Here, wait one second." Alexis ran out to the kitchen. She returned a second later with two paper plates, two plastic spoons, and two plastic forks. "Here." Alexis handed me a plate. "I brought spoons and forks, didn't know which one you preferred."

"A fork is good, thank you."

Alexis handed me a fork. She quickly snapped her fingers. "I almost forgot, what would you like to drink? Coffee or orange juice?"

"Coffee is good for me. Thank you."

Alexis ran out to the kitchen again. She returned with a pot full of coffee and two mugs. After pouring the coffee she asked if I wanted any cream or sugar, I declined. With everything going on in my life, I think I needed the most potent version of caffeine.

Alexis and I ate, talked, and laughed the entire morning. I truly enjoyed spending time with her. After breakfast, Alexis demanded that I look for a job. She pulled her small computer out and hooked up the internet. Alexis went on a website called *Indeed,* she told me this site had tons of jobs on it. Before I could apply, I had to write up my resume... oh boy, how do I get out of this one? I can't really say that I worked at a candy factory back in 1980...

"Joe, I asked, what is your job history?"

"Ah, yeah. To be perfectly frank, I don't have any history of work."

Alexis' eyebrow shot up again. Even though I felt crazy about this woman, her eyebrow really started to bug me.

"What do you mean you don't have any work history? You never worked a day in your life?"

My mind raced through many answers. Finally, I settled on what I believed to be a good answer. "Of course I worked before, don't be silly."

Alexis crossed her arms and sighed.

My hands gripped the pillow on the couch. "I worked with my dad at his business plenty of times. He would pay me under the table, though. So I can't really use that on a resume."

This, of course, was a big fat lie... but a good one at that.

"Okay, that's cool," Alexis said. "So what did your Dad do?"

"What did he do?"

"Yeah, Joe. What was his business?"

My mind went back to a situation that changed my life... the death of John Lennon. That day at the Dakota, the reason I was there to begin with. I remembered being on a job, cleaning the floors of the mighty apartment building.

"My Dad had a floor cleaning business."

Alexis grabbed her hair, fixing the ponytail she sported. "Oh, that's cool. Okay, well, then we will leave your work history blank."

I nodded, but Alexis shot me a look. "This might hold you back from getting a job. At least the good-paying jobs."

"Well, all I can do is try, right?" I said, shrugging my shoulders.

Alexis nodded her head. She reached out and squeezed my shoulder. Oh, how I loved her touch.

The next hour passed and Alexis went to work on finding me a job. After setting up my profile, she sent my resume to a hundred jobs, or at least it seemed like a hundred jobs. Later on in the day, I told Alexis that I'd leave and try to get some money for a hotel room, but she declined that notion. She told me I could stay with her as long as I needed too, or at least till I got a job. Now the waiting game began, nothing I could do till an employer reached out.

Later that night, Alexis and I were watching a movie on the television. It was a romantic movie called *The Notebook*. Now, I personally found the movie boring, but Alexis loved it. She kept crying throughout the movie, which made it good for me, since she kept grabbing my arm.

After the movie, she put on a cartoon show about four boys that live in Colorado. This show made me laugh so hard, yet when I glanced back at Alexis, she fell asleep. Her head lay on my shoulder; she snored slightly. I found this to be incredibly cute. Not too long after Alexis fell asleep, I did as well.

In the morning, I woke up to an empty couch. I figured Alexis must've woken up during the night and headed to bed. After a few minutes, I sat up, rubbing my eyes. On the coffee table in front of me were two things. A cranberry muffin and a folded note. The muffin smelt great, but I grabbed the note first. I opened the note and read the message. *Hey Joe, I had to go to work early today and I didn't want to wake you. I just wanted to thank you for a great last two days. You are such a sweetheart and I'm glad I've got the chance to know you. Good luck on the job search today! XoXo- Alexis.*

The grin on my face after reading Alexis' letter would make *The Joker* jealous. This couldn't be real. How could me, Joe Miller, travel through time and up in the future? Then, in the future, I meet and fall head over heels over a woman. This entire situation was insane. I started to pinch my arms, trying to see if I'd actually wake up... I didn't. Yup, this wasn't no dream, just the new reality that overtook my life.

After letting my emotions run wild for a few minutes, I ate the muffin (it tasted great). After filling my belly, I grabbed Alexis' computer. Now, I should have been looking for more jobs, but I decided to take advantage of my alone time and look up more information about my unique situation.

First, in the search bar, I typed the monster's name again. Seeing pictures of this goon really pissed me off.

Once again I saw the name of the facility where they kept this piece of garbage. *Wende Correctional Facility, Wende Correctional Facility, Wende Correctional Facility.* This kept running through my head. I couldn't stop my mind from screaming it.

Next, I looked up the society that might know about the glowing orange ball. The Outer Space Conspiracy Society. I clicked on their website and a beautiful animation of the solar system appeared. *Whoa, neat.* On the webpage, it literally showed the planets orbiting around the sun. On the right side of the page, just after the animation, a picture of a man appeared. This man had gray hair and wore glasses. He had a part in his hair and a thick mustache. *Hmm, he somewhat resembles someone I've met before,* I thought as I scrolled down the page.

Underneath the photo, I saw the name of the man; Barry Frey. *Yup, I knew he looked like someone. He looks like the man I met on the motorcycle... I knew they were related.* My mind raced with all these thoughts. After some more searching on the page, I found the address of The Outer Space Conspiracy Society. Next to the address, I saw a phone number. *Shit, I need a phone.* As I glanced around the room, looking for a home phone (there wasn't a home phone), a message popped up on the computer.

An icon of a letter blocked my screen, it read *new email.* Under the new email, two more buttons appeared. *Open* and *decline.* I dragged the cursor to the open button and clicked on it. A response to one of my job applications appeared on the computer screen. The message came from *New York Penn Station*; the rail station here in New York City. To be perfectly frank, I didn't recall applying to this position, but Alexis did most of the applying for me.

Working on a train excited me. I clicked on the link to find a surprise. *Custodian for Penn Station. Job includes cleaning the areas of the terminal. Cleaning includes outside of the restaurants/shops, but does not include inside of those businesses. Starting pay is $12.50 hr. Click reply if you are still interested.*

My dreams were crushed, I wouldn't be working on a train, just in the terminal, cleaning up after all the slobs. *Oh, well, it's a job,* I thought as I clicked on the *reply* button. A form popped up, asking for my phone number. Of course, I didn't have a phone number. So I left the computer alone and figured I'd wait for Alexis to get home. She'd probably let me put her number down.

Into the kitchen, I walked. On the counter sat a coffee maker. A smile formed on my face as the thought of a hot cup of coffee would be good right now. After snooping around Alexis' cabinets, I found the coffee. A box of plastic spoons sat on the kitchen table, I took one out and scooped out the coffee. After placing the coffee in the filter, I grabbed the coffee pot, and filled it all the way up with water.

Dumping the water in the back of the coffeemaker, I placed the pot down, and the filter in the correct spot.

An orange button on the side of the coffee maker caught my eye. I clicked the button and it glowed a bright orange color. A slight shiver hit me, but that quickly dissipated once the smell of coffee hit the air.

Now, with the tutorial of making coffee out of the way, I'll get back to the heart of my story. On the front porch, I stood, sipping on the freshly made hot coffee. My eyes squinted to see the sun. A few things swarmed my mind.

Number one: when will the *other* orange glowing ball in the sky return?

Number two: how in the hell do I get to the *Wende Correctional Facility?*

Number three: what does Barry Frey from Red Lion, Pennsylvania, really know?

Number four: why does Alexis trust me enough to have me stay in her house alone?

These questions I hoped to find answers to, and soon...

Chapter 12

Later in the evening, a little after five, a car pulled into the driveway. I sat on the porch in the big rocker. Another fresh hot cup of coffee by my side (I made six cups of coffee throughout the day). The car belonged to Alexis, of course. She jumped out of the car and waved; the way a little kid would wave at a friend they haven't seen in a week.

She ran up on the porch, holding a bag. "Hey, Joe! How was your day?"

"Good, to be perfectly frank."

Alexis giggled. "That's good." She held up the bag. "I grabbed us some burgers. I hope that's good."

"Hey, if you're getting food, I'm not going to complain." I rocked in the chair, slowing down to let Alexis sit. The rocking chair wasn't that big, but she could fit next to me.

She crossed her right leg over her left. A part of her leg sat on my thigh; this I didn't mind. "So how did your job searching go today?" Alexis asked.

"Great!" I shouted.

"Great? Did someone contact you?"

"As a matter of fact, they did," I said. "The only problem is they wanted my phone number... I don't have a phone."

Alexis jumped up from the rocking chair. "That is great news!" She dug her hands in the pockets of her scrubs, pulling out her cell phone. "You can use my phone."

I took another sip of my coffee. "Thank you, Alexis. I'll make sure I call them."

Alexis pushed something on her phone. "You can call now, Joe. They still might be in."

Jumping off the rocker, I stretched. "Okay, I can do that. The number is on the mail they sent me."

"Mail? They sent you a letter?" Alexis asked.

I bent down and picked up my cup of coffee. "Yeah, on the computer they did."

"Oh, you mean through an email?"

I sipped my coffee. "Ah, yeah. If that's what you call it, sure."

A funny expression formed on her face. She shook her head and dusted off my comments. "Anyhow, so Joe, what is the job?"

Alexis walked inside the house; I followed. "It's at the *New York Penn Station*."

She jumped up and down, clapping her hands. "That's great, Joe. It's for the custodian position, right?"

"Yeah..." I scratched my head. "How did you know?"

Alexis laughed. "Well, silly, I did apply for you."

"Oh." Rubbing the back of my head, I let out a small giggle. "I thought the job was going to be me, working inside of a train."

Alexis leaned up against the railing of the steps. "Joe, you have to start out somewhere. One day, maybe you'll be the conductor of a train."

This didn't provoke an answer from me, as I didn't care about becoming a conductor. What I wanted to do was far bigger than some job.

"I'm going to run upstairs to get changed. Once I come back down, we'll call the job. Okay?"

I nodded and smiled. Alexis returned a smile and ran up the stairs.

She returned in less than five minutes. We went to the couch to sit down. Alexis found the phone number for the job and called it. She handed the phone over to me once it rang. To be perfectly frank, I got nervous holding the phone up to my ear. The thought of applying for a new job, in this time, scared the willies out of me.

"Hi, yes, I'm Joe Miller. I applied for the custodial position."

A deep, scruffy voice answered on the phone. "Yes, Joe, it's nice to meet you. So tell me, are you still interested in the job?"

"Ah, yeah, I am."

"Good." The man cleared his voice in a disgusting phlegmy way. "How about you stop by tomorrow morning around nine?"

"Ah, yeah, I'll be there. Thank you."

"Good, see you then, Joe. Oh, by the way, the name is Randy."

Randy abruptly hung up the phone. Alexis clapped her hands. "What did he say?"

I held the phone away from my face, glancing at it. These things were still weird to me. Alexis grabbed the phone out of my hand.

"He told me to meet him tomorrow morning, at nine."

"Great, this is what we can do," Alexis said, glancing out the window toward her car. "You get up early in the morning and I'll let you drop me off at work. Then, you take my car and get to your interview."

"You sure you want me to take your car, Alexis? We still don't know each other completely, that's a lot of trust."

Alexis clapped her thigh as she let out a glorious laugh. "Sweetie, I'm letting you stay in my house, even when I'm not here. I think you borrowing my car will be fine."

You know what? She certainly had a point there.

The rest of the evening Alexis helped me get ready for my interview. First, we went out to a shopping mall and she bought me a nice dress shirt and a pair of slacks. Once we got back to her house, Alexis performed a bunch of mock interviews, pretending to be my potential boss. Damn, she looked so cute while she did it. By the end of the night, I felt ready.

The next morning, I showered and put on my new outfit. Alexis put on her light blue scrub outfit, which she looked so adorable in. She let me drive her to work, which went well.

After dropping her off, I headed to the *New York Penn Station.* Back in my time, in New York, before my little predicament, I never set foot at the *New York Penn Station.* This would all be new to me and I can't lie, it excited me. I've heard about the station before and always wanted to go. Now I'd get my wish.

After a nice long struggle to find a parking spot, I finally did. Stepping out of the car, I took a deep breath. After my exhale, I trotted inside the station, feeling pretty confident as of now. *This job will be mine. I've got this.* I repeatedly said this to myself for the entire walk. Now, inside of the station, my nerves started to return.

First, I didn't know where to go to meet Randy, he never told me. Second, I already forgot everything Alexis told me to say from our mock interviews. I truly hated these one-on-one interviews, but whatever, it needed to be done. While walking around the station, I found an information desk. Behind the desk, a middle-aged, partly balding man sat.

"Hi," I said.

The balding man smiled at me, exposing his front gold tooth. "Hello, sir. How may I help you?"

"Ah, yes. I'm here to meet Randy..." Then it hit me, Randy never told me his last name. "Ah, I'm not sure of his last name, but I'm here for an interview."

The balding man sat up in his chair. "Yes, you want Randy Morris. I'll call him right now."

Less than five minutes from the balding man's phone call, I found myself shaking Randy's hand. He told me to follow him back to his office. The entire walk to his office, Randy kept pointing around the vicinity, explaining to me what I'd be cleaning. In his office, Randy basically asked me if I wanted the job. He explained how the last cleaner just up and quit, so they needed someone right away. This all happened so quickly, but I accepted the job and would start tomorrow morning at seven.

That night Alexis jumped in my arms when I told her the good news. She wanted to celebrate, so she took me back out to the Japanese restaurant. We laughed, ate, and drank the natural hot green tea. It was a great time, for sure. There was only one thing missing from that night: no Yoko or Sean.

The new problem we faced was the *how to get to work epidemic*. We both started at seven, and only Alexis had a car. But Alexis, being the kindred spirit I started to find out she was, told me I could drive her car. I'd drop her off at the hospital a little earlier, and then I'd drive myself to work. I asked, "What happens if you get off earlier than me?" At that time, I didn't know how long I'd actually be working during the day. But Alexis told me if I thought I'd be working late, she'd just call an *Uber* to drive her home. This sounded great, but I asked, "How would I let you know?"

After the restaurant, Alexis took me to the store to buy me a cell phone. This felt strange, having my own phone, one that didn't have a cord, or connect to the wall... strange indeed. The remainder of the night, she went over how to use the phone. If I told you I got the hang of it, I'd be lying.

The next morning, I woke up feeling groggy. I hated waking up early, as I'm definitely not a morning person. But I got up (thanks to Alexis) and got ready for work. After dropping Alexis off at her job and receiving a big hug, then, I drove to the station. Inside the station, Randy met me at the information desk again. Like yesterday, for the entire walk down the hallway of the station, Randy pointed at what I'd be cleaning. He explained to me the job function, which didn't seem hard at all. Heck, I used to strip floors... back in 1981.

I got started on my job, cleaning the area. Randy left only an hour after I started, which I liked. I didn't mind working by myself, not one bit. The job wasn't hard at all, I even had some downtime to sneak off to one of the custodian closets to relax. My downtime grew larger the more I worked. After two months, I knew when and where I could sneak off to relax.

Of course, I didn't just sit around and do nothing. I started to get good with this cell phone. It's basically a pocket computer, pretty far out, huh? You could get on the internet and search for things just like you could on a computer. That's exactly what I did. I dug deeper into the mystery of the glowing orange ball, and I came up with a brilliant idea.

One day, I'll hop on the train and head down to Pennsylvania. I found the route maps, and discovered the train goes to Harrisburg, Pennsylvania. Harrisburg is only about a forty-five-minute drive from Red Lion. Once in Harrisburg, I'd order an *Uber* and have it take me to Red Lion. Then, I'd find The Outer Space Conspiracy Society, and get to the bottom of this entire thing... they must know something.

That day came on the third month anniversary of me starting the job. I told my boss the day before I had a doctor's appointment, so he gave me off. By this time, Alexis would drop me off at work in the morning and I'd take an *Uber* home since I had some money now.

The day of my planned trip to Red Lion arrived. Alexis drove me to work and dropped me off. I walked in, like every other day, but on this day, I bought a train ticket (forty-seven dollars, for the cheapest seat). On the train I walked, finding my seat. The seats were a blue color and made from some sort of soft material. Once in my seat, I stared out the window, feeling a little antsy.

What if Barry Frey doesn't know a thing about the orange glowing ball...? What if he does? These thoughts bounced around in my head as the train took off.

The ride was amazing, I must say. The scenery outside the window was simply breathtaking. They brought food and drinks to me, which both tasted good. Also, I played a game on my cell phone throughout the ride. I enjoyed this game very much. In the game, you take this bird and you fling him at pigs... simple, yet effective.

After about three and a half hours, the train pulled into the Harrisburg station. By now, I was ready to get off the train. Once off the train, I clicked on the *Uber* app that Alexis downloaded for me and I requested a ride. My driver showed up about twenty minutes later. He seemed like a nice guy, just a little old. His hair was snow white and the glasses he wore were thicker than the Earth's crust. But he drove the speed limit and kept up the chatter.

Forty-five minutes later, my driver dropped me off in Red Lion, at a small grocery store. I thanked him and tugged on my ears. That dude could talk your ears off... literally. Now, I would be off to meet Barry Frey. The grocery store where I had the driver drop me off was only a five-minute walk from the Outer Space Conspiracy Society headquarters.

First, I ran into the grocery store and bought a pop. It tasted good, refreshing, to say the least. Then my short walk to the Outer Space Conspiracy Society began. The day was beautiful, the bright orange sun sat in the sky, not a single cloud in sight. Even though I enjoyed my walk, the closer I got, the more my nerves bounced around. This truly would be the first real *step* of me figuring out my situation.

At the end of the street, a small, deep purple colored hut sat. I called it a hut because it truly looked like one. On the door hung a sign saying: *Welcome to the Outer*

Space Conspiracy Society. After about a million deep breaths, I opened the door. Inside, my eyes immediately locked on the walls. They were painted, beautifully in fact, with planets, stars, and everything outer space.

A small desk sat about five feet from me, but no one appeared to be around. On the desk, a call bell sat. Since no one seemed to be around, I tapped the call bell... repeatedly. Behind the desk, a deep purple colored curtain hung; the color matched the walls. After my few rings on the call bell, a man appeared.

"Hi, may I help you?"

This man indeed was Barry Frey (I recognized him from the picture on the website).

"Ah, hi, my name is Joe Miller."

Barry smiled. "Hello, Joe. What brings you to the Outer Space Conspiracy Society?"

While staring at Barry, I noticed he truly had the slickest part I've ever seen in one man's hair. Just as I was about to open my mouth, the door opened from behind me. I turned around to see a woman walking in the door, carrying a box.

"Hey Dad," the woman said. "I got a bunch of stuff from the yard sales today. Like you said, *grab all the free stuff.*"

Barry chuckled, gesturing for his daughter to bring him the box.

I cleared my throat, trying to regain his attention. "Ah, Barry, if possible, I'd like to talk to you in private."

Barry dug into the box at an intense rate. He seemed like a man on a mission.

His daughter looked at me, but apparently, he didn't hear me. "Ah, can I speak to you in private?"

Barry's head whipped up toward me. In his hand, he held an old *Slinky* toy. "Joe, you got kids? Give them this toy, you can have it."

I waved my hands around. "No, I don't have any kids. Barry, I have something to talk to you about... It's about the bright glowing orange ball in the sky."

Barry's eyes narrowed. "You talking about the sun?" His eyes glanced over to his daughter.

"Ah, no," I replied.

A low chuckle exited Barry's mouth. "Here, Sara." He handed his daughter the *Slinky*. "Take this toy, give it to one of your friends. One that has a kid."

The daughter, Sara, laughed. "Sure, Dad."

Barry gestured for me to follow him. "Joe, come with me."

We walked back behind the curtain. In the back were a bunch of boxes and what I'd call *junk* lying around. We approached a door; Barry opened it. Inside sat a small desk and a barstool. Yeah, that's right, a barstool, not a chair.

"Have a seat," Barry said as he sat down behind his desk.

"Thank you, Barry." I sat on the barstool, it spun sideways (I nearly fell off). "Nice place you got here."

Barry chuckled. "Yeah, great. So get to the point of your visit."

Damn, I thought. *This guy doesn't mess around.* "Yes, I see you run this society about outer space. I want to know if you know anything about a mysterious glowing orange ball? And, no, not the sun." Barry sat silently, not saying a word. He held something in his hand and he tapped it on his desk. I glanced down at his hand to see he held a silver dollar. "Do you know anything about an orange glowing ball or no?" I asked again.

Barry flipped the silver dollar through his fingers. His eyes bounced back and forth between me and the silver dollar.

I jumped off the barstool. "Okay, well, I'm not wasting my time. Good day."

My hand gripped the door handle, ready to pull the door open till Barry's voice echoed out. "What have you experienced?"

I turned around, meeting Barry eye to eye.

"Have you had any experiences with the orange ball?" Barry asked.

Back on the barstool, I sat, nearly falling off. "Ah, yes I have... a lot in fact."

Barry reached down at his desk. He opened the drawer and pulled out a Dictaphone. "Here," Barry said, clicking a button. "Explain everything to me."

I proceeded to do just that. Even though this was the first time I've met this man, something told me to trust him. He watched me as I explained the very first time I saw the orange glowing ball. I explained to him what I believed to be the connection between the mysterious light in the sky and the murder of John Lennon. Then, I finished by giving him my memories on the orange glowing ball sucking me into the future. Most people would stare at me and roll their eyes, or laugh. A normal person possibly would have called the psych ward on me, but not Barry Frey. He listened and stayed focused on my story. This man appeared to believe me, so I must have been at the right spot.

After I spilled the beans of what I've experienced with the orange glowing ball, Barry told me his mission in life.

"Joe, I want you to know that I believe every word you say. You want to know why I believe you?"

I nodded my head.

"Because it has become my life's work to find this orange light and enter it."

My heart seemed to skip a beat. It startled me that someone else actually knew what in the hell I was talking about.

"Go on, please," I muttered.

Barry nodded. "Back in 1980, I was twenty-five. My studies into outer space intensified. I love everything about space, my dream was to become an astronaut one day."

My leg jumped from a nervous tick. I wanted him to get to the point, and fast.

Barry continued. "Well, on December 8, 1980..."

The day Lennon got shot…

"While looking through my telescope, I saw the orange ball. I maximized the magnification, and what I saw, startled me," Barry said.

Sweat beads formed on my forehead. My leg's tick became more intense. "What was it, Barry?"

"In the orange glowing ball, I saw what appeared to be eyes… blinking eyes that locked directly on me."

"Jesus," I muttered.

"Yeah, but it gets even crazier. The eyes started out very fuzzy, hard to see. But once the eyes seemed to lock onto me, everything became clearer. Once the fuzziness was gone…" Barry took his glasses off, he wiped his forehead with his sleeve. "A face appeared, but not just any face."

Barry started slamming his silver dollar into the desk, harder and harder. The silver dollar flew out of his hand, I reached down and grabbed the coin before it hit the ground.

"Here," I said, handing the silver dollar back. "What face did you see, Barry?"

Barry took the coin, held it up in front of my face. My eyes locked on the *heads* side of the coin. The design of a woman in a dress, holding something, maybe flowers. Barry flipped the coin around and the same image appeared… *Double-headed coin?*

"The face I saw was mine, it was fucking me, man," Barry bellowed.

I gasped and leaned back, falling off the barstool. My back slammed on the floor, the barstool kicked up, chipping a part of the desk.

Barry jumped up, walking over toward me. "You okay, Joe?"

While grabbing for my back, I responded, "Are you okay? Why in the hell was your face in the God-forsaken thing?"

Barry grabbed my hand; he helped me up. I assured him that I felt fine, and he picked up the barstool. Reluctantly, I sat down on the barstool. My back still ached, but I didn't pay much attention to the pain. This mysterious orange glowing ball was a lot more serious than a hurt back.

"That's the thing, Joe. I don't believe this orange ball of light is forsaken."

"What are you saying, Barry?"

"Well, in my opinion, the orange ball might be God or some form of authority." Barry adjusted his glasses and reached back into his drawer. He pulled out a Bible, throwing it down on the desk. "To be perfectly clear, I don't think this orange ball is the God you may have read in this book. Or in any other religious books out there."

My eyes locked on the Bible. It appeared to be old, and it even had an orange faded tint to it.

"God in the Bible or the Quran, or any of these other books, was created by man. To me, these Gods aren't real. Man is an ignorant species, and I believe they used what they didn't understand to control others."

To be honest, I couldn't take my eyes off of this orange-tinted Bible. They stayed locked on it the entire time he spoke.

"I think this orange ball is what really created the universe and I've made assumptions that it's sort of a protector," Barry explained.

Finally, my eyes left the Bible and locked back onto Barry. "Protector of what, exactly?"

"Protector of all things good in the universe." Barry leaned forward in his chair. "The orange ball is connected to me... to my family."

My eyes blinked hard as I tried to follow along with him.

"I believe that John Lennon was some sort of beacon of hope, some kind of force of good that the universe needed. When he got shot, everything in the universe got flipped upside down," Barry explained.

I cracked my neck to the left, then the right. "How can you be so sure? I loved John Lennon and admired his peaceful message. To be honest, I'm his biggest fan. But for one man to be that important to the universe? That's hard to believe. Plus, what about the fool who killed him? Is he a force of evil?"

Barry smirked. "Yes, like in every story, there's good and there's evil. The killing of John Lennon set off the evil in the world, making it more powerful."

My head started to hurt from all this information. I closed my eyes and rubbed over them.

"Have you seen the red light, Joe?"

I opened my eyes, glaring at Barry.

"The ball, have you seen it change from orange to red?" Barry asked.

"Orange changing to red?" I said. My mind started to replay the night Lennon was shot.

"Maybe you haven't seen it, but I have also witnessed a glowing red ball of light," Barry said. "In my opinion, that's the evilness of the universe. Or, as in the man-made religious books, this would represent the devil."

My memory brought me back to when Lennon was shot, how the orange ball expanded and changed more to a red color. I then thought of the other occasions where the ball changed to red. That's when things seemed to truly get bad.

"Barry, where did you see the red ball? Have you seen it as many times as the orange one?"

Barry shook his head. "No, I've only witnessed the red ball one time..." Barry reached down and picked his silver dollar back up. He began to flip it between his fingers as he did before. "When I was looking at the orange ball, after my face appeared, it quickly vanished."

I scratched my head, listening to Barry's story.

"The thing I forgot to mention was on the night I saw the orange ball, I was in New York City," Barry said.

Jeez, he was in New York when Lennon got killed…

"Why were you in New York on that night? To stop Lennon's assassination?" I asked.

"I wasn't, no… but my father was…" Sadness grew on Barry's face. "It was my father's life goal to track this thing down."

My mind raced. I tried to remember if I saw anyone else on that night that was trying to stop the monster from shooting Lennon.

Barry chuckled as he rubbed his hands through his hair, destroying the perfect part he had. "Now it's my mission. Like father, like son, aye?"

"How did your father know this? And why was he tracking this thing?" I asked.

Barry took a deep breath. He sat straight up. His eyes narrowed, locking onto mine. "The reason I have been tracking it, every single day since the eighth of December 1980, is to find my father, James Frey, who vanished into the light."

"James Frey…" I mumbled under my breath.

"The image of my face in the orange glow faded away and it turned red, a blood shot red, and I swear, just for a second, a set of darker red eyes flashed at me," Barry said.

I felt sick to my stomach all of a sudden. This information scared me, even though I was already living through it.

"I was watching it through my telescope because I was following my dad. He told me the light would shine over Dakota sometime in December. He thought this meant the state, and he didn't want to travel to New York, but I made him."

"You made him? How?" I asked.

"I told him some guys at the convention knew about the orange ball and that since he didn't know when in December it would show up, that he should follow me."

Tears filled Barry's eyes. He took off his glasses to wipe them dry.

"What did these people know?" I asked.

Barry shook his head as he used his shirt to clean his glasses. "Nothing, I made it up so he could stay by my side. But he didn't do that, he snuck away after he stepped outside for some fresh air."

I felt even more confused now, but at least my sickness started to ease up.

"I went to go check on him and I found him jumping inside a taxi," Barry said. "Then I looked up at the sky and for the first time in my life, I saw the orange ball, and it wasn't the damn moon, man."

My mind went back to the night of Lennon's killing and I tried to think harder of seeing someone else there that stood out. Seeing the man I met on the motorcycle all of these years earlier. This I didn't remember, but a flash of orange light did enter my mind.

"I got into a taxi, we followed closely and I saw him get out a couple blocks from the Dakota building. That's when it hit me. This was the Dakota my dad was supposed to be at."

"How'd he hear about the Dakota being the place to be at in December?" I asked.

"He said in his dreams, from his friend."

I didn't know what to think of this statement. What friend was James referring to? Then I remembered my encounter with James at the gas station. I remembered how nice he was to me and how I felt a strange connection to him. Then, I thought of him riding away on his motorcycle.

"Your dad, James, he liked to ride motorcycles, right?"

Barry sat straight up. He now looked confused. "Yes, how did you know that?"

A small smile formed on my face. "I met him back on Thanksgiving Day, 1974. He stopped at the same gas station my father and I stopped at. He was such a nice guy."

The tears I witnessed fell from Barry's eye before returned. "Yeah, he was the best man ever."

Barry and I sat in silence for about three minutes. Finally, I decided that this might be a good enough time to leave. "Ah, thank you, Barry. Thank you for all the information, but I best believe I should get going."

Just as I stood up from the barstool, Barry promptly stopped me. "Wait! Joe, there's more."

Ah, shit, I have had about enough I can handle for one day.

I never told you the reason why my father was tracking this thing in the first place.

My head tilted to the side. "Why was he tracking it?"

"A man named Ollie Oggy. He was an astronaut back in the sixties," Barry said.

I tried to think if I remembered that name, but it didn't ring a bell.

"Ollie was my father's best friend growing up. Those two were inseparable. Then, on one mission, up in space, Ollie disappeared."

My mind started to understand. I knew at that moment that Ollie must have been taken by the light.

"Despite his disappearance, my father kept telling me that he was seeing Ollie in his dreams and that Ollie was telling him to follow the orange ball of light, to bring him back."

My stomach wasn't hurting any longer, but now my head started to hurt. All of this information was too much at once.

Barry stood up as he continued his story. "Ollie told me he saw a big, bright glowing orange ball. He even said it gave off a loud *ringing* noise," Barry explained.

"Wait, I thought you said he disappeared?" I said. "How did you speak to this Ollie guy?"

Barry walked to the door, "Wait here." He exited the room.

I sat on the barstool, twiddling my thumbs.

Barry re-entered the room in about a minute. He held a half folded newspaper in his hand. "Here, read this. I kept it and I'm glad I did, all the other newspapers of the article mysteriously disappeared."

I grabbed the paper and read the article: *Commander Ollie Oggy, missing spacecraft pilot found alive nearly forty years after he disappeared. Ollie looks like he hasn't aged a bit. Mr. Oggy explained that he got sucked through some sort of orange wormhole. He was placed on a new planet, in a new universe. Mr. Oggy said the orange wormhole returned shortly after his landing and destroyed the planet, shooting him back to Earth, into the future. As of now, Mr. Oggy is being held by the Military.*

I glanced up at Barry. "What happened to Ollie, is he still alive?"

Barry nodded. "Yes, the last time I saw him he was, at least."

"So, you did see him."

Barry nodded once more. "Yes, I have. I needed to see if he knew where my father was." Barry lowered his head. "But he didn't."

I clapped my hands, still holding the half folded newspaper. "Where's he living at? We should go together and talk with him."

Barry shook his head. "No, I can't visit him any more. These *men* in suits told me not to come back."

His statement struck me as odd. "Wait, come back to where? What men in suits?"

Barry shrugged. "I honestly don't know who the men were, but they didn't seem to like all the questions about the orange ball and time travel that I was asking. Oh, and Ollie lives in a nursing home now, in the psychiatric unit."

A sense of sadness struck me. "So he's crazy, huh?"

"Yeah, that's what they are saying, at least. These men know about this entire thing, and they must be covering it up."

Two quick knocks banged at the door. "One second," Barry shouted.

"Your dad, what happened after he got out of the taxi?" I asked.

"I used my telescope to spy on him. He was kneeling down in the darkness, right before the archway of the Dakota. As John's limo pulled up, the orange ball of light swooped down and snatched him up... he was gone, simply gone," Barry said.

This now made me more confused. "Wait, so the orange ball is bad? It didn't let your dad stop that fat monster."

Barry calmly shook his head. "No, I think it was protecting him."

"From what?" I quickly asked.

"A second before the orange ball took my father, a shadowy figure appeared behind him, I could see red glowing eyes on it."

Knocks continued at the door.

"Come in," Barry shouted.

His daughter, Sara, opened the door. "Dad, there are some people out there that would like to see some of the paintings of the planets you did. They said they saw them online."

Barry smiled. "Okay, tell them I'll be right there."

Sara smiled and left the room.

I turned back to face Barry. "Does your daughter know about this?"

"No, she knows nothing at all…"

I glanced at a clock on the wall and noticed the time: 2 PM. *Shit, I better get back in time to be at the station for when Alexis comes to pick me up.*

"Barry, this truly has been a pleasure, you've helped me a lot with my situation and I hope to keep in touch. But I really need to get going now."

Barry smiled. "It was great meeting you too." He placed his hand on my shoulder. "It's nice to know that I'm no longer alone in this thing."

I smirked, not so sure that this was a good thing.

Barry handed me a business card. "Here, keep this, it has my number and email. Keep me updated if you find out anything new."

"Will do," I said, as I slipped the card in my back pocket.

As I almost reached the door, Barry called me again. "Joe."

I turned to face him.

"Can I get the newspaper back?"

I glanced down to see that I was still holding the paper. "Ah, yeah, sorry."

As I walked over I unfolded the paper and saw underneath the article showed a picture of a man lying in a hospital bed. The picture appeared to be an amateur snapshot of Ollie Oggy. Men in military uniforms stood around the bed.

My mouth dropped open. I brought the paper closer to my face. The two military men were the FBI agents. My face went ghostly white.

"You okay, Joe?"

I looked up at Barry, gulped, half-smiled and handed him the paper. "Sure, ah, yeah."

Barry smiled, and finally, I left his small office. As I walked out, his daughter and I said our goodbyes. I opened the main door to leave the building to discover a major shock...

"Hello, Joe, why don't you come with us?"

Huh? The FBI agents?

Chapter 13

That's correct, everyone. Standing outside of the Outer Space Conspiracy Society was none other than my *friends,* Agent Jones and Agent Carter.

"You're coming with us, boy," Agent Carter said as he grabbed my wrist; I jerked back. "Don't you resist, I'll hurt you."

Agent Jones laughed. "You better do what he says, he's a loose cannon sometimes."

Reluctantly, I turned around and let Agent Carter handcuff me. "What's going on? I didn't do anything."

Agent Carter pulled me along, Agent Jones helped. "You will find out, let's take a ride in my car first," Agent Jones said.

The FBI agents tossed me into the back of their car. My head smacked into the backseat; it hurt. These corrupt agents drove me all the way back to New York City. The entire ride I kept asking *why are you arresting me?*; they did not answer. Agent Carter turned up the radio, blaring it so loud that it gave me a headache.

Once we arrived in New York, they took me back to the prison. Now inside of the holding cell, both agents lit cigarettes, filling the air with their toxic smoke. A burning sensation hit my eyes from all the smoke. They watered and I wiped them dry.

"You crying, pussy?" Agent Carter asked, leaning against the small table in the room.

"Leave the pussy alone," Agent Jones laughed.

These *agents,* if that's what you want to call them, really started to get on my nerves. "Please, you have to tell me why you're arresting me."

"Who said we're arresting you?" Agent Jones snapped.

I glanced around the cell; Agent Jones uncuffed me.

"Maybe we have a few questions, that's all," Agent Carter said.

These fools brought me all the way back to New York to ask me a few questions? Thanks for the free ride.

"Why were you in Red Lion, Pennsylvania?" Agent Jones asked.

"And specifically, why were you talking to Barry Frey?" Agent Carter snarled.

"Huh?" I asked. *How did they know his name? And why do they care?*

Agent Carter slammed his fist on the table. "Are you deaf? I swear I'm going to fuck you up."

Agent Jones grabbed Agent Carter. "Easy, let the little punk speak. Tell me, punk. Why were you meeting with Barry Frey?"

The light in the cell started to flicker. The color changed from a white to an orange tint. "He is a friend, I knew his father and I wanted to check in with him."

Agent Carter made a *pfft* sound. "A friend, my ass. You're a lying sack of shit."

"No, it's the damn truth, I swear on it." Anger overtook me. I slammed my fist on the table. "Why are you guys harassing me?"

Both of the agents looked at each other and laughed. "Harassing you?" Agent Carter asked. "Boy, I'll show you harassing."

Agent Carter reached for his waistband. He pulled out a nightstick, which he flung open. Agent Carter swung the nightstick toward the side of my head. I saw all this unfold from the corner of my eye. My head bobbed down underneath the nightstick. I jumped up from the chair; the nightstick slammed on the table, denting it. My fist balled up, I swung a right straight directly at Agent Carter's face, connecting perfectly. Agent Carter spun downward, and his head smacked on the table.

This prompted Agent Jones to pull his gun out. "Hold it right there, you piece of scum!"

My hands raised up in the air, my heart pounded a mile a minute.

"I should kill you right now, you motherfucker! I'd say you grabbed my gun, I shot you in self-defense." Agent Jones licked his lips while looking at his gun. "How does that sound, bitch?"

"Argh, ugh," Agent Carter groaned. He reached his hand up, grabbing onto the chair.

Agent Jones glanced down at his fallen comrade, he reached his left hand out to help him up. As Agent Jones grabbed Agent Carter's hand, I saw he tilted the gun down toward the floor. My mind raced through many different scenarios. One that felt certain was that if I didn't act, I would end up dead. In a blink of an eye, I reached out, grabbing the gun out of the hand of Agent Jones.

His eyes widened as I cocked the gun, pointing it at the back of the head of Agent Carter. "I'm sick and tired of you two fools harassing me. This shit is going to end now."

Agent Jones held his hands up to me. "Listen, Joe, you don't want to do this. Hand me the gun."

The gun shook in my hand, my emotions ran high. My mind replayed the night John Lennon was murdered... *If I ever get a second chance, I'll be a man and stop that monster.*

Agent Carter started to turn around, his right hand drifted toward his waist.

"Hold it right there, bitch man," I screamed. "If your hand goes any lower, I'll shoot you in the back of your head, I swear on that."

Agent Carter's hands shot up, his face still pointed away from me. "Please, what do you want? There must be something."

"Yeah," Agent Jones said. "What do you want? Money? A private jet? I'll get it for you-"

"Shut the fuck up, both of you." The gun did not shake in my hand anymore. My confidence shot to a new high. "You." I pointed at Agent Jones. "Move over to the wall, face away from me."

Agent Jones followed my commands. I approached Agent Carter. My hand gripped the gun, I slammed the back of the barrel into Agent Carter's head; he fell to the floor. Agent Jones turned around, I swung the gun in his direction.

"Turn the fuck around, asshole," I said; he obliged.

I made my way to the asshole agent on the floor and dug in his back pocket. As I pulled out his handcuffs, a big smile formed on my face. After clicking the one end of the handcuff on Agent Carter's wrist, I glanced around the cell. My eyes locked on a small radiator in the far corner of the cell.

"Hey!" I shouted. "You, fuck face standing against the wall. Make your way over to the radiator."

"You're making a big mistake, boy," Agent Jones said, slowly making his way to the radiator.

"Yeah, yeah. I've got too much shit going on for me to care what you think." My eyes glanced at the back pocket of Agent Jones. "Grab your handcuffs and lock yourself to the radiator."

Agent Jones shook his head. "No fucking way. You'll have to shoot me first."

"No problem," I said, taking a few steps toward him. The gun pointed straight at his face. "Guess I'll see how much of your brains will splatter on the wall."

Agent Jones ducked down, waving his hands. "Okay, shit, don't shoot." He grabbed his handcuffs and cuffed himself to the radiator.

"Good," I said. Now, turning back around, I made my way over to Agent Carter. He still lay unconscious on the floor. I dragged him over to the radiator. After handcuffing him to the radiator as well, I dug through his pockets. A set of keys were in his back pocket. I took them, since they must have been the handcuff keys.

"You won't get away with this," Agent Jones said.

"Shut up." I slammed the barrel of the gun into Agent Jones' face, knocking him out. Into his pockets I went, confiscating his keys.

Now, standing up, glancing around the cell, I had to figure out what my next move would be. I snuck out, tiptoeing down the hallway. Down the hall and to the left I found a door that read: *Custodian*. I opened the door and found a bunch of neat things. This included a spare custodian outfit, neatly hung up on a hook. A cleaning cart sat in the middle of the closet. On this cart, I found a roll of duct tape. After putting the custodian outfit on (it was a little big), I pushed the cart down to the holding cell where my two buddies were. Inside the room, both agents were still knocked out. I ripped off two pieces of duct tape and placed the tape around both agent's mouths.

After dusting my hands off, I snooped around on the custodian cart. Inside a side compartment, I found a sign that read: *Closed for Cleaning*. Back outside of the cell, I closed the door and placed the *closed* sign on the door. I tossed both of the guns inside of the cleaning cart, not wanting to set off the metal detector at the front of the prison. On the cart, I also found the real custodian's badge. When I passed the front area of the prison, I held up the badge from far away and smiled... *what a great disguise,* I thought as I casually walked out of the prison.

Now outside the prison, standing in the sun, I felt great. I was a free man, and I knew from this moment on I'd be on the run. Like an older woman walking in the park, I power-walked down the steps and off the prison property. Once I got around the corner (out of sight), I ran as fast as I could. A few blocks away from the prison, I stopped in a pizza joint. While sitting in a booth, I pondered my next move. *Shit, what do I do now? I have to get out of the city, but how? Those FBI fucks took my cell phone. I cannot call for an Uber...*

Alexis entered my mind. *Damn, I guess I'll never see her again. Shit, I must call her.* I tried to think of her number, but I couldn't. Since the cell phone automatically saved phone numbers, I never took the time to remember it. *I cannot stay here, no way...*

"Hi, are you ready to order?"

"Huh?" I glanced up to see a teenage girl standing, holding a notepad.

"Are you ready to order?" the teenage girl asked. "Or, do you need a few more minutes?"

I took a deep breath. "Ah, just get me a pop, please. Any kind will do."

The teenage girl smiled. "Sure thing."

She walked away and my eyes shifted to the outside of the building. As I looked through the window, I noticed a car pull up. A teenage boy jumped out carrying a pizza warming bag; he ran inside the restaurant. What caught my attention wasn't necessarily the teenage boy, but the fact he left his car running.

"Here you go, sir."

The loud sound of a plastic cup smacking the table startled me. "Oh, ah, thank you."

The teenage girl smiled. "Would you like to pay now? Or are you still considering getting some food?"

"Ah, umm."

"I'll let you in on a little secret. Stromboli is to die for!" the teenage girl said.

My eyes bounced back and forth from the window to the teenage girl. "Give me a few more minutes, I'm still deciding on what food to get."

"Sure, I'll check back in with you in a few minutes."

The teenage girl walked away and I took a large sip of my pop. It tasted good, very refreshing. Now, glancing back toward the kitchen, I didn't see the teenage boy; I made my move. Like a cheetah, I sprung up and ran out the door. In one fluid motion, I jumped inside the running car, placing it into drive and taking off down the street. The car was a red *Pontiac Sunfire* and it drove nicely.

At first, I drove fast, but quickly I realized that wasn't such a good idea. In no way did I want to draw attention to myself. I didn't see any cop cars driving around up to this point, which was good. *Maybe those two FBI bozos were still locked up in the holding cell.* The thought of this made me laugh.

Then it crossed my mind. *If the cops don't know about the FBI agents, they should be swarming around the area soon from me stealing the pizza boy's car.* With this idea in my head, I turned the car down a back alley. Behind some business, I found a large dumpster. Parking the car in front of the dumpster, I jumped out. For the rest of the day, I wandered the streets of New York City, trying to stay undetected.

By nighttime, I made it to Chinatown. Now, I know what you're thinking, *won't you stand out like a sore thumb in Chinatown?* Maybe, but I believe this may be one of the safest places for me right now. I went door to door, knocking on people's homes. Most didn't answer. Others shut the door in my face once I asked them if I could spend the night. Hell, most probably didn't speak English either. At probably the twentieth home, an older Chinese gentleman opened the door. "Neih hou?"

Shit, I don't speak a lick of Chinese... well, other than what I learned from watching Bruce Lee. "Jeet Kune Do!"

The older Chinese man laughed. "You don't speak a lick of Cantonese, do you?"

What in the hell is a Cantonese? "Ah, no, other than Jeet Kune Do."

The older Chinese man laughed again. "You're a funny guy. What you're saying is the way of the intercepting fist. That's the martial art of the late great Bruce Lee."

I rubbed the back of my head, *oh, so that's what that means.*

"What I said was Neih hou, which means hello." He chuckled once more. "But luckily for you, I do speak English... as you can tell."

After my little Chinese lesson, I told him the reason for my visit. "Sir, I hate to bother you, but I'm homeless and have no place to go. Is there any way I could stay the night? I'll pay you, I have some money."

The older Chinese man glanced behind me, looking up and down the street. "Sure, you can stay the night." He gestured for me to enter his home. "By the way, what is your name?"

"Joe, what's yours?"

"You can call me Bob."

I let out a small chuckle. "Okay, Bob." To this day, I still don't know why I laughed, maybe just ignorance on my part.

Bob asked me about my situation, and, of course, I lied and made something up. He gave me some stern life advice, which I still hold dearly to this day. Bob was one of the nicest men I've ever met. He cooked me up a homemade meal, which tasted amazing. In a back bedroom, he had one of those beds which pulled down from the wall. It was funny to see, but the bed sure was comfortable.

I ended up staying at Bob's house for an entire week. He loved the company, as he normally didn't get any visitors. Bob told me all of his family was either back in Hong Kong, or moved to Seattle. To be honest, Bob wanted me to stay longer, he didn't mind one bit. I figured one week was long enough, plus, I needed to find the orange glowing ball. Which, again, I figured the only way I'd find it was by giving that monster who killed John Lennon a visit.

One thing I hated about being on the run was not being able to talk to Alexis. I grew fond of that woman, and now I couldn't even tell her I was safe. She must have known I was on the run. Well, if she watched the news, she definitely would. One night while watching the news with Bob, a story came on about me. The news anchor said I assaulted two FBI agents and viciously (that is the word he used) stole a pizza boy's car. The news said that I was armed and dangerous... what a crock of shit.

After my week stay at Bob's house, I left early in the morning. During my stay, I asked Bob to run out to the store to buy me a new cell phone (I did pay for the phone). So now, I had a phone again, but unfortunately, I still did not have Alexis' number. Even though I couldn't contact Alexis, I could call an *Uber* driver. This time, a woman in her forties picked me up. She had dark black hair and wore the brightest red of lipstick I've ever seen.

I got the woman to drive me to my old job; *The New York Penn Station*. After saying my *thanks* to the driver, I snuck inside the station. Inside the station, people scurried all around me. I kept my head lowered, trying to keep unnoticed. You may be asking, *why would you go back to your place of employment?* The answer was simple.

My plan was to jump aboard the train and ride it up to Alden, New York. This, if you remembered, was where the monster who killed John Lennon was being held. I would sneak inside the prison and kill that son of a bitch, once and for all.

Thanks to my time working at the station, I knew places to sneak off too. I wouldn't pay for a train ticket, in no way did I want to leave a paper trail. Instead, I'd sneak on the train. A set of doors, near the front area bathroom's, would be my starting point. I snuck through the doors, being careful to not be seen. Once in the back, I made my way to the loading dock. This was where items were dropped off for the businesses. Out back at the loading dock, I didn't have to walk far to reach the back area of where the trains would sit. Now, after doing some research online, I'd wait for the train that's heading north. Once the train arrived, I'd sneak aboard.

My wait wouldn't be long. The train I wanted arrived only ten minutes later. Once the train came to a full stop, I snuck on through the backdoor. Now on board, I made my way to the kitchen area, there, a few extra aprons hung up on a hook; I took one. Back in the kitchen, I found a small break room with a table, six chairs, a refrigerator, and a microwave. The farthest chair away from the door was where I sat. Slouching down, I turned to face the wall, pretending to sleep. This was my plan, to keep people away from the *sleeping* worker; it didn't work. About a half an hour later, someone nudged me on my back.

"Hey-yo. Wake up, man."

My head rose up slowly to see a chubby man wearing one of those funny chef's hats.

"I noticed you over here sleeping for the past half an hour. Time to get back to work."

I nodded. "Sure."

The chubby man led me to a table, and he asked me what job was mine. Glancing around the kitchen, I saw a sink with a bunch of dirty dishes piled up. "I'm the dishwasher."

The chubby man glanced over to the sink; he gasped. "Well, damn. Get your ass over there and clean that mess up."

After a smile and a nod, I made my way to the sink. For the next two hours, I washed dirty dishes. Once done with the dishes, the other kitchen workers and I sat around. A small TV hung in the break room. The guys turned on a funny cartoon show. We ate, laughed and had a good time. After about a two-hour break, the workers got back up. They started to prepare for lunch. For me, the new dishwasher, I grabbed a broom and swept the area up. In no way did I want to attempt to cook any food. After sweeping the kitchen, I headed back to the break room to watch more TV.

The train ride ended up being about eight hours. We arrived at the Buffalo Depew Station. After doing some research on my phone, I discovered that I was about twenty minutes away from Alden.

My next move: get an *Uber*. After using the application to order my ride, the dude showed up about a half an hour later. I told the dude to take me to Alden, to a hotel or motel; he agreed. The ride up from *Buffalo Depew Station* to Alden only took about twenty minutes.

My driver, an older Indian man, dropped me off at a small motel named Forrest's Motel Chain. The rates were dirt cheap, only ten dollars a night. The room was tiny, a twin bed barely fit inside. A small one drawer dresser sat at the end of the bed, with a teeny TV set on top. But for ten dollars a night, what do you really expect, right?

My first night in Alden was quiet; I didn't leave my room. After my trip up here, I decided to relax. An idea came to me as I lay in my small motel bed. While living with Alexis, I remembered her getting on those social media things. On the internet, I searched for different social medias; I came across *Facebook*. This was one Alexis frequently used. The website made me create a profile before I could search for anyone. So that's what I did. Personally, I thought it was weird to want to create a website and put all my information out to the world. But hey, that's what people do in this time.

After putting in my information (I made up facts about myself), it asked me to upload a picture. This I did not do; I kept it blank, not wanting my image out there for anyone to see (especially the law). Now, with my created profile, I searched for Alexis Brown. I typed her name in the search bar and a bunch of results popped up.

An entire page of *Alexis Brown* profiles were in front of me. I scrolled down the entire page, finding a lot of beautiful *Alexis'* but none were my Alexis. At the bottom of the page, there was a button saying, *click to next page;* I clicked the button. The next page popped up, full of more *Alexis Brown* profiles. Scrolling down the page, I ran into the same problem as page one. So I clicked on the button to page number three.

Page three turned out to be the same as the first two. In fact, I ended up on page forty-five before finding, halfway down the page, a profile with my Alexis' face. My eyes hurt from the constant glancing at the tiny phone screen, but I was overjoyed to find my girl. Now I ran into another problem. Alexis' profile said it was *private*. I could only see the one main picture. I found a *message* button, but it wouldn't let me send a message.

Only one choice remained; click the *Add friend* button. This is what I did, I clicked the button. Now I had to wait for her to accept it. After clicking the button, I threw myself down on the bed. My eyes wouldn't look away from the phone. I kept hoping to see Alexis' profile pop up. What I wanted wouldn't happen on this first night. The next morning I woke up, immediately grabbing my phone. I clicked it on, opened the *Facebook* application and nothing. Alexis didn't accept me. Either she turned me down, or she hadn't seen it yet. *Yeah, she must not have looked at her phone. Yeah, that's what it is.*

My next day played out the same way the previous ended. I stayed in my room all day and night. While watching the evening news, a story came on about me.

"Good evening, Alden. I'm your news anchor, Barron Williams." This man, Barron Williams, appeared to be in his sixties with bright, snow-white hair. He donned a stone-cold expression on his face. "Tonight's top story on the ongoing search for Joe Miller, the man who assaulted two FBI agents and a pizza delivery driver."

Assaulted? Yeah, right, those FBI clowns assaulted me.

"Joe Miller is reported to be armed and dangerous-"

Armed and dangerous? I placed those damn guns in the cleaning cart.

"Anyone who sees this man." The news showed my picture from the first time those FBI agents arrested me. "Should not approach him, just call nine-one-one."

I laughed; this entire situation seemed to be a bad dream.

Barron Williams paused for a second, staring directly into the camera. "Boy, I don't know about any of you other Alden residents, but I'd like to punch this guy square in the face."

Huh? What is wrong with this newsman?

"You don't assault people in high authority, you just don't. I hope to see this man in Alden," Barron Williams said.

Maybe you'll get your wish, newsman...

The camera switched to a new angle and this cheese weasel continued on with the news. "Also in the news, Sir Paul McCartney will be in concert tomorrow evening at the *Canalside*, in Buffalo."

Sir Paul McCartney? When did the Queen knight him?

"It is rumored that Ringo Starr may show up as well. What an exciting *Beatles* reunion if it happens," Barron Williams said.

Paul McCartney... Ringo Starr... The Beatles...

"The two surviving former band members haven't been seen together in a very long time. I think both George and John would smile down from heaven if those two would reunite in Buffalo."

Wait, George Harrison died? On my cell phone, I performed a search on the former *Beatles* lead guitarist and found that George passed away in 2001. *Damn, George, how did this happen?* After doing some more research, I found the cause. *Lung cancer... shit, rest in peace, George...*

Grabbing the remote, I clicked off the TV. I had enough of listening to this turkey give the news. Then my mind thought about Buffalo. *I know I've seen signs to Buffalo on the drive up here.*

Now, on my cell phone, I found the map application. After opening the map application, I typed in Buffalo. A search result popped on my screen; forty-one minutes from Alden. *Maybe I could go see Paul in concert... I'd love to see him.* From here, I didn't really know what to do. So I went back to the search page and typed in *Paul McCartney Buffalo Concert.* A result popped up, giving tomorrow's date; I clicked the link.

To my surprise, tickets were still available. After clicking on the *seating* button, I found a few different tickets. They were all for different sections of the stadium. Now, I didn't have much money to survive on, so the only ticket I could afford was the fifteen-dollar ticket. After bringing the cursor over the *Buy Tickets* button, an option to type my credit card information came up. I proceeded to type in my debit card (I did not possess a credit card). Now with my information in place, I clicked to buy the tickets; success! Tomorrow evening at eight, I will be sitting in the back (yes, the back, but at least I'll be there, right?) at a Paul McCartney concert. *Damn, I hope Ringo shows up too.*

The next morning I arose to find a message on my phone... *Who are you?* This message came via *Facebook,* and it was from Alexis. She added me to her page, so my plan worked, but now, I felt scared to message her. *What do I say? Does she even want to talk to me?* A small green circle (thank God it wasn't orange) sat underneath her profile image. *I suppose this means she's on right now.* After three deep breaths, I clicked on the area to write a message.

Hello, Alexis. I hope you are doing great. I miss you so much. This is Joe Miller. Please talk to me. It's a lie those FBI guys assaulted me. My finger hovered over the *send* button. Sweat beads formed on my forehead as my heart skipped a few beats. After three more deep breaths, I clicked *send.* A sense of relief hit when I sent my message. This didn't last long, though. Less than a minute after sending my message, a new message came in from Alexis; this brought back the nerves. This time there weren't any deep breaths; I dived right into the message.

Omg is it rely u? Y havent u called me u asshole! I'm worried sick bout ur punk ass! Her message actually made me laugh. For one, the way she typed was silly. Second, she seemed more relieved than mad... or at least that's how I took it. After a few minutes of debating what to say, I messaged her back. *Sorry, Alexis. Those FBI bozos took my cell phone, so I couldn't contact you. I'm doing fine though. I'm currently in Alden, if you don't know, it's in upstate New York, near Buffalo. I miss you and hope to see you again.*

A message from Alexis entered my inbox almost immediately. *U need to get a phone n call me ASAP.* I flipped the cell phone around in my hand, glaring at it. After letting out a small chuckle, I sent a message back. *Hey, I bought a new cell phone the other day, you can call me here...* I gave my phone number (sorry folks, I don't want any of you to call this number) and less than ten seconds later, an incoming call came to my cell phone.

Now my trembling nerves returned. They hit me so hard that I didn't answer the call. Once the incoming call ceased, the same number called back a second later. This time, I answered. "Ah, hello?"

"You son of a bitch, it really is you!" Screaming and crying shot into my ear. The voice belonged to Alexis. "I thought you ended up dead, I was worried sick!"

"Ah, Alexis... My intentions were never to leave you. Those FBI turkeys arrested me for nothing-"

"Why did they arrest you? For what reason do they want you, Joe?"

Oh, how I wanted to tell her the truth, I truly did... but I couldn't. "They contacted me before, they mixed me up with somebody else. Then, back in the jail, they assaulted me in an interrogation room."

"Joe... are you some sort of master criminal? When I first met you in the hospital, you had cops and the FBI after you."

All this time living together, Alexis never asked this, which I was happy she didn't. But now, the time has come.

"No, I'm not, Alexis. I have wrongfully been accused of something that I didn't do. You must believe me, I wouldn't lie to you." Silence followed. "Please, Alexis..."

"Joe, I believe you, I truly do."

A smile formed on my face as I let out a big sigh of relief.

"Joe, give me your address, I'm coming up to be with you tonight."

Even though I didn't want to involve Alexis in my plan to sneak into the jail and kill the monster, I needed to see her. To be perfectly frank, I was falling in love with her.

"Okay, Alexis... okay."

I gave the address of the motel to Alexis. She told me she would leave right away. We stayed on the phone for the next forty-five minutes, talking and laughing. It felt like I never left... too bad I did.

After our forty-five minute talk, Alexis decided to hang up since the traffic started to pick up. Then an idea struck: I *could take Alexis to the Paul McCartney concert.* Then the tickets entered my mind. Flipping open my *Google* application, I searched for the concert as I've done before. Then I found the ticket section. After performing a short search, I came across my seat. Happiness hit when I saw the seat next to mine was still vacant. I clicked *buy* and now I possessed two tickets to the Paul McCartney concert. Now, these tickets weren't real physical tickets. It said that all I had to do was show the *electronic* ticket to the people at the front gate. I jumped up and rushed to the tiny shower in my motel room.

After finishing up my shower, I stood, observing myself in the mirror. *This guy needs to go shopping,* I said to myself. That's right, I was feeling myself. I hit up the

Uber application and in less than ten minutes, my driver arrived.

"Take me to any shopping mall that's near here. This guy needs to get a new outfit," I said to the driver, smiling ear to ear.

"Sounds good, my man." My driver took off, driving about fifteen minutes away to a small shopping mall.

The mall truly was small with only four stores, a food court, and a gaming room. I went into a clothing store that appeared to sell clothes for men (the first store I walked into only sold clothes for women). After checking out a few different outfits, I settled on one that was pretty far out. I only hoped that Alexis would dig my new look.

Let me describe to you my outfit, it was the perfect outfit to wear to the concert. First, I found a groovy *Beatles* tee shirt depicting the cover of the *Let It Be* album. All four members were on the shirt, including John Lennon. Next, I found these jeans, they were black and fit well. To be perfectly frank, these jeans were the only jeans I could find that weren't skin-tight.

The last piece of the outfit was maybe the coolest (even though I loved the shirt), it was a black fedora. I looked dapper, ready to take on the night. Soon, I'll be with the girl I'm falling for, and I'll be at the concert of one and possibly two of *The Beatles...* life is starting to feel good again. As I left the store, Alexis called and told me that she was getting close, only four hours away.

This, I laughed at it, "Jeez, only four hours? Yeah, you're close."

"Hey, I started eight hours away, so I am close," Alexis said.

We talked and laughed for about five more minutes before Alexis hung up, she needed to follow her GPS. Now, I had four more hours to kill... what to do? By the time Alexis would arrive, it would be right before seven. The concert started at eight, and Buffalo was about a forty-minute drive, depending on the traffic. To kill some time, I walked into the game room, basically a small arcade. This arcade rocked. It didn't have too many arcade machines, but the arcade machines it had were a lot cooler than the ones I played back in 1981.

There was another game I found that looked all so familiar. In the back of the arcade sat a TV, and not just any TV but a TV that looked to be from back in my time. Hooked up to the TV was a gaming system and it just so happened to be the system I saw the guy playing on the computer at the library. I ended up playing a game called *NBA Jam*. It was so good. Then I played a game called *Super Mario World*. This game also rocked. I've never played anything like it. The crazy part was the guy who worked at the arcade told me this wasn't a new system. In fact, it came out in 1991. Of course, I skipped that year thanks to the orange glowing ball. He went on to tell me about all the newer systems. The arcade worker also asked how I didn't know about the *Super Nintendo*. I came up with a story that my parents were missionaries and they moved us to Africa when I was little… it worked; he bought it.

Two hours later, I left the arcade, feeling exhausted by now. I headed over to the food court to buy a burger and some fries. After eating, I ordered an *Uber* and waited for my driver. He showed up about a half an hour later and took me to my motel room. Alexis wasn't too far away now. We spoke on the phone for a few minutes while I rode in the back of my driver's car. Things were going well on this day, but that would all change when my driver turned down the street that led to my motel. As we approached the motel, five cop cars were parked around the motel. When we got closer, I saw the car those FBI clowns had. It was parked right in front of my room's door.

"Hey, driver!" I reached up and tapped my driver on his shoulder.

He glanced up in his mirror; our eyes met. "Yeah?"

"Can you take me back to the mall?"

My driver's eyebrow raised.

"I just realized that I forgot my wallet."

"Oh, yeah, don't want to leave that, no worries," my driver said.

He drove past the motel; I dipped my fedora down over my face. Glancing out, I saw my door open. Both FBI agents walked out with a police officer. They all had a pissed-off demeanor about them.

I pulled out my phone and sent Alexis a text: *Hey, change your GPS to the mall here in Alden, it's called Alden Mall.*

An incoming call from Alexis came in a second later; I answered. "Ah, hello?"

"Yeah, Joe. Now you want me to go to a Mall? I'm getting close, why don't I just go to the motel?"

"No, no, please, no. I can't talk about it now but meet me at the mall and I'll explain everything, okay?"

A second of silence followed. Then Alexis responded, "Umm, okay, sure. Let me get off of here so I can get the mall's address."

Alexis hung up the phone, and I sat quietly for the rest of the ride. Back at the mall, my driver asked if he should wait for me to get my wallet. At first, I gave him a dumbfounded look, then I remembered the lie I gave to him. "No, I'm going to meet a friend here now, but thank you."

My driver nodded and drove off. I went straight to the bathroom in the mall, too afraid to be out in public. Like a scared child trying to escape a beating from a parent, I sat on the toilet, trying to stay quiet.

Finally, Alexis called. "Hey, I just pulled into the mall. Where are you at inside? So I can find you."

"No!" I shouted. "Ah, stay there, I'm coming."

"Okay..."

"Hey, Alexis, where are you parked at?"

"Umm, I'm parked near the sign that says *A*."

I jumped off the toilet and made my way out of the bathroom. "Could you pull up to the front? I'm coming out now."

"Sure, Joe. I hope everything is okay."

I power-walked down the Mall, probably looking like a madman. "It will be, I'm coming, keep the car running."

After making my way through the mall (and gaining a lot of stares), I pushed open the door to find Alexis' car parked right in front of the entrance doors. Alexis waved and I grabbed the door, opening it and jumping into the seat.

"Drive, I'll explain everything." She gave me a scared look and took off down the parking lot. "Alexis, we can't go to my motel, I drove past it to find the cops and those FBI agents standing at my door. They found me somehow."

A frown grew on Alexis' face. "Joe, what is going on?"

I didn't hear Alexis, as my mind was running a mile a minute. "Shit, they probably hacked my phone. When they talked to me, they took my phone to check all my messages and everything. Those sons of bitches must've hacked me."

Damn, now I've involved Alexis in my mess... This thought shook me. "Damn, I'm so sorry, maybe you should go back home."

Alexis shook her head. "No fucking way, I'm sticking with you, Joe."

She placed her hand over the top of my hand. We smiled, and I gently rubbed the hair out of her eyes... she looked amazing.

"Joe, you need to be perfectly honest with me. If you're hiding something from me, you better come clean right now."

This struck me hard. There wasn't anything more I wanted to do than tell Alexis the truth, but I couldn't. She wouldn't believe me anyway, plus she's already been involved enough. Then Alexis changed everything by saying, "Joe, I'm going to come clean to you. There's something I've been hiding as well."

"What are you talking about, Alexis?"

"Joe... I love you."

Whoa, did she really say what I think she said?

The car stopped at a red light. Alexis blushed. She glanced at me, smiling. "I know I shouldn't since we haven't known each other that long, but I don't care. Ever since we first met in the hospital, I felt something special with you. Joe... I fucking love you."

The light changed to green, and she started to drive. I rubbed my hand through her hair again. "Alexis."

"Yeah, Joe?"

"I love you too..."

Chapter 14

What I said to Alexis was real. What she said to me, I believed to be genuine as well. Even though I didn't want to tell her the truth, I felt obligated to.

"Alexis, I will tell you everything, but I will warn you. What happened to me is very unbelievable."

Alexis rolled her eyes and shot me a smile. "Oh, please, just tell me, Joe. Whatever it is, it can't be too crazy."

Well, you might change your mind after I tell you.

"Oh, also, where do you want me to drive too?" Alexis asked.

This put a smile on my face. "Go to Buffalo, I got us tickets to the Paul McCartney concert."

"Oh, that old *Beatles* guy?"

I laughed. "Ah, yeah, I guess."

"Wait, didn't he get shot in the eighties?" Alexis asked. "I thought he died."

I sighed. "Sweetie, that wasn't Paul who got shot. It was John... John Lennon. And to be perfectly honest, he's sort of the reason why I am here."

Alexis glanced at me, her eyebrow shot up. "Huh? Joe, you better get talking, I want to know everything. And you better get the directions to the concert on your phone."

What Alexis wanted, she got. First, I typed in the address to the Paul McCartney concert and we followed the directions. Next, I told her my entire story, starting from the beginning. I spilled the beans, not leaving anything out. A few times, I noticed Alexis glancing over at me, giving me a concerned look. But I kept telling my story.

By the end of my story, Alexis sat in silence. This scared me, maybe I made a mistake. I wanted to say something more to her, but the words wouldn't come out. Her silence stopped me dead in my tracks. We didn't say anything else to each other till we reached the concert. We found a parking spot, but it was far back from the building.

"Wow, this place is packed," I said.

"Yeah, it is, Joe."

I turned toward Alexis; she smiled at me. "Alexis, do you believe me? Or do you think I'm some sort of nut job?"

Alexis leaned forward and kissed me. The kiss was something special... amazing, in fact. Often I thought about what our first kiss would be like. But I never would've imagined it being in the parking lot of a Paul McCartney concert.

"Joe, I believe you." Alexis glanced past me, looking out the window. "We better get moving, the concert will be starting soon."

I nodded, and we both stepped out of the car. We walked side by side, not holding hands, though. I wanted to hold her hand but felt too timid to grab hers. As we reached the entrance, I remembered the electronic tickets. After pulling them up on my cell phone, we walked inside the building. Two enormous bouncer dudes asked for my tickets; I promptly showed them. They let us inside and a smaller dude escorted us to our seats. This place was packed, so many people were there. A good feeling came over me. The fact that in this new year that I found myself in, one of *The Beatles* would still be this popular amazed me. *John, if you're watching this, I bet you're cheering along with the rest of us...*

"Joe? Did you hear me, Joe?"

Alexis' voice snapped me out of my trance. "Huh, what?"

"Joe, I said I'm going to go to the bathroom quick."

"Oh, okay."

Alexis stood up and walked past me.

"Hey," I said, grabbing her hand (yeah, now I grabbed it). "You want me to walk with you?"

"No, it's okay," Alexis said with a smile. "I'll be right back."

She left, and a loud roar from the crowd bounced around the arena. My head whipped over toward the stage. Even though I sat far back, I could see a man walking out on the stage.

"Hello, all you beautiful people!"

The oh, so familiar voice of Paul McCartney rang in my ears. What was blackness behind the lit-up stage clicked on to reveal a large screen. On this large screen, I could see an older-looking Paul McCartney.

"Before I start this little shindig, let me get some help on the drums..." Paul turned around, looking to the back of the stage. "Any drummers back there that would like to assist an old man like myself?"

A voice appeared in the speakers. This voice I also knew. "Yes, there is a drummer back here. I'll help you if you don't mind it being from an old chap like myself."

On the large screen, Ringo Starr, former *Beatles* drummer, walked out from the curtains, carrying two drum sticks. Paul trotted over and the two former band members hugged. It was great seeing them, yet weird seeing how old they were. As I watched the two *Beatles* get themselves ready to start the concert, I realized Alexis hadn't returned yet. I stood up, wanting to go find Alexis, but I found something else.

Standing at the end of my aisle were three police officers, all staring in my direction. Behind the officers, toward the area of the bathrooms, I saw Alexis standing, watching. *What in the fuck?*

The police officers made their way down the aisle. I looked around the entire area, trying to find an escape route. The only choice I had was to jump down over the next aisle; this, I attempted to do. I pushed my way through the people, jumping down to the next aisle. Paul McCartney and Ringo Starr jammed in the background. Just as I started to make my way through the next aisle of people, someone grabbed me from behind. A large forearm wrapped around my neck, pulling me backward. The back of my head slammed on the ground; I felt woozy. Atop of me stood a large man in a purple button-down shirt. He wore a *Beatles* baseball hat. *A fellow Beatles fan brought me down?*

The large fan sat his knee into my chest; it hurt like hell. The next thing I knew, police officers surrounded me. They jumped on me, pushing the large fan out of the way. The officers flipped me over on my stomach, slamming my face into the ground. They cuffed me and lifted me to my feet.

As they dragged me out of the concert, I passed by Alexis. She stood near the bathrooms, crying. Tears filled my eyes as I stared at her. "Why, Alexis? Why?"

"I'm so sorry," Alexis shouted. "You need help, Joe. They will get you the right type of help."

I lowered my head, not wanting to see her anymore. The girl from the future that I started to fall for just pulled a fast one on me. My story of how I came to this time must have scared her. She probably thought I was some nut case. In a way, I didn't blame her, but calling the cops was still a low blow.

The next part of my plan, in a roundabout way, would start now. My goal was to sneak into *Wende Correctional Facility* as some worker. Maybe a laundry or kitchen worker. Now, I would get my wish to go to the prison, but as a prisoner. The officers threw me into a small jail cell. No door on this, just bars. The good thing was nobody else occupied the cell. I didn't want to share a cell with another prisoner. Too many problems could occur... unless the cellmate was the monster. Then, I could put my plan into motion and kill that son of a bitch.

Inside my tiny cell, I sat for about an hour. Then two familiar faces approached my cell.

"There's our old buddy. How you doing, Joe?" Agent Jones asked.

I sat up in my little cot. The two FBI clowns stood, glaring at me.

"My partner asked how you were doing?" Agent Carter said.

I didn't answer.

"Pretty neat trick you pulled on us," Agent Jones said. He started a slow clap. "I give you props, boy. You got me and my partner good."

Agent Carter grabbed the bars, he brought his face right against the iron. "Now you're going to fry, you son of a bitch. You're going down for the assault on a federal agent. How's that sound, fucker?"

I still didn't say a word.

"He probably is afraid that we will come into the cell and get him," Agent Jones said.

Agent Carter laughed.

"No, we aren't going to do that, old buddy," Agent Jones said.

"Yeah, don't worry about us. You are going to have bigger problems in here," Agent Carter said with a laugh.

This caught my attention.

"You better grow a pair of eyes in the back of your head," Agent Jones said.

Finally, I spoke. "Why? What in the hell did you do?"

"We let the leader of the Bailey Boys gang know that you snitched on their entire operation," Agent Carter said. "They will be coming for you."

Both agents laughed as they walked away. I placed my head in my hands, not sure what to think. I wasn't sure what the hell a *Bailey Boy* was, but it didn't sound good.

That night, I didn't sleep an ounce. In the morning, bright and early, a guard screamed into my cell. "Get the fuck up, inmate"

I stood up, rubbing my eyes.

The guard smirked and walked away. I heard him scream *get the fuck up, inmate* over and over. After a few minutes, a loud *buzzer* roared and the cell door slid open.

"Everyone get the fuck out!" the guard screamed.

I stepped out to find every other inmate stepping out of their cells. Three guards stood down on the floor with us. Up top, I found three more guards with rifles pointed in our direction. As I watched the other inmates, I thought of two things. *Which one of these people are involved with that gang? Where is that monster at?*

The guards ordered us down to the cafeteria. We all lined up to get a breakfast tray. A slob of oatmeal and a hard biscuit was on the menu today. They also gave us a bag of orange juice. I found a chair at the end of a long table and sat down. All the inmates walked by me, staring hard. *Any one of these guys could be associated with that gang.* I didn't feel safe one bit, I knew I had to act and fast.

A large monster (not the monster I wanted) of an inmate sat down at the table across from mine. I stood up with my tray in hand and approached him. With his back to me, I swung my tray, smacking him in the back of the head. The inmate jumped up and turned to face me. His eyes narrowed, a snarl grew on his face. I swallowed hard, thinking maybe I made a wrong decision here.

The inmate pounced on me, taking me down to the floor. He repeatedly punched me in my face, knocking me out ice cold. I awoke sometime later in a dark cell. This cell had a door and no bed. Just an old dirty blanket lay on the floor and a toilet sat in the middle. *This must be solitary confinement... Good, my plan worked.* After using the toilet to perform a bowel movement, I discovered the toilet didn't flush. *Great, now the cell stinks worse than before.*

I sat in that old dirty cell for the rest of the day, not seeing one guard. At night, I surprisingly fell right to sleep...

"Rise and shine, pussy!"

I woke up to a loud scream and a *squeaking* sound. As I sat up from my *blanket* bed, I noticed the tiny window in the door was open. Something stuck through the tiny hole. It appeared to be a hose... a large one at that. Just when my mind realized what stuck through the hole, a cannon blast of water sprayed out, smacking into me. The water was cold... ice cold, in fact. The guards sprayed the water on me for about two minutes. To me, it felt like days.

"There, maybe you won't stink anymore," the guard said, laughing. He threw something into my cell and slammed the window shut.

After wiping some water out of my eyes, I crawled over to the *thing* the guard tossed into my cell. Something wrapped in foil lay on the ground. I grabbed and opened it. Two pieces of bread was what I found. *I guess this is my meal for today.* The guards kept me in solitary confinement for two weeks before pulling me out. This wasn't exactly good. Now, back in the general population, I'd have to deal with the gang members and the big brute I hit with my tray. Not good, not good at all. I have also heard nothing about when my court date will be. Hell, I haven't seen those FBI clowns since the first day they threw me in here. Alexis hadn't visited me either...

Back in the general population, I walked, being led by a guard. He took me outside since it was the afternoon and that meant *yard time.*

"Can I please go back to my cell?" I asked the guard.

"No, get the fuck outside." The guard shoved me from behind.

I stumbled out into the yard. The guard slammed the door, abandoning me out in the yard with murders, rapists, and God knows what else. After scanning the entire yard, I couldn't find a guard. *Did they really let us all outside by ourselves?*

"Yo!"

"Huh?" I said, jumping back. Something smacked me on my lower leg, startling me.

"Yo, a little help?"

To my left, I found a basketball court filled with a bunch of guys. I looked down at my leg and discovered a basketball.

"Yo, throw the ball back."

I smiled, picked the ball up and tossed it back toward the basketball court. The guy who stood nearest to me, the one screaming, nodded as he picked the ball up. The guys went back to their game.

"Ouch!" I screamed. An intense pain entered the right side of my lower back. I fell to my knees. The pain grew larger. Looking up, I saw an inmate walking away from me hastily. Blood dripped from my mouth, my lower back started to become numb. The next thing I knew, everything faded to black...

A *buzzing* noise entered my ears, nothing I could see but blackness. Yet, the *buzz* became more intense. Suddenly, in the center of the blackness, a small orange ball appeared. The *buzz* grew louder and the orange ball grew in size as well. Now, my vision switched to me seeing myself standing in the blackness. The view slowly panned toward me. A look of terror was on my face. My eyes showed the reflection of the orange glowing ball. I tried to scream, yet no sound came out.

Suddenly, a figure stepped out from the orange glowing ball... It was Ollie Oggy.

"Please, save us, you must save us!" Ollie bellowed.

I held my hands above my eyes, shielding the bright orange glow.

"You must kill the assassin to save us!" Ollie screamed.

"Who? Save you and James Frey?" I asked.

"All of the good in the world, the orange, save us before the red destroys Earth, as it destroyed many planets before!"

"Destroyed many planets before?" I asked, still shielding the light from my eyes.

"Humanity, save us all!" Ollie screamed.

Suddenly, the orange light changed to a blood red, and a bright red flash blinded me...

"Ah!" I screamed. I jumped up to find myself in a bed. A pain shot from my lower right stomach to my lower right back. I discovered my left wrist was handcuffed to the bed railing. Yes, I was in a hospital. The pain returned to my lower right stomach and back. Blankets covered my lower body. As I pulled the blankets down, someone cleared their throat from behind me.

"So you're awake now, inmate."

A police officer walked into my view.

"What happened?" I asked. A large bandage covered my lower right stomach.

"You were stabbed in the yard. We rushed you here to the hospital to have emergency surgery."

"Damn," I said, touching over the bandage; it hurt. "What surgery did they have to do? Was I bleeding nonstop?"

The officer stared at me, his look didn't feel too comforting.

Suddenly, the door to my room opened. In walked a doctor. "Oh, you're awake now, Joe." The doctor turned to the police officer. "May I have a moment alone with the patient?"

"He is a criminal. I must stay with him," the officer said.

"Well, in all due respect, officer, this patient still has privacy rights."

The officer lowered his head.

"Give me five minutes to go over some things with the patient, then he's all yours again," the doctor said.

The officer nodded and left the room.

The doctor turned and shot me a smile. "Hello, Joe. My name is Doctor Clifton. Let me catch you up to the reason why you are here."

I nodded.

"You were stabbed in prison, the knife ruptured your kidney. There wasn't anything we could have done to save it. So we took out your right kidney."

"Damn," I said, lowering my head.

"But don't you worry any, Joe."

I glanced back up at Doctor Clifton.

"You only need one kidney to live, and nothing else was damaged by the knife. So you are going to be perfectly fine."

"Really?" I asked.

"Yes. You will need to be in the hospital for another two or three days. Then, afterward, you will be released back to prison."

A frown grew on my face.

"And don't you worry, Joe. I've already talked to the warden at the prison. When they take you back, you will be placed in a special unit, away from the hardened criminals."

"Really?" I asked, tilting my head to the side.

Doctor Clifton nodded.

"Ah, thank you."

The door busted open and the police officer entered. "Okay, time is up."

"Take care now, Joe," Doctor Clifton said and exited the room.

Glancing back down at the bandage, I couldn't help but think, *wow, I only have one kidney now... damn.*

After two more days in the hospital, Doctor Clifton told me I was good to leave. Of course, this wasn't what I really wanted to hear. Two loud knocks thumped at my door. "Surprise, fucker!"

The person standing in my doorway was no other than Agent Carter. "Ah, shit," I said.

"Ah, shit is right, little man. I'm the one who will take you back to prison." The smile on Agent Carter's face was scary. It didn't look right at all. "So get your ass up, now!"

I stood up as far as I could go before the handcuff pulled against my left wrist.

"Turn away from me, dickhead," Agent Carter said.

I turned away from him, not sure if he would smack me in the back of the head; surprisingly, he didn't. The FBI agent grabbed my right arm, pulling it behind my back. Then he unlocked the cuff on the bed rail and swung my left arm to my back. There, he handcuffed my hands behind my back. He dragged me out of the room, pushing me forcefully.

Doctor Clifton stood out in the hallway. "Hey, sir, you can't transport him like that."

Agent Carter stopped dead in his tracks. "What do you mean?"

Doctor Clifton approached us. "What I mean is the patient had kidney surgery, he needs to be wheeled out of the hospital." Doctor Clifton walked behind the nurse's desk in the hallway. He grabbed a wheelchair and pushed it toward us. "Here, let him sit in this."

Agent Carter didn't yell, to my surprise, he smiled instead. "Sure thing. Here, Joe, sit."

I sat down in the wheelchair.

"Have a good one, Joe. Take care," Doctor Clifton said.

"You too, Doc."

Agent Carter grabbed the back handles of the wheelchair and pushed me down the hallway. "Let's go, Joe."

He wheeled me outside and up to his car. I glanced inside and didn't see the other agent. "Where's your partner at today?"

Agent Carter opened the back door of his car. He grabbed me hard on my shoulder, squeezing it tight. The next thing I knew, I flew in the air, smacking down in the back of the car. I landed on the right side of my stomach, where the doctor took my kidney.

"Ah, shit!" I screamed.

Agent Carter slammed the door and walked to the driver's side; he opened the door and sat down. "Hope that hurt, you little fuck. And to answer your question, my partner took the day off to spend with his family. Something you'll never be able to do again."

Fear entered my mind as Agent Carter revved up the car. He made it *roar* so loud. The next thing I knew, he stepped hard on the pedal, and the car took off. Since I wasn't strapped down by a seat belt, I bounced around in the backseat, smacking all over. I smacked against the cage that separated the front and back seats. Then I flew back, smacking into the backseat of the car. Every smack hurt like hell. When I hit the cage, it hurt where the doctors cut me open. When I hit the backseat, it hurt where the inmate stabbed me.

The entire ride back to jail went like this. The FBI clown drove like a madman. He'd go really fast down the street where the light would be yellow. Then he'd hit the brakes so hard as the light turned red. Clearly, he did this on purpose. When we arrived at the prison, he opened the back door and grabbed me around my neck, pulling me out of the car. For a few seconds, I couldn't breathe. I thought I was going to black out again, till the agent let go of my neck, letting me fall hard on the ground.

"Get the fuck up, pussy," Agent Carter said, picking me up.

He dragged me into the prison and handed me off to a couple of correction officers.

"See you later, Joe. I'll be in touch," Agent Carter said with a smile.

I didn't respond, just looked away from that turkey.

The correction officers led me down a different way than I remembered. "Hey, officers. Where are you taking me?"

The correction officer on my left, a young Asian fellow, responded. "We are moving you into the protective unit. Since you were stabbed and apparently have the attention of the Bailey Boys."

"Jeez, thanks, guys."

The correction officer on my right, an older, maybe mid-forties, white man, responded. "Shut the hell up, you criminal."

This, I listened to. In no way did I want to ruin my chance at moving into the protective unit. After a decent walk (it still hurt me to walk from my surgery), the correction officers opened a steel door that said *P. Unit*. As I stepped through the door, I found a pleasant surprise. This area looked to be like a community. There were a bunch of beds separated by curtains. No cells at all, just one big open area. It reminded me of a gymnasium that opened its doors to homeless people.

The correction officers led me to a bed in the far back corner of the room. This I loved. Most of the beds had a bed on each side (of course, separated by curtains). Mine had only one bed next to it. On the other side was the wall. The correction officers told me they would bring my stuff (items the prison provided for me) later. I sat down on the bed, and it certainly felt better than the bed in my original cell (and the blanket from solitary confinement).

As I lay down on the bed, a pain shot up through my back to my stomach. My hands gently rubbed over my incision area. In no time, I fell asleep…

"Dinner time, get the fuck up!"

The loud yelling from someone woke me up. I sat up, rubbing my eyes. Down the aisle walked two correction officers pushing a rolling cart.

"Dinner time, everybody back to your beds and for you all sleeping, wake up!" The correction officer, who was not pushing the cart, screamed.

They stopped at everyone's bed, handing them a tray of food. From where my bed was, I received my tray of food last. The correction officer handed me the tray of food and it shocked me. This meal looked and smelt

Titan Frey

delicious. It was a thick hamburger, fries, and a bottle of soda.

"Thank you, officer," I said. "Man, this food is a lot better than the food we get in general pop."

"Yeah, yeah. Just eat, okay?" the correction officer said and walked away.

I took a bite of my burger, oh how it tasted so damn good.

"Yeah, new neighbor, the food is much better in here. Glad you could make it."

The voice came from the other side of the curtain. For some reason, my stomach turned when the voice entered my ears. It sounded eerily familiar.

"Ah, yeah, thank you," I said.

The curtain ripped back in front of me. There sitting was the older version of the monster who killed John Lennon.

Chapter 15

I was at a loss for words. This monster, the motherfucker I've been after, the one who basically got me into this mess, now sat in front of me. There wasn't any doubt this was him. When researching this pig, I saw updated pictures of him. So I definitely recognized his face.

"Hello, new neighbor, what's your name? My name is-"

He told me his name, but as you already know, I will not repeat it. "Ah, my name is Joe."

The monster slapped his thigh. "It's nice to meet you, Joe."

He stuck his hand out to me. I stared at his hand. *This fucking hand pulled the trigger which killed John Lennon.* Reluctantly, I reached my hand out to meet his. We shook hands and I must say, this monster shook hands like a woman. No strength in the grip at all, a real *pansy shake* as my friend's would have said back in my day.

"Yeah, ah, nice to meet you too." I started to squeeze this pansy's hand harder, which prompted him to pull it back.

"Well, I'll let you be. Enjoy your dinner," the monster said with a smile... an evil, disgusting smile.

"Ah, yeah, you too."

The monster grinned once more and ripped the curtain back. Oh, how my blood boiled, I wanted to kill him right then and there. But could I? That was the big question on my mind. *Damn, he's right there, next to me. I have the perfect opportunity to do what I believe I need to do. Yet, I'm over here in pain. Being stabbed and having a surgeon take my damaged kidney out, really puts me in a bad spot here.* I slammed my fist on the pillow. *Ugh, I cannot let this opportunity slip by me. There's no way I'm staying here. Alexis is a traitor, my father is dead and I have one fucking kidney. No, I'm going back to where I belong.*

The rest of the night I pondered ideas of how to kill this motherfucker. The thing that held me back was my physical condition. *Yeah, Joe, you're hurting. But this cock sucker is old. You can do it,* I thought, lying on my bed, staring over at the curtain. The monster had a small light turned on, I could see his silhouette... frightening and disgusting at the same time. I heard what sounded like the pages of a book being flipped over. *What you reading you son of a bitch? The Catcher in the Rye?*

The next morning, the correction officers woke us up for breakfast. They would bring every meal to our beds, which was nice, to be honest. This unit also had private bathrooms. Hell, in this unit you could piss in private, shit in private, and even shower in private. I walked to the bathroom with my toothbrush and toothpaste. As I reached the bathroom, the door swung open.

"Oh, hey again, neighbor. Did you enjoy your breakfast?"

This ape of a man stood in front of me with the stupidest smile I've ever seen. "Yeah, ah, great, just great."

"Well, see you later," the monster said. He walked by me and I turned to stare at him. Even the way he walked pissed me off.

After brushing my teeth, I found one of the correction officers. "Say, officer, can I make a phone call?"

The correction officer laughed. "Boy, in here you can call as much as you want. Well, as long as you put enough money on your books, that is."

Now, for those who may not know what this means, *money on the books,* in prison it's basically an inmate's own trust account, which the prison maintains. Inmates can use this money to buy snacks, get more soap or shampoo. Now, I found out that this money can be used to make phone calls. The prison gave every inmate a number, which they used to get into their account. I walked over to where the correction officer pointed and found an entire roll of payphones.

Most of the phones were filled up with inmates, but two at the far end were empty. I picked the phone up and a *machine* voice told me to type my account number in; so I did. The *machine* voice told me I had enough money to be on the phone for a total of eighteen minutes. So one call for eighteen minutes, or a bunch of different calls broken up till it equaled eighteen minutes. There were two people I wanted to call...

After losing Alexis' number the first time, I studied it hard when I got it back. Now I had the number memorized. After a deep breath, I dialed the number. *If*

Alexis answers, she will know it's me. She will have to accept the charges.

The phone rang three times, I almost didn't think she would answer, but she did. "Hello? Joe, is that you?"

"Yeah, it's me alright."

Alexis wept over the phone. "I'm so sorry, Joe. I never meant to cause you any trouble."

"Then why did you snitch on me? What the fuck were you thinking?"

"Joe! I-I thought you needed help. I mean, your story was pretty far out there. All I wanted to do was get you some help."

I laughed. "Well, sweetheart, you did help me in a way, so thank you for that."

"How do you mean, Joe?"

"Goodbye, Alexis." I slammed the phone down.

This woman really let me down, but her actions put me next to my target. So I supposed it worked out. Yesterday I noticed a few inmates with little computers, or *tablets,* as they called them. I walked over to an inmate named Eric Hake. When I found him, he was lying on his bed, using his tablet.

"Say, Eric. Is there any way I could use your little handheld computer for a few minutes?"

Eric glanced down at the device. "You mean my tablet?"

"Yeah, tablet."

Eric sat up in his bed. "Well, whatcha got?"

In prison, if you ever want to borrow something from another inmate, you must give up something first. "Ah, well, I have a pack of instant noodles I could give you."

Eric smiled. "Deal."

As I walked back to my bed, I saw the monster lying on his bed with a pair of headphones on. He hummed along to whatever he was listening to. Just the mere sight of him angered me. *How hasn't any of these other inmates killed this motherfucker already? They must know he killed Lennon.*

As I passed by, the monster waved at me; I nodded back. I found my pack of instant noodles and headed back to Eric's bed.

"Here, Eric. Take the noodles."

"Good shit, Joe. Now, give it back after..." Eric rubbed his finger on his chin. "Twenty minutes."

I nodded. "Thanks."

Now, with the tablet in hand, I headed back to my bed. As I approached my bed, the monster stood up. "Hey, neighbor."

This stopped me dead in my tracks. He walked straight up to me. "Ah, yeah?"

"Sorry to bother you, neighbor, but I couldn't help but notice the way you are walking."

I bit the inside of my gums. This asshole really pissed me off. "Yeah, and?"

The monster looked me up and down. "Well, I was just wondering if you were injured? You walk with a limp and I noticed you hold the right side of your stomach."

Why is this monster of an asshole being so nice?

"Ah, well, another inmate snuck up and stabbed me in the back. I guess he hit my kidney, so they rushed me to the hospital. There, doctors had to take my kidney out."

The monster's eyes widened. "Oh, my. I'm so sorry, Joe. That's terrible. Are you in a lot of pain?"

I glanced down to my stomach. "Ah, yeah, my back and stomach does hurt. But it will get better, no worries."

The monster reached his hand out to me; I jumped back slightly. He stepped closer and gently placed his hand on my shoulder. "Joe, have you found Jesus in your life?"

What is this monster asking? A man who killed a legend, now believes his soul is saved by Christ?

"Sure, yeah, I believe in Jesus."

He gently rubbed my shoulder. "Good. Now, if you ever want to read the *good* book, I have one. You're more than welcome to borrow it."

"Ah, thanks."

The monster patted me on my shoulder. "You're welcome. I'll say a prayer for you, my friend."

He turned and walked back to his bed. My face felt hot, a sickening feeling hit my stomach. *Why in the hell is this asshole so nice? And he called me friend? What the fuck?*

Back in my bed, I lay staring at the curtain that separated me and the monster. I shook out the cobwebs and pulled up the tablet. I found *Google* and typed in *Outer Space Conspiracy Society.* There, I found Barry Frey's number. He gave me his card with his number, but that was unfortunately lost when they brought me into this shithole.

I wrote Barry's number down on a napkin. After getting what I wanted, I dropped the tablet back off to Eric (he was eating my pack of noodles when I gave the tablet back). Then I headed straight for the phones. I picked the same exact phone I used to call Alexis; this time I placed a call to Barry Frey.

The phone rang three times. *Please, Barry, pick up the damn phone.* A fourth ring echoed in my ear. *Shit, he's not going to answer.*

"Hello?" A woman's voice answered the phone.

This must be Barry's daughter. "Ah, Sara? Sara Frey?"

"Yes, may I help you?"

"Ah, yes. My name is Joe Miller, I met with your father a little while ago."

"Yes, I remember. You scared me, Joe. When the operator asked if I wanted to accept charges from a prison, I thought it was my father calling."

I laughed... slightly. "Sorry about that. Say, the reason I'm calling is to talk to your dad. Is he in?"

Sara let out a sigh. "No, sorry. He's been out all day, that's why I thought it was him calling."

My fist clenched tight. "Do you know when he will be back?"

A computerized voice spoke through the phone. "Five more minutes of talk time, only Five more minutes. Add more money."

Shit.

"Sorry, Joe. I'm not sure to be honest. He didn't tell me where he was going."

Shit!

"Oh, wait. My father just walked in, here he is."

I heard some whispering, but couldn't tell what they were saying.

"Hello, is this Joe Miller?"

"Ah, yes, this is Joe Miller."

"What are you doing in jail, Joe?"

"Listen up, Barry. I don't have much time and I'm not sure how secure this line is."

"I'm listening," Barry said in a serious tone.

"Okay, good."

The computerized voice shot through the phone once more. "Three more minutes of talk time. Only three more minutes. Add more money."

"Shit, okay, listen closely, Barry. I've been arrested by some punk ass FBI agents-"

Even though I said *listen clearly*, Barry interrupted me.

"Joe, I saw those guys arrest you after you left my shop. I'm sorry I couldn't stop them. But I wanted to tell you that those two agents were the same two men who stopped me from talking to Ollie Oggy."

Ollie Oggy? Oh, yeah, the astronaut.

"Yeah, that's correct… they were also in the photo with Ollie in the newspaper." I leaned against the wall, rubbing the phone against the side of my head. "Damn, who are these guys?"

"I'm not sure but they must know something about all of this."

The computerized voice shot through the phone for a third time. "Two more minutes of talk time, only two more minutes. Add more money."

"Barry, before my time runs out, I have to tell you something."

"What is it, Joe?"

"The monster who killed Lennon... he's lying in the Goddamned bed next to me!"

"You're shitting me, Joe."

"Barry, I shit you not. They took me to the same prison he's in. Now, they moved me to the same area he's at."

"Damn, that's heavy," Barry said.

"One more minute of talk time, only one more minute. Add more money."

"Listen Joe. I think the only way to fix all of this and get my father back is to kill that fat bastard."

"I… should I do it now, or wait? Maybe the orange glowing ball will return."

"No! You do it and do it now. You got that, Joe?"

"Ten seconds remain."

"Okay, Barry-"

"Nine, eight, seven, six-"

"Good, Joe."

"Five, four-"

"If everything works out, I think we'll both know," Barry said.

"Three, two, one, goodbye."

"How will we both know?" I bellowed.

The phone clicked off, an empty dial tone buzzed in my ear. I hung up the phone and turned around. My eyes focused on the monster's bed, my fist clenched once more. *I'm going to get you, once and for all.*

After the phone call, my back and stomach started to hurt. Standing for long periods wore me out. I certainly wasn't at full strength. But I couldn't let this hold me back. No… I will fulfill my destiny tonight.

I limped back to my bed, holding on to the lower right side of my stomach. As I passed the monster's bed, I saw him lying down, reading the Bible. He lowered the Bible, "I'll say a prayer for you tonight, neighbor."

I nodded, "Thank you, I'll return the favor."

The monster smiled and went back to reading the Bible. An image shot through my mind… it was of the monster as a younger man, sitting and reading *The Catcher in the Rye.* As soon as my head hit the pillow, I passed out.

Later on that night, exactly at 10:50 PM (the approximate time that Lennon was shot) I awoke from my nap. The lights were off in the unit, even the monster's light didn't shine against the curtain. I sat up in my bed, I could hear snoring coming from where the monster lay. *You have to do it now, please, don't back out, Joe.*

My mind raced, my heart pounded. This would be the most important duty of my life... hell, of the universe; or it seemed. Now, the question arose, *how do I kill this bastard?* Unfortunately, unlike my attacker in the yard, I didn't have a knife, or *shank*, as my fellow inmates would call it. Then I glanced down at my pillow. *Yes, the old pillow over the face trick.* A smile grew on my face, yet it didn't last too long. *Shit, am I even strong enough to hold the pillow down on his face?*

A pain shot from my lower right back to the lower right part of my stomach. I grabbed my back, then my stomach, wincing in pain. I looked around the unit, trying to see if there was anything I could use to bash the fucker's brains in; but there was nothing. My mind focused back on my pillow. *This has to work, right?* I picked up my pillow and examined it. *This will work.*

Slowly, I walked over toward the curtain. At the end of where the curtain hung, I peeked into the other side. There, I saw the monster, fast asleep, lying on his back with the Bible placed promptly on his chest. *Joe, can you really do this?* I juddered my head. *Yes, damn it! I can and will do this!* As I finished yelling at myself, something above caught my eye. The lights, that were all turned off, came back on. These lights were a white light, yet now they appeared to be orange... bright orange. The lights were so orange; I felt like I stood in a horror movie.

I inched closer; the monster snored louder. My hands gripped the pillow, my arms shook. I've never been so nervous in my entire life. The way the monster looked, lying under the distinct orange glow, frightened me. *Get it together, Joe. You must act now, before someone sees you.*

Slowly, I approached the monster. Now, I stood next to his bed, looking straight down at him. "This is for John Lennon," I whispered; the monster did not wake up.

I lifted the pillow above my head. When I stretched my arms up, a pain hit me in my stomach. The pillow lowered as tears filled my eyes. *No, Joe. Fight through it!*

The pillow lifted above my head, higher than before. Saliva dripped from my mouth, an intense rage came over me. "Huh?"

The lights promptly changed from orange to red... a deep blood red.

"Argh!"

Someone screamed from my left side. My head whipped to the left, a figure ran toward me. I couldn't tell what this figure was. The bright red light mixed into the night made it hard to see. Gripping the pillow, I lowered it down, covering my stomach.

"Shit!" I screamed as the figure ran into me, tackling me onto the floor. We flew back, hitting the curtain and ripping it off its hinges. My back slammed on the concrete floor as the figure fell on top of me. Pain jumped from my back to my stomach.

The monster jumped up from his bed, scratching his head. "What in God's name?"

The figure shoved its hand under my chin, pushing my head back. Pain now grew in my neck. "Ah, get off of me!" I screamed.

Every inmate in the unit jumped up from their beds. They all stared in amazement, from the scuffle, to the glowing red lights. The next thing I knew, the monster's head appeared overtop of the figure. Then, like a weight being lifted off me, the figure got yanked back. I jumped up, holding onto my stomach. The monster held the figure in a Full Nelson type hold. The figure's face hid in the light.

"Calm down, buddy. This isn't the way," the monster said.

My head tilted sideways, *the monster I'm supposed to kill, is saving my life?*

"Get off of me! I'm protecting you, damn it!" The figure screamed.

The voice of the figure rang a bell. "I know that voice, I fucking know who you are," I bellowed.

"Go to hell, that's where you belong!" the figure screamed.

I ran over to the figure, grabbing him on the face and titled his head up in the air. "It's you, what the fuck do you have to do with this?"

The figure... the man being held by the monster was Agent Carter.

"Tell me, what the fuck do you have to do with this?"

Agent Carter spat in my face, hitting me in my left eye. "You're going to burn in hell." He turned and looked up at the monster. "And you, I'm here to protect you, you fucking idiot."

The monster let go of Agent Carter's right arm to scratch his head. "Huh?"

Agent Carter threw an elbow into the monster's gut. He reached down at his waistband. Glowing in the blood-red light was a handgun.

"Shit, he's going for his gun!" I shouted.

"Ha-ha," Agent Carter laughed. He grabbed the gun, lifting it up toward me. "Die!"

I closed my eyes and covered my head. What I heard next wasn't a gunshot, but the sound of something hitting the floor. My eyes opened to see the gun on the floor. Agent Carter bent over in front of the monster, he held the back of his right shoulder. The monster stood above Agent Carter with his fist balled.

I jumped for the gun, Agent Carter pounced toward it as well. My hands grabbed the back of the gun, Agent Carter grabbed the front.

"Let it go, motherfucker!" Agent Carter screamed. His eyes glowed red from the reflection of the lights.

"Fuck you, asshole!" I answered while simultaneously pulling the trigger.

Blood sprayed over my face as I watched Agent Carter's head split open; he fell to the ground. My breathing grew to an intense rate; my hands shook. While trying to catch my breath, my eyes fixated on the FBI clown.

"Ugh, err."

Two moans snapped me out of my gaze. I glanced up to find the monster holding onto his neck, blood spraying out from both sides of his hands. *Damn, the bullet that split open the FBI turkey's head must have flown into the monster's neck.*

I approached the monster, watching him as he struggled to breathe. A few different emotions ran through me. First, sadness struck. This monster of a man was actually nice to me. Hell, he even saved my life from the FBI bozo. Second, anger flew through me. Of course, this came from the fact this fucker killed John Lennon and sent me into the future (it had to be because of him, right?). The third and final emotion was satisfaction. A mission that was given to me now appeared to be, well, almost complete.

The blood-red glow of the lights faded back to orange. The monster fell to his knees, looking me square in my eyes. *Should I? Or shouldn't I?* A smile formed on my face.

"Yes, I fucking should." My finger squeezed the trigger, the bullet flew out, hitting the monster right between the eyes; he fell over.

The orange lights went out, the unit faded back to darkness. A bunch of chatter could be heard through the darkness, but I didn't pay it any mind. I did what I was supposed to do. Even though during the short time I've actually met him, he treated me nicely. Hell, I had to kill him. This *nice* guy I met in jail was still the cold-blooded monster I saw back in 1980. The younger, fatter, and meaner version of this dude was still there. And he caused this entire mess. Yeah, there is no doubt in my mind that I did the right thing.

After killing the monster, no other guards entered our unit (thankfully), so I decided to take a nap. And damn it, that's what I did. I fell asleep like a baby.

Chapter 16

Something woke me up from my nap. A loud *buzz* pierced my ears. A rumble shook my bed around. My eyes opened and I found the unit's lights were still off. As I sat up, I glanced around, finding the bodies of both the FBI agent and the monster. *No guards came in yet?* The *buzz* sounded louder. The intensity of the rumble picked up; I fell off the bed. The ceiling of the unit partially tore off and flapped around, banging, causing a loud *screech* every time it smacked down. To be percent frank, I thought we were having a tornado.

My eyes glanced around the unit to find every other inmate fast asleep, not bothered by any of this. More of the ceiling ripped off. Up in the sky, in the opening, I discovered a glowing orange light. *It's here...* I thought, watching in amazement. The ceiling ripped back more. Now my eyes fixated on the orange glowing ball. *Come and get me, take me back to where I belong.* With one last yank, the ceiling ripped off, flying out into the sky, disappearing inside the orange glowing ball. I raised my arms up into the air. *Take me now!*

The next thing I knew, my ears rang with such an intensity that I lost my hearing. The orange glowing ball expanded; the light grew brighter. All that surrounded me was orange... nothing but orange. By now, I seemed to be floating in mid-air, still surrounded by an orange background. I tried to move, but I couldn't. *This must be what astronauts experience.* Then Ollie Oggy crossed my mind. *The astronaut who got sucked into this thing... James Frey got sucked into this damn thing...*

"Where are you taking me? I want to go back to my time!" My screams weren't answered. I hopelessly floated in the air. My head started to hurt, I became dizzy. My consciousness started to fade. "Help me." My voice came out weak, I was losing it.

What happened next looked like a movie cutting to a new scene. From floating around in an orange glow, I suddenly found myself standing in a wheat field. It was nighttime and the sky sat clear as a picture. No moon, but the stars were bright and they twinkled magically. *Where am I?* I thought as I began walking through the field. Not another person in sight, just me and the stars. After walking for about ten minutes, I came across a large tree. This tree sent off some sort of energy. The energy shot through my body, very powerful. It also struck me as odd since this large tree was the only tree in the entire wheat field.

I stood in silence, taking in the tree. The bark appeared to be tinted with an orange color... *Orange, it has to be orange.* On the leaves of this tree were pieces of fruit. Can you guess which type of fruit? If you answered oranges, then you would be correct. My hand reached out, grabbing the orange. While staring at the piece of fruit, I couldn't deny my hunger. My mouth opened wide, and I made my way to the orange. With one strong bite, I ripped off a big chunk of the fruit. I spit the skin out, only chewing on the juicy middle. Damn, it tasted so good, the best orange I've ever eaten.

An intense breeze blew… cool and refreshing. Glancing up, I watched as the leaves blew in the wind. They seemed to be dancing. To this day, I'm not sure if what happened next was real. While the wind blew, I heard what sounded like someone's voice. The voice spoke in a whisper, and I only heard it when the wind would gust.

"Hello?" I called out.

The wind picked up its speed. *Joe… Joe Miller.*

"What? Is anybody there? Show yourself!"

The breeze seemingly blew around my head, passing by my ears. *Joe Miller…*

I spun around, looking in every direction. The tree's leaves bounced around. It looked like the tree was standing in the middle of a hurricane.

"Who are you?"

The wind gusted harder.

"What is all of this? Are you involved with the orange and red glowing balls?"

A harder gust blew.

"Can you at least tell me that?"

The wind hit my face so hard that my eyes watered. *The universe needs balance. Good trumps evil…*

After wiping the tears out my eyes I screamed, "Are you, God?"

The wind seemed to howl this time. *I am the holder of good in everything. Anything and everything good is me.*

I smiled, the thought of me talking to *God* or some sort of God felt like an honor. The wind blew so hard, my prison uniform almost flew off my chest.

But know this, Joe. There is evil in everything as well. Some such evil is so pure that it threatens the existence of the universe.

"But I killed that evil... the monster who killed Lennon, right?"

The next gust knocked me back a few steps.

Joe, the evil isn't dead. You must make it right. Save the good in the universe, before it's too late!

The most intense gust of wind blew, knocking me off my feet. The beautiful tree lifted up from the ground, exposing its roots. The tree tilted forward.

"No!" I screamed, holding my arms up. The tree's roots completely popped out of the ground; the tree fell toward me. Covering my head, I couldn't do anything but cry. A loud *bang* roared in my ears. The ground shook, then, silence. I kept my arms over my head for a few more minutes. Then I lowered them.

"Huh?" To my surprise, I wasn't in a wheat field or under a large tree. I lay in some dark alley. A cool breeze did blow, but not like in the wheat field. *Where am I? What's going on?* I picked myself up and off the ground. After dusting my pants off, I came to realize that I wasn't wearing the prison outfit anymore. *Holy shit. I'm wearing my work uniform, the one I wore the night John Lennon got killed.*

This gave me a sense of hope. *Maybe I'm back in my time.* I ran out of the alley. Out on the main street, I discovered I was back in New York City. A coin-operated newspaper machine sat to my left. I leaned over to glance at the newspaper. The date in the newspaper read: *December 8, 1980.*

Shit, I'm back on the exact night that Lennon will be killed. My mind replays what the magic wind told me; *Joe, the evil isn't dead. You must make it right. Save the good in the universe, before it's too late!* I snapped my fingers and kicked the newspaper machine. *That's what it meant. Even though I killed the monster, John Lennon was still dead. It wants me to kill the monster in his true form and save John Lennon!*

Down the street, I ran. By now I needed to find out the time. After checking all my pockets, I realized I had no cell phone. *Damn, how did we live without cell phones?* An older man, maybe sixty, walked down the street in my direction.

"Hey, sir, do you have the time by any chance?"

At first, the older man jumped back. I appeared to have startled him. Then he let out a small laugh.

"Yes, sonny, let me check for you." He reached into his pocket and pulled out a shiny gold pocket watch. He flipped it open and brought the watch up to his eyes. "Hmm, it's five on the dot."

"PM?" I asked.

The older man shot me a look. He closed up his pocket watch. On the front of the gold watch was a beautiful sculptured picture of a bald eagle.

"Ah, yeah. Of course, it's PM. Are you crazy, mister?"

"No, sorry. Real sorry." I slapped him on his shoulder. This time, he jumped back farther. "Thanks for telling me the time. Bye now."

This was it. The real dance would start in less than six hours. I would be ready. I've killed this fucker already, and I'll do it again.

My mind was clouded with thoughts. Ideas of how to finish this and regrets as well. For one, while in the future, with the assistance of the wonderful internet, I should have looked up the monster's whereabouts before the murder. Then, I could sneak to wherever he was staying and kill him there. If I could kill him and keep him far away from Lennon, that would be ideal. Unfortunately, while studying up on the monster, I did not look that up.

Another regret I had was my dissipating relationship with my father. We used to be so close, now; he let a woman stand between us. But was it all his fault? No, I could have made more of an effort to see him, but I didn't. In the future, my father passed away. The worst thing was, I couldn't find out when or why he passed. Now being back in the past, back in my time, I wanted to make things right between us.

That's exactly what I did first. I stood on the main road, whistling for a cab. About eight cabs passed by and none of them stopped. How I wished I had my cell phone right then, I could have called for an *Uber* (if they existed). After three more cabs zoomed by, the fourth cab stopped. Inside the cab, I gave the cabbie my father's address and off we went. My leg jumped like a Mexican jumping bean. It was safe to say I was nervous. The cabbie pulled up to my father's place. I sat in the back, twiddling my thumbs, staring out the window.

"Eh, you gonna get out, mister?" the cabbie said.

This shook me out of my trance. "Ah yeah, sorry, buddy."

I opened the door just to hear the cabbie scream. "Hey, mister, that be $9.66."

Into my pocket I reached. Luckily, my money from the night still sat inside my wallet. I paid the cabbie and hopped out of the taxi. My eyes fixated on the door of my father's place. My memories replayed my trip to this house in the future, where it wasn't my father answering the door. This time, I hoped he did.

My right fist pounded three solid times on the door. After waiting for only about five seconds, three more solid *pounds* shot out, thanks to my fist. Then, the sound of a bolt unlocking sounded behind the thick wooden door. My nerves struck harder… *this is it, Daddy, I'm home…*

The door opened and it wasn't my father, nor was it the blond haired man from the future. The person standing in the doorway was my father's apparent wife, Rose.

"Joe? Is that you?"

A small chuckle exited my mouth. "Well, I sure hope so."

Rose rolled her eyes. "Well, your dad isn't home. He's out grocery shopping."

"Ah, well, do you mind if I wait inside till he gets home?"

She rolled her eyes again. "Yeah, I sort of mind, to be honest. I'm doing some cleaning and you'll just get in the way."

What a bitch.

"I'll tell your dad that you stopped by. How's that sound, Joe?"

"Ah-" Before I could finish, Rose slammed the door in my face.

Bitch! I walked around to the window and peeked inside. There I found Rose, sitting down watching the TV, with what appeared to be a bag of chips. *What a lying bitch, she isn't cleaning.*

This had me steaming. I squeezed my fist tight and slammed it against the brick siding; this hurt like hell. While shaking my fist out, I remembered being stabbed in jail. Also, I remembered the surgery to remove my damaged kidney. I lifted my shirt to see my large scar, yet it was gone. While rubbing over my lower right stomach, and my lower right back, a voice entered my ears.

"Joe, is that you?"

Slowly, I turned around to see my father standing, holding two plastic bags full of groceries.

"What's going on, Joe? Why is your hand bleeding?"

Without saying a word, I ran over and hugged my dad.

"Ah, Joe?" my father said, holding the bags of groceries up in the air. I held on to my father for a couple of minutes. Finally, I backed up with tears in my eyes. "Joe, you're scaring me."

"Dad, I'm sorry for ever being a bad kid. Anytime that I ever went against your wishes, I'm truly sorry."

My father bent down and sat the two plastic bags on the ground. "Joe, I don't know what you're talking about. You never did anything bad to me, or upset me in any way."

"Then, why have you blocked me out of your life?"

"Joe, I-ah-"

"Dad, you did block me out, don't even act like you didn't."

My father glanced past me, looking up at his home. I turned around to see Rose standing in the doorway, watching us.

"You chose her over me and I want to know why? If I didn't do anything to upset you, then why?"

My father looked up at the door again.

"Dad, forget about her. I'm your son, fucking answer me!"

He stared at me, the look in his eyes spelled out *regret*.

Tears filled my eyes, my bottom lip trembled. "Dad, I love you, I really, really love you."

My father grabbed me, this time, he held on to me tight. "Son, I love you too..."

Chapter 17

My father invited me inside, despite what Rose said. He sat me down and actually told Rose to leave; which she did. After she left to go out with her friends, my father and I talked about everything. He explained to me how he admitted he picked this new woman over me. At first, I didn't understand, but he told me how after my mother treated him, to find someone who seemed to care, it meant a lot to him.

Again, like I said in the beginning of my story, I was really happy for him. It was great to see him with a woman who cared so much for him. I don't doubt that she does for a second. The only problem was that Rose wanted my father all to herself. My father told me from this point on, he would make time for me and explained to Rose, who had no children, that time with me was precious.

That's exactly what time with my father was, precious. After seeing the future, a future without my father, I wanted to spend as much time as I could with him. It killed me knowing my father passed away and I wasn't there to be by his side. Of course, now with this knowledge, I'm going to make sure my father eats right, exercises, and does anything he can to keep his heart strong. Can history be changed? Well, if I can get to the Dakota before John Lennon does tonight, then I'll find out.

I spent two hours with my father. We laughed and had a great time. To be perfectly frank, I didn't want to leave. But I knew I had to. So I left my father's place and he even gave me the keys to his car. I told him I had something important to do tonight, and how I was going to call for a cab. I'd get the cabbie to drive to my job. Then, I'd borrow the work van (I supposed I still worked at the same job). My father wouldn't have it, so he gave me his keys... thanks, Pops.

My father's car, thanks to Rose, was a *1980 Chevy Camaro*. Boy, was this car fancy. The only problem I had with the car was the color. Can you guess? Yeah, it was a blood red; I'd prefer it to be orange, at this point. My first stop after leaving my father's place was at a gun shop. I knew of this place, which wasn't too far from where I lived, but I've never been in it. Today, I will go there. Inside, I found an older gentleman with large and thick glasses standing behind the counter.

"May I help you, sir?"

"Hi," I said, glancing around at all the guns. There were rifles, other larger guns, and a bunch of handguns. For me, I needed something I could hide in my pocket. "Yes, how much are your handguns?"

The gun shop worker adjusted his glasses and looked around at all the handguns. He reached down and picked one up.

"Here's a *Beretta 92.* It's a very good semi-automatic pistol."

He handed me the gun, I flipped it around, getting a good look at it. "Very nice."

The gun shop worker adjusted his glasses. "You planning on buying it, or what?"

"Ah, yeah. This will be my new gun."

The gun shop worker smiled. "That'll be three hundred dollars, mister."

Damn, three hundred dollars? No wonder I don't buy firearms. In my back pocket, my hand went, reaching for my wallet. I pulled the wallet out and opened it. *Shit, only fifty-three dollars.* This wouldn't be enough to buy any gun, and I needed a gun. Trying to suffocate the monster with a pillow wouldn't be an option this time.

"Ah, how much are bullets for this gun?" I asked.

The gun shop worker adjusted his glasses and ducked back under the counter. He returned a second later with a box in his hand.

"Here you go, mister. These are the bullets." He shook the box around. "These are ten dollars."

Damn, only two-hundred-and fifty-seven dollars short.

"Ah, can you grab one more box of bullets for me?" I asked. "Just so I can have them in stock."

"Sure, mister." The gun shop worker adjusted his glasses and ducked down under the counter.

Right then and there, I made my move. I grabbed the gun and lifted it up. As the gun shop worker lifted his head up, I slammed the gun down, smacking him right on the head. The poor bastard fell to the floor. This, I can't say, was my brightest moment. Honestly, this wasn't what I wanted to do, but the universe depended on me and I needed a gun.

Now, with the gun shop worker knocked out, I grabbed the one box of bullets and ran out the door. As I exited the shop, a man about my age walked toward the door. After breezing past him, I jumped into my father's *Camaro*.

In the car, driving down the street, I noticed the time. 8:30 PM. *Less than three hours till Lennon is shot. Damn, the monster is at the Dakota. This I know... It is time.* My foot pressed harder on the pedal; the car roared. The closer I got, the slower the *Camaro* went. Suddenly, 1 West 72nd Street appeared on my right. Yes, the Dakota Building... my battleground. As I drove slowly, I tried to get a glimpse of the monster, but I couldn't tell where he was. So I kept on driving. My job now was to find a parking spot. Then, I could sneak up and end that fat bastard's life for a second time.

Around the block, I found an empty spot. After parking the car, I sat in silence for ten minutes, replaying everything. From the first time that I witnessed the orange glowing ball, to taking my first steps into the Dakota. From seeing John and Yoko, to walking past the monster. John's death played over and over in my mind. Tears fell, then they fell harder when I thought of Alexis.

I've seen the future. There were good things, no doubt about it. The technology was out of this world. A million years could pass by and I would never have thought we would come up with such things. But there were many horrors as well. Horrors that were caused by the red glowing ball.

Yes, the orange glowing ball scared me. Shit, still to this day it scares me. But what talked to me in a gust must be the good in the universe. If not the good, at least the protector of the universe. It wanted us, humans, to do the right thing, to try to rid the world of pure evil.

The red glowing ball resisted anything good, that I'm sure of. It would resist what I had to do on December 8, 1980, approximately at 10:50 PM. This moment would change our history, and *it was all up to me*.

After my thoughts passed through my mind, I grabbed the gun and tucked it away in my waistband. Then, out the door, I went. While standing on the sidewalk, a block away from the Dakota, I saw the orange glowing ball of light hovering above the apartment building. It appeared to be small like it was far away, yet it was there, watching me.

Down the street, I walked, keeping my eye on the orange glowing ball. It appeared to be growing in size. It was like the closer I got, the bigger it would grow. The street was empty, nobody on this block at least. Now, I reached the block where the Dakota sat. People were standing around in the distance, in front of the Dakota. I didn't notice any large man as of yet, but he most likely sat in the archway. Yes, sitting, and reading *The Catcher in the Rye*... tonight, I would be Holden Caulfield.

Inching closer, my hand placed deep in my waistband, holding on to the gun. The orange glowing ball continued to grow... I almost made it.

"Psst."

Someone in an old clunker of a car pulled up next to me.

"Psst." They called again. The car stopped and jumped. It made a horrible noise.

"What? Who are you?" I called out, but received no answer.

My hand gripped the gun harder. This person in the car could be bad news. A bright light caught my attention from the corner of my eye. This light glowed in an eerie red tint.

Suddenly, the presence of someone standing next to me could be felt. My head turned over to the right, toward the road.

"Oh, my God," I said frighteningly.

"I'm not God, boy."

Next to me stood Agent Jones. He grabbed me around my neck so fast that I couldn't react. My hands reached up to my neck, letting go of the gun. He dragged me over to his car and opened the backseat. Before throwing me inside, he reached into my waistband, pulled out my gun, and threw it down a storm drain.

The ball in the sky glowed red, an evil, blood toned red. My ears started to ring as my breathing almost stopped. Agent Jones threw me inside his beat-up old car, slamming the door shut. I noticed a cage separating the front and back seats, just like his car in the future. He jumped inside the driver's seat and slammed his foot on the pedal. I jumped up, glancing out the back window. The now red glowing ball of light grew three times in size. It appeared to resemble a full *blood moon.*

I kicked the cage as hard as I could. "What are you doing? Let me the fuck out! You don't understand, I have to stop pure evil tonight!"

The old beat-up car pulled down a dark alley. Agent Jones slammed on the brakes, making me fly up against the cage, the same way his partner did in the future. The agent turned around and his eyes were glowing the same bright evil tint of red as the glowing ball.

"Jesus," I muttered.

"I ain't God or Jesus, sonny boy. I'm not even Agent Jones, as you know it. I'm the protector of all things evil, and I've been sent here to KILL you."

"This isn't real, you're not real."

Agent Jones smiled, large fangs appeared in his mouth. A ghostly grin grew on his face.

"Oh, I'm real, boy. I'm as real as it gets. You, on the other hand, won't be real for much longer."

This agent, demon, or whatever the fuck he was, reached down on the passenger seat. "My partner wasn't strong enough to stop you. Pure evil started to change and went against its core values. Well, in this time pure evil is at the height of its powers. I'm also at the height of my powers and I'll kill you so fast, boy."

Agent Jones pulled up a shotgun. The evil grin on his face grew larger.

"Shoulda killed you earlier, the same with the astronaut and the biker. I won't make this mistake any longer."

Agent Jones cocked the gun.

"Holy shit!" I screamed.

I rolled down as far as I could on the floor of the backseat of the car. A loud *bang* echoed out. My eyes were closed when I heard the bang. I opened them and checked all over myself. *I wasn't hit, he didn't hit me.* Another bang rang out, again I wasn't hit. The cage stopped this demon fuck from getting a perfect shot at me. A sinister growl exited the agent's mouth. Glancing up, I noticed Agent Jones reloading the shotgun. This was where I made my move. I reached up and pulled up on the lock. Thankfully, these old cars were easier to unlock than the cars of the future. I busted out of the car, ducking and running as fast as I could.

"Get the fuck back here!" Agent Jones snarled.

The sound of footsteps scurrying across the ground followed me down the alley. The sound of the clip being smacked into the shotgun nearly gave me a heart attack. To my left sat a large dumpster. Without thinking, I opened the dumpster and jumped inside. Two more *bangs* rang out. The sound of crunching metal destroyed my eardrums. I lay underneath a pile of trash, holding a large piece of wood over my body. My hearing went numb. All I could hear was an eerie *ring*.

The lid of the dumpster started to lift. My hands gripped the piece of wood tightly. Just as the hideous agent's face appeared, I swung the piece of board, smacking him directly in the neck. The agent fell backward and a wet *gurgling* noise followed. A loud *bang* followed. This, I assumed, was the gun going off when the agent hit the floor. I climbed up and peeked out. The agent lay on the ground, rolling around and holding his neck. The gun lay away from the falling demon and I pounced on it like a lion pouncing on a zebra.

I grabbed the gun and pointed it at the demonic agent.

"You son of a bitch, whatever you truly are, you're going to die tonight."

The demonic agent stumbled to his feet, still holding his neck. His red glowing eyes seemed to dim, just a bit.

"You won't win, boy. In no way can good defeat evil, not in this universe and especially not on this planet!"

"I've killed your partner and I'll kill you. But before I do, tell me, are you the devil?"

The demonic agent laughed. "Please, I'm whatever your human brain thinks I am. My form depends on you."

"Huh?"

Before I could think of what this *thing* meant, it pounced toward me. Without thinking, I pulled the trigger and a loud *bang* followed. Splatter flew everywhere, hitting me on my face. It looked like *Gallagher* smashing a watermelon. It took me a few seconds to recuperate from this incident. After I regained my composure, I checked to see how many more bullets the shotgun had; none. *Damn, now I have no gun to shoot the monster.*

I ran over to the old beat-up car. *Shit, no.* I found where the inadvertent gunshot went; it hit the rear left tire. Inside the car, I turned the engine on. After attempting to drive the car down the alley, I realized this wouldn't work. The car wouldn't drive too well, but the clock worked: 10:18 PM.

Shit, only around thirty minutes till Lennon is shot. Damn, I have no idea how far away I am from the Dakota now. I tossed the empty shotgun in the dumpster and paused for a second, placing my left hand on the dirty trash collector. *Thank you for saving me.* Oh, one thing I didn't mention was the odd color of this dumpster; it was bright orange.

While running down the street I said to myself, *orange good, red bad.* This, I repeated over and over again. I came to the end of the alley and tried to figure out which direction the Dakota was. To be perfectly frank, I felt lost. With the intensity of being kidnapped, I didn't take notice of which direction the agent drove down. After some self debating, I headed left. *Orange good, red bad, orange good, red bad...* my running picked up, my breathing became more intense. But a smile formed on my face as I realized I was headed in the right direction.

I turned the corner of the street at Columbus Ave. Now, I stood, catching my breath, staring down toward the Dakota. *Shit, I'm close but not close enough. It's around fifteen minutes here, I believe. I'm not sure what time it is, but I must hurry!* I picked up my speed and ran as fast as I could down the street. This reminded me of the time in the future, where I ran to the library. In the sky, the orange glowing ball started to reappear. It started small, but the closer I got, the bigger the orange glowing ball grew.

The sound of a vehicle driving down the road caught my attention. While running, I glanced back to see a limo. This wasn't any old limo either, this was the limo bringing John and Yoko home.

"Hey! Please, stop!" I screamed while waving my arms. The driver of the limo didn't seem to notice me. "Please! You must turn around!"

The limo continued on its way down the street. This made me feel hopeless. The limo now passed me and headed straight for the Dakota, straight to the danger.

"John! Don't go home!" My legs felt weak. After the fight with the demonic agent and now the run, I was worn out. But I had to continue, the monster needed to be stopped.

I got closer to the Dakota. The orange glowing ball almost filled the entire sky. The limo stopped out front of the Dakota; the backdoor opened.

"Hey! Yoko! Get back in the limo!"

Yoko Ono stepped out of the limo. She glanced in my direction, but quickly looked away. To be perfectly frank, I probably scared her with my running and screaming. Next, John Lennon stepped out, hands filled with cassettes.

I inched closer to the Dakota, almost reaching the entrance. At that very moment, I saw the monster. He stood in the shadows of the archway, the orange glowing ball immediately turned red. The monster, whose face I couldn't see from being blocked by the shadows, took one step forward. There, I saw a part of his face. That evil grin, those large glasses. The top of his head was still covered by shadows. Yet, I could have sworn I saw two pointy horns sticking straight up in the air.

"John! Mr. Lennon! Please get back in the limo!"

John turned to face me. The red glowing ball became brighter. An evil red tint filled the night sky. Now, I could see the monster completely.

"Hey! What are you doing?" the doorman screamed, running toward me.

John picked up his speed, walking faster, passing by the monster.

"No!" I bellowed.

This I didn't want. The monster waited for John to pass last time so he could shoot him in the back. My mind replayed the shooting in that split second. I remembered how I walked outside of the Dakota after working on the floors. Then, I remembered seeing the monster sitting on the ground, reading *The Catcher in the Rye.*

My memory replayed the limo pulling up and me standing still, in awe of the moment. Yoko, then John stepped out. Not too far from me the monster jumped up after John passed, firing five shots, hitting him four times. I did nothing, but I couldn't do anything to stop him, right? I had no idea this sorry excuse of a man would shoot my idol.

Now fast forward to this moment. With the knowledge of what would happen, I found myself struggling to stop this senseless killing.

"John, go back to the fucking limo!" I bellowed.

John picked up his speed even more, he now jogged down the archway.

The monster jumped out of the shadows, landing in a combat stance.

"No! Stop you fucking monster!" I cried out.

The monster faced John Lennon, yet for a split second, the back of his head formed an evil glowing red face. It smiled at me with the same fangs Agent Jones had.

"Senor, you must leave now!" the doorman screamed, stepping in front of my path.

"Mr. Lennon," the monster softly said.

"No! Stop now, you son of a bitch!" I screamed and simultaneously pushed the doorman in the direction of the monster.

The doorman flew back at a rapid speed. He smacked into the back of the monster. A loud *bang* erupted in the night. John Lennon screamed and jumped around. Yoko Ono now screamed, peeking her head outside of the door.

I glanced up, looking at John. To my surprise, I didn't notice any blood. John looked back, locking his eyes onto mine.

"John, get inside now! That monster on the ground has a gun!"

The gun lay a foot away from the monster. I realized this and made my way toward it. The monster saw what I was up to and began to crawl toward the gun.

The doorman swung his arm up, grabbing a hold of my right leg. "Senor, you must stop now!"

This slowed me down, preventing me from grabbing the gun first. "Hey, get off of me, I'm trying to save John!"

The monster grabbed a hold of the gun. John Lennon wasn't inside yet, almost but not yet. Weird grunts exited the mouth of the monster. After kicking the doorman's hand off my leg, I dived toward the monster.

"Fuck you!" I screamed, landing on his back.

"Ugh!" the monster bellowed, still holding the gun.

John had one leg inside the Dakota, but the other half of his body was still vulnerable. The monster's finger started to squeeze the trigger. This I took notice too. I Karate chopped down on his hand, the one holding the gun. Another loud *bang* roared in the night. My head whipped up, staring down the archway... John wasn't there, he made it inside. A sense of relief hit me, but that changed immediately.

"Err," the monster growled.

He swung his body over to face me. The gun was still in his hand, my right hand still holding his hand. For a second, the barrel of the gun pointed directly at my face.

I bobbed and weaved just like Muhammad Ali, barely missing the next shot the monster took. My left hand now grabbed the gun as well. I slammed my right knee into the groin of the monster, he yelped like a small dog.

Even though the monster still had a grip on the gun, I gained control of the gun. Lowering the gun toward the monster's face, my mind replayed the first time I shot this monster.

Now centered directly between his eyes I muttered, "This is for John, motherfucker."

My finger squeezed the trigger. A single shot flew out, causing a hole in between the eyes of the monster... as it did in 2023.

I sat the gun down on the now-dead monster's chest. Standing up, I stretched and glanced up at the sky. The red glowing ball faded before my eyes. First, it faded to an orange glow, then it faded away.

Heavy breathing hit the back of my neck, I spun around and found the doorman standing, watching me.

"Senor, I'm sorry for trying to stop you. I didn't know this man had a gun and was trying to kill Mr. Lennon."

I placed my right hand on his shoulder. We didn't say another word, just nodded to each other. Then his face looked up and a startled expression formed on his face. This made me jump around and what I saw formed the same expression on mine. Standing, looking down at the lifeless body of the monster, was none other than John Lennon himself.

"Senor, John. Are you okay?" The doorman asked.

John's eyes never looked away from the monster. "Yeah, I'm okay." John kneeled down, examining the lifeless body. "Call for an ambulance, if this fella is holding onto any sort of life, he's going to need help, and fast."

John now stood up slowly, a look of sadness in his eyes. Then his eyes met mine. His glasses must've fallen off during his scurry to get inside the Dakota because he wasn't wearing them. John walked around the lifeless body of the monster, he placed his hand on my left shoulder. I was at a loss for words. My idol stood in front of me, touching me, just after I saved his life.

Then, what happened next, I'll remember for the rest of my life. John uttered some special words to me.

"Thank you for keeping me around, so I can watch my two sons grow up."

Finally, I found three words of my own to say. "You're welcome, John."

Chapter 18

The cops showed up less than ten seconds after John and I shared our words together. Yoko approached, putting her arms around John. This made me smile. She wouldn't have to mourn her husband; she could continue on with loving him. The police escorted me down to the station. Now, I wasn't in trouble. They just wanted to get a statement from me. The doorman, John Lennon, and Yoko Ono all vouched for me. They all told the cops that I showed up screaming, trying to warn them about the monster.

Then, how I wrestled with the monster and the gun *accidentally* went off, striking the big brute in between his eyes. This struck curiosity from the cops.

"Hello, Joe. My name is Detective Carter, and my partner here is Detective Jones..."

I leaned back in my chair, crossing my arms. "Of course it is."

"Huh? What?" Detective Jones asked.

"Oh, nothing," I said while checking these two men out.

They certainly weren't the FBI bozos, but were their names just a coincidence?

"We are grateful for the deed you did, saving Mr. Lennon's life," Detective Carter said. "But we have a question."

"Oh, yeah? Asked away, detective."

Detective Jones leaned forward toward me. "How did you know that the perp was planning on shooting Mr. Lennon?"

"Yeah, you weren't friends with him, were you?" Detective Carter asked.

"Yeah, you didn't plan this all with him and back out at the last second?" Detective Jones asked.

Boy, did these two detective clowns not only share the last names with my future FBI pals, but they also shared their personalities.

"Please, I wasn't friends with that monster, not one bit."

"Then, how did you know, boy?"

There it was, the word, *boy*, the same term this *Jones* doppelganger used against me in the future... oh, how I hated to be called that.

"Listen, officer, that monster wasn't my friend at all. In fact, I met him only yesterday when I walked out of the Dakota."

"Are you a resident of the Dakota?" Detective Jones asked.

"No, not at all. I work for Martin's Building and Maintenance (Jeez, I hope I'm still working for Martin's). We work on the floors in different businesses. These past few days I've been working in the Dakota."

Both Detectives glanced at each other and nodded.

"Last night, when I left the job, that man approached me. We started talking, and I didn't want to be rude, so I stood there to listen to him."

The two detectives focused on my story... they were buying my bullshit.

"Then, this guy told me how he planned on coming back tomorrow night, which is tonight, to kill Lennon."

The two detectives looked at each other. Detective Carter stepped toward me.

"If he told you this, why didn't you go straight to the police?"

"Yeah, why didn't you call the police?" Detective Jones asked. "Sounds pretty fishy to me. What do you think, Detective Carter?"

"Yeah, a little fishy, indeed."

These clowns irritated me, to say the least.

"Please, you can look my job up in the phone book and give them a call. Then, you'll believe that I was at the Dakota doing a job."

Detective Carter smirked. "Sure, we will look that number up. Say, Joe. What did you say the company you work for is called?"

"Martin's Building and Maintenance."

Detective Carter nodded at his partner and Detective Jones left the room.

"Hey, seriously, I don't think the person who saved John Lennon's life should be treated this way. Like, this is ridiculous."

"Calm down, Joe. You aren't in any sort of trouble and we're happy you saved Mr. Lennon." Detective Carter leaned closer and whispered in my ear. "I'm actually a huge *Beatles* fan."

Detective Jones reentered the room. "Whelp, I checked it out and yes, Joe does work for Martin's Building and Maintenance."

"Yup, see," I said, nodding my head.

"Yeah, Joe." Detective Jones walked around me, finishing up back in front of his partner. "He did have a job tonight and yesterday. I think I believe Joe." He turned back around, kneeled down and stuck his right hand out. "Joe, I personally want to thank you for saving John Lennon's life."

My hand grasped the detective's hand. "Ah, no problem."

This version of *Jones* and *Carter l*et me go. Once I left the jail, a limousine pulled up out front. The back window rolled down and Yoko Ono's face appeared. "Hello, Joe Miller."

My mouth dropped. "Ah, hi."

"John would like to invite you to our apartment tomorrow afternoon... you know, in the Dakota."

"Ah, really?"

Yoko giggled. "Yes, so will you join us? We'll have food and drinks."

"Yes, of course, Yoko. What time shall I stop by?"

Yoko smiled. "Make it one o'clock."

That night, I couldn't sleep. I lay in my bed, in my small apartment, thinking... *with what happened tonight, is it truly over? Will the world grow up the same way as it did? Or will things get better? Shit, what if things get worse?* Then my mind thought of a thing called *The Butterfly*

Effect. For those who don't know this *coined* term, let me try to explain it. For starters, if you look the term up in the dictionary, you'll find this: *butterfly effect – noun. A cumulatively large effect that a very small natural force may produce over a period of time.*

In layman's terms, if someone went back in time and did something as small as killing a butterfly, that could cause a drastic change in the future. When you hear stories about *the butterfly effect,* it's always something bad happening in the future. So with my deed done, would everything get better? Or would things get far worse?

The next day arrived, and 1 PM came in a flash. I drove my work van down to the Dakota, finding a spot right out front. Once out of my van, my eyes fixated on the large, beautiful, yet, mysterious-looking building. I walked halfway up the archway and saw the doorman from last night walking out to greet me. "Senor! It's great to see you."

"Hey, it's wonderful to see you, ah, I never caught your name."

"Senor, the name is Jose Perdomo."

We shook hands, and he led me inside the Dakota. "It's nice to meet you, Jose."

"Yeah, I wish it wasn't under such a crazy scenario, but I'm glad you were there to save Mr. Lennon."

"Me too," I said.

A worker inside the Dakota greeted me and took me straight up to Lennon's room. Now, standing in front of

John and Yoko's door, the Dakota worker knocked three times. A bolt inside snapped and the door opened slowly.

"You made it!" Yoko Ono screamed. She jumped toward me, grabbing and hugging me tightly. "Come in, come, please." Yoko gestured for me to follow, so I did. Inside the big and fancy room, I found it to be swarmed by people. So many people filled the room you could barely walk. Yoko cleared her voice, quieting down the commotion. "Excuse me, hello, everyone. I have Joe Miller with me. Joe is the man who stopped the gunman!"

The silence and stares made me feel awkward. It felt weird having an entire room filled with people looking at you in silence. This would change in a mere second. Someone in the crowd started to clap. One by one, the entire crowd clapped. Then, roaring, whistling, and plenty of *thank yous* came my way. By now, I didn't feel as awkward but proud. What I did wasn't just to save an icon who may or may not make the future better. No, what I did was save a human being, a man. Someone who had friends, a wife, and kids...

A teenage boy approached me. "Hello, um, Joe is it?"

"That's right." I stuck my hand out. "Joe Miller."

"Nice to meet you, Joe. My name is Julian Lennon-"

"I knew you looked familiar, your John's older son."

Julian smiled. "Correct."

Julian was John's son from his first marriage. John married a woman named Cynthia Powell. She and John attended Liverpool College of Art and met in their calligraphy class.

"I want to thank you, Joe. Thank you for saving my father's life."

"No, problem, Julian."

Julian lowered his head, a frown grew large on his face.

"What's wrong, Julian?"

His head popped up. Tears filled his eyes. "I'm truly grateful for you saving my father, but yet, anger still resides as well."

"Anger toward who? The shooter?" I asked.

"No," Julian responded while giving me a stern look. "Anger toward my father."

I nodded my head, remembering the stories I'd heard in the media about John's relationship with his first son.

Julian pointed to an empty couch. "Here, do you mind taking a seat?"

I smiled. "Not at all. Lead the way, Julian."

John's first son did exactly that. He sat down on the couch, a leather couch that had a *brand-new* leathery smell to it.

After sitting down next to Julian, he gave me a look that reminded me of a scorned puppy. "Can I explain to you what I meant by saying anger toward my father?" Julian asked, and I nodded. "My father wasn't around much when I was younger. Now, I understand that he was busy touring with *The Beatles* and making a career for himself. But to not make much time for me or my mother wasn't and isn't right."

Indeed, I saw the hurt in young Julian's eyes.

Julian continued. "Like one time my father said I came out of a whiskey bottle on a Saturday night. Who says that type of shit? Not someone who preaches peace and love."

Damn, I'm sorry, Julian. This thought popped into my head.

"When my baby brother was born, my father changed. He gave him all the attention. Hell, he even quit music to be a full-time stay-at-home dad..." Julian's tears grew thicker. "Why didn't he do that for me?"

I went to speak, but for a moment, I was at a loss for words.

"Don't get me wrong, I love Sean, he's an amazing little kid. I'm just jealous, I suppose," Julian said.

"You have every right to feel that way, Julian." My words finally showed up.

"I don't know, maybe I do."

"You do, man," I said with a smile. I wanted to cheer this kid up. He certainly deserved it.

Julian took a deep breath. "After hearing the news that someone tried to kill my father, I begged my mother to fly me here to New York. So she bought me a ticket and sent me here."

"She didn't come with you?" I asked.

"No, she couldn't do it."

"Why?"

"Because her heart ached too much. The idea of someone almost killing John, the first love of her life, tore at her from the inside."

I didn't say anything, just nodded my head.

"This entire situation also tore at me because even though my dad is sort of a hypocrite, he's still my damn dad. For that, I'll always love him."

Not only did tears fill Julian's eyes, but I felt as if a case of the sniffles would soon come my way.

"Things have been better between Dad and me. Especially when Dad was seeing May Pang." Julian lowered his head. "I honestly don't know what I would do if I lost him... hell, what would Sean do if he'd been killed?"

Without thinking, I reached over and grabbed Julian, hugging him tightly. "But he wasn't killed. Your father is alive and well."

We hugged tighter until a voice over the top of us caught our attention.

"Hello, Joe. May I have a seat?"

Both Julian and I swung our heads up to see John standing behind the couch. "Ah, no, I don't mind at all."

John smiled and walked around the couch on Julian's side. "Hello, Son."

Julian stood up, still with tears in his eyes.

John cocked his head to the side. "Julian, what's a matter?"

The moment Julian and I shared, now belonged to father and son. Julian grabbed John, hugging him. At first, John looked startled, but a soft smile quickly formed on his face.

Julian rested his head on John's chest. "Dad, I almost lost you, I don't want to ever lose you."

John rubbed his son's back. He kneeled down in front of Julian, wiping away his tears with his thumb. "Julian, my son, you won't ever lose me. Even when I'm gone physically, my spirit will always reside with you."

This was a sight to see. To have a front-row seat to this moment, a true father and son moment, is one of my fondest memories.

"Julian." John rubbed his hand through his son's hair. "I'm sorry for not being there for you and your mother when you were younger. I was a part-time dad, thanks to my career. This isn't any excuse, though. From now on, I want to be by your side as much as I can."

"I would like that," Julian responded.

"And for those times where maybe I can't be exactly by your side, I'll call you every night to say goodnight. And remember, if I'm not around when you need me, I'll be there the next day, blowing in like a white feather floating in the wind."

Father and son hugged again. After what seemed to be five minutes, Julian glanced back at me; his eyes widened. "Joe, oh my, I have forgotten you were back there."

I threw up a small wave and put a silly smile on my face (damn, I must have looked like an idiot). "Yup, still here. No worries, guys."

Julian looked back at his father. "Dad, I'll let you go so you can have a chat with Joe."

John nodded and Julian stood up. He started to walk away before John called out to him. "Say, Julian."

"Yeah, Dad?"

"I love you, Son."

Julian's smile grew from ear to ear. "I love you too, Dad." His eyes then met mine. "Nice to meet you, Joe... and thanks for everything."

"It's nice to meet you too, Julian. And, no problem at all."

Julian left the area. I watched as he found his baby brother and the two started playing with toys on the floor. A smile formed on my face. Then my head shifted over to John, he sat with a smile on his face.

"Great kid, he is," John said, pointing back toward Julian. "Both my sons are great and thanks to you, I'll have many more days to spend with them."

I blushed, still in awe of this entire situation.

"Thank you, Joe. Thank you for being there to warn me."

"Oh, no problem, Mr. Lennon. I'm just glad I could be there at the right time."

John smiled. "Call me, John. None of this Mr. Lennon crap, okay?"

I nodded.

"Can I ask you a question, Joe?"

"Sure, John. You can ask me anything."

John smiled again. "Tell me, how did you know this man was going to shoot at me?"

My eyes lowered, my mouth opened.

"The police told me that you didn't know him. So you being a friend of his is out of the question."

"Yeah, he was no friend of mine." Then I told John the same story that I told the cops. "Well, I work at a floor maintenance company called Martin's Building and Maintenance. They assigned me to work on a few floors in the Dakota."

John raised his hand and pointed his finger toward me. "That's where I've seen you before. I knew you looked familiar."

I smiled and continued on with my story. "The night before the shooting, when I left the job, that man approached me. We started talking, and I didn't want to be rude, so I stood there to listen to him. Then, this guy told me how he planned on coming back tomorrow night, which was last night."

John stared at me, listening to every word I said. At that moment, I realized John wasn't wearing his glasses (they fell off when he ran from the monster). I stared into his eyes, seeing into his soul. This man wasn't the most perfect man, but what man is? There's no such thing as perfect, not in our world at least. But John was someone of importance, handpicked by the orange glowing ball.

His eyes told me right then and there, that saving him would make the world a better place.

"He told me he wanted to kill you," I continued to say.

John gulped. "Did he say why he wanted to kill me?"

"Yeah, he did."

"What was his reason?" John asked.

"That monster wanted to be famous. Nothing more and nothing less."

John lowered his head. "Wow, that man would have taken me away from my family. All in an attempt to be famous."

"Yeah, but he didn't, John."

He glanced up with tears in his eyes. At that moment, I couldn't help but notice how much John and Julian looked like each other. "Thanks to you, he didn't."

John stuck out his hand, I met him with mine and we shook hands. "Joe, you'll always have a friend here with me."

"Thank you, John. I'm truly grateful to call you a friend."

"As I am to call you a friend, Joe."

Chapter 19

I stayed at Lennon's apartment till about 8 PM. It was so much fun hanging with them, I personally didn't want to leave. Once I did leave, I didn't head home. The conversation I had with Julian really stuck with me. He had a rocky relationship with his father, just as I did. Now, with the powers of the mysterious orange glowing ball, Julian and I would each get a second chance. Boy, would we each make the most of it, I'm assured of that.

I drove to my father's place and he welcomed me in with open arms. We hung out and watched TV till about 3 AM. That's when my father fell asleep on the couch. I got up, gave him a small peck on his forehead and left for the night. On my ride back home the night sky was clear, not a single cloud in the sky. Now, I didn't see any orange or red (thankfully not red) glowing balls of light, but I did witness something.

While driving, my eyes kept looking up in the sky, just in case something would happen. All of a sudden, the biggest shooting star I've ever seen shot across the night sky. It shined in a bright orange tint... I made a wish, watching the shooting star fade away. A small smile grew on my face as I pulled up to my apartment.

Are you wondering what wish I made? Well, if you are, I'll tell you. I wished that what I had done, killing the monster and saving John Lennon, truly would turn out to be the right decision. I prayed the butterfly effect wouldn't happen and everything in the world would become worse... but; I supposed there wasn't anything I could do now but live life and see how everything played out.

Now let's *time travel* back to the future, to my present day. 2023, the current year of this writing. I have lived life to the fullest ever since that night. Well, to be perfectly frank, ever since the orange glowing ball first took me in. That's when my life changed. It gave me a real purpose in life. It asked if I could live up to it, and I think I have.

Now I bet you're wondering if I've seen any orange or red glowing balls since the night of December 8, 1980. My answer to that question would be no. It hasn't appeared, at least to me, since that night at the Dakota. I'm glad not to have seen it because if I had, then maybe I made the wrong choice of killing the monster. Not seeing it makes me feel like I made the right choice.

But why should I just tell you I feel like I made the right choice? I can do better than that. How you may ask? Well, I can explain to you everything that has happened since the killing of the monster. When the orange glowing ball transported me to the future, I discovered the internet. I read up on the history of the world since the night Lennon had originally been killed. This, I felt I needed to discover, to know what I missed.

So I had a basic understanding of important events from that day on. Now, maybe there are some things I didn't learn about during my readings on the internet.

But the things I did read about and now lived through and saw a difference, I can tell you, the reader, all about. Once I explain to you the differences, you can be the judge if saving John Lennon made the world better, or worse.

First, let's dive into the book the monster was reading on December 8, 1980. That's right, *The Catcher in the Rye*. This book inspired the monster in a roundabout way to shoot John Lennon. Less than four months after the monster originally killed Lennon, another shooting occurred that somewhat involved the book. Do you remember me saying how some wacko shot President Regan in the first timeline? Well, it happened on March 30, 1981, and yes, the book wasn't really the reason behind the shooting. But the police did find *The Catcher in the Rye* in the shooter's hotel room. A man named John Hinckley Jr shot at President Regan, wounding him but luckily not killing him. Hinckley shot President Regan in an attempt to get the attention of actress Jodie Foster.

Pretty sick world we lived in, huh? Well, in this new timeline, after saving John Lennon's life, John Hinckley never shot at President Regan. He wouldn't get a chance to. Yes, I read an article saying how Hinckley was still obsessed with the young actress. He still wanted to gain Foster's attention, but in this timeline, on March 26, 1981, something happened. Four days before the previous timeline's assassination attempt, Hinckley spotted Jodie Foster and her mother leaving a restaurant. Now, during the last timeline, I have no idea if Jodie Foster was in Washington D.C. on March 26, 1981. In this new timeline, she was. Maybe this was the work of the orange glowing ball, or maybe she was always at that restaurant.

One thing is for sure, Hinckley did not see her during the first timeline. In this one, he spotted her. Hinckley jumped in his car and raced after Jodi and her mother. This resulted in Hinckley speeding through a red light and meeting a semi-truck. In case you're wondering, Hinckley did not survive. This also set off a chain reaction to the previous timeless. Since I got zapped into the future back in 1981, I never got to see how President Regan's tenure went. But I read that President Regan got reelected in 1984 after dominating the Democratic nominee, Walter Mondale. The new timeline had an entirely different scenario, as you may know. Since President Regan never got shot, he didn't win any sympathy votes from the American people.

President Regan's policies were basically the same. The American people saw past his charm and focused on the policies. In both timelines, President Regan gave the people *trickle-down* economics. Basically, this meant the government would give the upper-class enormous tax breaks. Then, these upper-class people will become even richer. Then, because they've got these breaks and made more money, their idea was the money would eventually hit the lower class.

Now, from my Internet reading, during my first time in 2023, I found the rich did get richer, yet the poor never saw any of it. The election of 1984 didn't turn out so well for President Regan. Which, in the first timeline, President Regan destroyed Walter Mondale. In the new timeline, President Regan still faced off against Walter Mondale. But the opinion for President Regan wasn't so high anymore. Even John Lennon, who was friendly with Regan, came out against him in 1984. And I'm telling you, people listened to John Lennon. Ever since Lennon's assassination attempt, America fell madly in love with the boy from Liverpool.

In 1984, America made history. President-elect Walter Mondale's vice president would become the first woman to hold the VP position. Geraldine Ferraro jumped up and down behind Mondale during the election party as the results came in. She seemed to be the happiest woman alive. Unfortunately, not everyone in America would be happy. The 1984 election would be the closest election in the history of the United States. Ronald Reagan actually won the popular vote over Walter Mondale. However, Mondale would take the Electoral College vote, winning it 271 to 266.

I believe that every timeline is connected somehow. There are always pieces flowing through one and into the other. As in my situation, during my trip to 2023. I met FBI agents Jones and Carter. Then, once I traveled back in time to kill the monster, I met two detectives named Jones and Carter. Coincidence? I think not.

During my trip to the future, remember when I read about the 2000 presidential election? Yeah, the election was close, but, you want to know the exact numbers? Here, I'll tell you. In the 2000 election, George W Bush defeated Al Gore by winning the Electoral College 271 to 266... coincidence? Again, I think not.

The idea of a woman serving in the White House as Vice President angered many Americans. Which is sad to me, because, in my opinion, we are all human and all capable of doing great things. Now, I wish I could say that saving Lennon would rid the world of all evil. That no red light would ever shine down on the Earth. Well, even though I never saw the red light again, the world certainly was still filled with evil.

December 25, 1985, Christmas day. President Mondale was attending a Christmas banquet in New York City. Vice President Ferraro also attended. She laughed and seemed to be having the time of her life. The good mood would quickly be changed. A man entered the banquet, posing as a member of the press. He pulled out a .38 Special revolver, firing three shots toward Vice President Ferraro. The first shot struck the VP in the shoulder, the last two shots missed. Well, the last two shots missed Ferraro, but they struck the man who stood behind her... President Mondale.

Two shots entered into the President's back, the second shot punctured his left lung. He never saw it coming. President Mondale stood with his back to Ferraro, speaking to a few members of Congress. Just as

Lennon was shot in the back in a different timeline, Mondale suffered the same fate. Oh, and the shooter shared an eerily similar name to another assassin. The man's name was Jerry Oswald.

While President Mondale wouldn't survive the attack, Vice President Ferraro would. After recovering for a few months, she was released from the hospital and sworn in as the first female President of the United States. This certainly was a bittersweet moment for America and for Ferraro, I'm sure. While being a historic moment in American history, the first female president was something to be proud of. But to have it come from an assassination was terrible.

Ferraro did an exceptional job filling in the remaining years for Mondale. The job she did, in fact, was so good that she was re-elected in 1988. President Ferraro faced off against a man named George H. W. Bush; she defeated him easily. After being re-elected, President Ferraro pushed for gun control. This became her main agenda. She clearly still felt shaken up from the killing of President Mondale. Many people wondered if she waited to push gun control after being re-elected. Not once did she speak on gun control during the finishing term that she took over.

Also, during her first term, the Republicans controlled the Senate. The Democrats controlled the House. In no way would the Republicans pass a gun control law. But by the time President Ferraro was re-elected in 1988, the Democrats controlled both the

Senate and the House. President Ferraro pressed hard and got the strictest gun laws the nation had ever seen passed. In order to own a gun in this new America, you had to follow these guidelines. First, you have to go through a lengthy process of background checks. This included drug and mental tests. So no previous conviction of any kind. This included traffic violations (sorry, my bad driver friends). If mental health problems ran through your family, you had to be subjected to even harder mental tests.

Once you pass these tests, then you'd have to get some formal training. This meant you had to go to either a police gun course or a military gun course. Here, you'd be taught the correct way to use the gun. Also, you had to write a two paged letter stating the reasoning of why you wanted to buy the gun. Once you passed all this, you had to apply for a gun license, which you would need to get renewed every year. The government also went door to door, confiscating all pump-action shotguns and high-capacity semi-automatic rifles that held more than five rounds. The government either paid you for your guns, or, if you refused to sell, they threw you in jail.

This seemed harsh by a lot of critics, especially Republicans. And I agree, it certainly was a lot to go through, especially if all you wanted to do was go hunting. But the fucking laws worked man. The homicide rate from firearms, hell the homicide rate period, dropped drastically. President Ferraro's approval rating did plummet during her second term, but she made America a little safer.

By 1992, a young, energetic candidate named Bill Clinton ran for president; he ran as a Democrat. His Republican opponent was businessman Ross Perot. George H. W. Bush started to run for a second try at the White House but quit halfway through the Republican debates. This drew controversy as he was leading in the polls for the Republican nomination. Once Bush dropped out, Perot sealed the nomination.

Are you wondering why George H. W. Bush dropped out of the race, even though he looked to be a shoo-in for his party? Well, it was never truly confirmed, but the rumor was he had some dark dealings with the President of Iraq, Saddam Hussein.

Bill Clinton won easily against Ross Perot in the 1992 election. Clinton had some success as president. He signed the Omnibus Budget Reconciliation Act of 1993, which increased the top federal income tax rate. It also increased the corporate income tax rate, raised fuel taxes, and raised various other taxes. The bill also included $255 billion in spending cuts over a five-year period.

President Clinton passed a law stating that openly gay individuals could serve in the military. He seemed to be doing a great job and the country loved him... well until we found out about Paula Jones. Paula was an Arkansas state employee at the time when Bill Clinton was governor of Arkansas. He supposedly called her into his office and proceeded to expose himself. This happened in 1991; she came forward in 1994. Her allegations against President Clinton brought out other women, who accused the President of some sort of misconduct.

Now, I read about this scandal involving President Clinton on the internet, during my trip into the future. It basically played out the same way other than one small fact. In the previous timeline, these *other* women didn't come forward till 1999, during an incident President Clinton had with an intern named Monica Lewinsky. Now, on this new timeline I've created, these women came out against the President in 1994. This hurt President Clinton's reputation, and it showed during the 1996 election.

With a rematch between Incumbent Democratic President Bill Clinton and businessmen Ross Perot, the nation saw a different result. Ross Perot narrowly defeated Bill Clinton to become the President. The newly elected President Perot went to work quickly, trying to end the Omnibus Budget Reconciliation Act. Being a businessman himself, he didn't favor the idea of raising the taxes on businesses. President Perot's presidency wasn't memorable, to say the least. The only thing he did was give big corporations tax breaks. In 1998, thanks to the Omnibus Budget Reconciliation Act, the United States saw its first budget surplus since the 1960s. This would quickly fade away by the year 2000, thanks to Perot's dealing. President Perot also canceled funding to public television. This move by President Perot would spark an unlikely candidate to run for president in the year 2000.

Television nice guy, creator, and star of the hit show *Mister Rogers' Neighborhood*, decided to put his foot in the race. Yes, that's correct, Fred Rogers joined the bid of the Republican party. Fred Rogers battled against the former timeline's Republican nominee, George W. Bush. In this timeline, Fred Rogers defeated Bush for the nomination. Now, he didn't win by much; it was a very close race between the two. Rogers won by only fifty votes, but as Bush discovered in the old timeline, a win is a win no matter how close it is.

The Democratic nominee once again was Al Gore. If Gore got robbed in the election during the other timeline, he wouldn't have to worry about that this time around. Fred Rogers won the hearts of the American voter, just like he won the hearts of America's children since the late 1960s. Fred Rogers, also known as Mister Rogers, dominated Al Gore in the election. Rogers received more electoral college votes than any other president ever. He won 530 of the 538 total electoral votes. Rogers was sweet, compassionate, and determined to make America a better place, especially for the children. Also, Fred Rogers had a very special and important supporter who campaigned hard for him. That special supporter was John Lennon.

Yes, John Lennon in the year 2000, alive and well. That point in time John was back on top of the world.

Just last year in 1999, *The Beatles* reunited and recorded a brand new album, their first since 1970. They named their new album Reunion of Hearts. Their first single off the album shot straight to number one. This hit me in a few different ways. For one, to have a brand new album by my favorite rock group was awesome enough. But that first single, which was written solely by John Lennon (credited to Lennon–McCartney), really hit my core.

The title John Lennon gave his song put goosebumps on my flesh. The title of the song was Time Traveler. This made me think, *does John know I traveled through time to save him?* But how could he know? It's surely not possible. Yet, at the same time, I would have never believed in time travel if I didn't experience it firsthand. So who knows, but the song itself is very beautiful.

Baby, you know when I'm gone, I'll never be gone. And when you're gone, I'll never give up to find you. Cause like glue, I'll time travel back to be stuck on you. Those were some of John's lyrics in the new *Beatles* song. It's a passionate love song with a great melody. I'm glad to say, thanks to what I've done, that John is around now to have *The Beatles* reunite.

Now, let's get back to the history of the new timeline. The year 2000 saw the beloved Fred, also known as *Mister Rogers,* win the presidential election. Rogers picked a former president's son as his running mate. Yes, John F. Kennedy Jr. would become the next vice president. Now, JFK Jr. was registered as a Democrat, as you may have thought. This marked the first time a President picked a vice president from the opposite party since 1864 (Republican Abraham Lincoln picked Democrat Andrew Johnson as his running mate).

Now, if you remember from my research, JFK Jr. died in a plane crash in 1999. Another sad tragedy to a family that saw so many tragedies. What really seemed sad was how JFK Jr. was just about to get into politics, but the plane crash also crashed that dream into oblivion. Now, in the new timeline, JFK Jr. never flew that plan on July 16, 1999. The son of Camelot and America's favorite neighbor took over a country that saw big business try to put a stranglehold on the middle class. This wouldn't sit well for President Rogers. He brought back the taxes on corporations, while lowering taxes on the middle and lower class.

President Rogers also made it mandatory for all children in school, regardless of family income, to receive free lunches. New learning programs and activities for children were funded by the Rogers administration. In 2003, President Rogers passed a bill making community college free across the country. In 2003, I took advantage of the new free college and attended The City University of New York. I majored in journalism as I liked to write. To be perfectly frank, I wanted to be a novelist, but when has being a novelist ever paid the bills?

So after enrolling in The City University of New York, or CUNY for short, I contacted an old buddy of mine. "Hello, John, how are you? It's Joe Miller."

"Joe, how have you been, old buddy? It's been a while."

"Yeah, you've been busy since you and the guys got the band back together."

John laughed. "Yeah, it's a lot being in a band and touring around. But it's been a great deal of fun."

"Yeah, I saw how at your most recent concert, Sean and Julian came out and played with you guys."

Once more, John laughed. "Yeah, my boys are great..." A sudden pause followed. I held the phone away from my ear, making sure it didn't hang up. "Joe," John's voice returned. "Thank you again for being there that night at the Dakota."

"John, you don't have to thank me. I just did what any other person would have done."

I could now hear John sniffling over the phone. "Anyway, I'm glad to have you call."

"Oh, yeah. That reminds me of the reason for my call. I'm currently enrolled in school for journalism and wanted to interview President Rogers."

"Oh, congrats, man," John said.

"Thanks, John. Now, I hate to bother you, but since I know you two are friends, I was wondering if you could set me up with an interview."

John's laugh returned. "Well, Joe, Fred is a busy man, but I'll see what I can do."

"Thanks, John."

"No problem, my dear friend. I'll be in touch."

Oh, I bet you may be wondering about George Harrison. Well, in this new timeline George did get diagnosed with cancer, as he did in the old timeline. His sickness put the reunion of *The Beatles* on hold for a little while. Then, in late 2002, he was diagnosed as cancer-free and the band began touring again. That's right, baby, George kicked that evil scum known as cancer right in the ass!

Three days after my phone call with John Lennon, I received a new phone call. My caller ID machine didn't help either, it said *incoming call from private number*. After the third ring, I answered the phone. "Ah, hello?"

The voice I heard over the phone brought back so many childhood memories.

"Hello, is this Joe Miller?"

"Ah, Mister Rogers? Ah, I mean President Rogers, is that you?"

"Please, Joe. Call me Fred. It's wonderful to hear your voice."

My arm shook while holding the phone. Even though I asked John to get me in touch with Mister Rogers, I still couldn't believe it. Growing up, watching *Mister Rogers' Neighborhood* with my father was some of the best times of my life. Just as John Lennon was my hero, so was Fred *Mister* Rogers.

"It's wonderful hearing your voice as well, ah, Fred."

"My dear friend John told me you are going to school for journalism and would like to interview me?"

"Ah, yes. Thanks to you for making community college free for all, I'm taking advantage of it," I said. Now, I couldn't see through the phone, but I imagined Fred was smiling. "I'd like to interview you and have a few questions already written down. If you have the time, President Rogers, ah, Fred."

"Joe, I have a better idea. How about I fly you down to the White House and you can interview me here?"

I gasped at this idea.

"I believe the most effective way to interview is by being face to face with the other person. Then, you can reach their soul," Fred said.

"Ah, yeah, that would be fantastic, thanks so much, President Mister Rogers, ah, sorry, Fred."

Fred laughed. "You're funny, Joe. Say, how about I send you the plane this Saturday and we can have our interview then?"

"That sounds wonderful, thank you again, Mister, ah, Fred."

"No, thank you for answering my call, Joe. Bye-bye."

The phone clicked off, but the smile on my face wouldn't fade away anytime soon.

Chapter 20

Saturday morning arrived and a man in a chauffeur outfit knocked on my door. The man told me he was here to take me to the private plane that President Rogers sent for me. So I obliged, and we left. Pulling up to a private airport, I saw a fancy jet with the official presidential logo on the side.

Wow, I thought as I boarded the private jet. Inside, the seats were made from leather and very comfortable. A TV played a DVD movie, which was wonderful to watch as I flew. A small buffet table loaded with food sat on the next section of the plane, and I was allowed to eat as much as I wanted. The plane ride only took about an hour. Once off the plane, a different chauffeur picked me up and drove me to the White House in his limousine. After a pretty extensive severity check, two secret service agents led me back to the Oval Office.

The agents opened the door and behind the presidential desk, I saw President Fred Rogers sitting, writing something down on a piece of paper. He glanced up at me and the largest smile I've ever seen on a person formed on his face.

"You must be Joe Miller." Fred stood up and walked over to me. He held his hand out for the entire walk. Now, he wasn't wearing his trademark sweater but a nicely fitted suit. "It's so, so nice to meet you," he said while shaking my hand.

"Ah, it's great to meet you too, Mister, ah, Fred."

Fred laughed. "You can call me Mister Rogers if you like. I'm just weirded out a little when people call me President Rogers."

"Why is that?" I asked as Mister Rogers gestured for me to sit in the chair he had so perfectly placed next to his chair.

"Well," Mister Rogers began to say. His eyes were fixated on a piece of paper that lay on his desk. No doubt this was the same piece of paper I noticed him using when I walked in the Oval Office. "Here, Joe. I drew you a picture. I'd like you to have it, a small token of my appreciation."

This confused me. *Why would Mister Rogers be appreciative of me?* "You shouldn't have, Mister Rogers." I grabbed the paper and saw a drawing; it was of two people. One person appeared to be wearing a red sweater and next to the person, it said *Fred*. The other person looked to be shorter and for some reason, wore a red baseball cap. Next to this person, it said *Joe*.

"I'm appreciative of the fact you wanted to interview me. I also love the idea of you going to college and taking advantage of the new laws. This makes me smile," Mister Rogers said with a smile on his face (he wasn't lying).

I looked at the picture. It was drawn in crayons and quite good, to be honest.

"Once I got done with some business this morning, I figured I'd draw you up a picture since I was waiting anyway," Mister Rogers explained.

I glanced up from the picture with a tear in my eye. "Thank you, Mister Rogers. Not only for this picture, or even for granting me this interview. But thank you for being my neighbor all those years."

Mister Rogers smiled. "Joe, it is my pleasure to be your neighbor."

We sat in silence for a few seconds, both seemingly touched by emotions.

"Now Joe, you asked why I get weirded out when people call me President Rodgers, correct?"

I nodded.

"Well, the answer is simple. I always was just your neighbor, an ordinary guy trying to make the world a better place, especially for our children."

"Then, what made you run?" I asked.

Mister Rogers leaned back in his chair. "Well, once the former president stopped the funding for public television it made me mad, hopping mad to be exact. This, I didn't like, public television is something I've fought for since the sixties."

I remembered the time a young Fred Rogers went before Congress and single-handedly won the right to keep the budget for public TV with a passionate speech.

"To be honest, I still had no plan to run," Mister Rogers continued. "But then my lovely wife told me I should and how this might be the best way to save not only public television but America."

Mister Rogers now leaned closer to me. He nodded with his head for me to get closer and continued on in a whisper. "Myself and my wife didn't trust George W. Bush. If he won the Republican nomination, he might have won the election. If he did, we believed something terrible might occur in this country. So she talked me into it and the rest I suppose is history," Mister Rogers said, now returning to a proper posture in his chair.

"Well, I think I can speak for most Americans and say how grateful we are to have you as our President."

Mister Rogers patted my hand. "That's such a nice thing to say, Joe. I appreciate that more than you probably know." We shared a smile. "Do you have any more questions that you'd like to ask me, Joe?"

I reached into my pocket and pulled out a piece of paper, which I wrote down some questions. The secret service took my note and looked it all over before giving it back. I supposed they thought I would ask bad questions, or maybe they thought I laced the paper with some sort of chemical.

Of course, I wouldn't do any of that to any president, especially not this one. "Ah, yeah. My first question was on the reasoning of why you decided to run. And you already answered that one. " My finger traced down the paper, finding my second question. "Okay, here's my next question. What made you pick John Kennedy Jr., someone from the opposite party as your running mate?"

Mister Rogers nodded his head and smiled. "What a great question, Joe." He placed his hands together, interlocking his fingers. "I want to unite the country as much as I can. That's what we all need as Americans, is a group of people united together."

This I agreed with, completely.

"Too many politicians fight with each other and divide themselves. That's why I picked John, who seemed like a good guy. This, I believed, has helped bring our country a little closer."

As I was about to ask my next question, Mister Rogers continued on with his thought. "All my life I fought against the separation of people. To me, I believe we deserve the same chances in life, no matter what color, creed, or even sexual orientation."

This man knew how to speak to people and get his message across. That's for sure.

"Under heaven, we are all angels to God. This message is what I've been trying to teach everyone since I first came on public television," Mister Rogers said.

"Mister Rogers, I think the message has gotten through," I said with a smile.

"That's very nice of you to say, Joe."

"You're welcome," I said, scrolling my finger down to my next question. "So Mister Rogers, what are some other goals you plan on trying to achieve as president?"

A stern look formed on his face. "Well, Joe. One thing that hurts me so much is when I see sick people, especially sick children, not be able to afford the proper health care. If a child is sick, or their parent, they shouldn't get turned away for not being able to pay. This, to me, isn't right."

"I agree, Mister Rogers."

"Thank you, Joe. Now, my next goal is to bring free universal healthcare for all."

"Great answer, Mister Rogers." I glanced at my paper and found I had only one question left. "I have only one more question and it's this. What do you want people to remember you for once you're out of office?"

Mister Rogers rubbed his hand through his hair. "Wow, another great question, Joe." His eyes locked on mine and the most sincere, trusting look formed on his face. "For me, it's not just about this presidency. It goes all the way back to when I started in public television, to all my work with children throughout the years."

As I sat listening to Mister Rogers, the theme song to his TV show played through my mind.

Mister Rogers continued on with his answer. "This entire experience, my goal was and is to show children and everyone else that you are special. People need to know that there's only one you in the world and that you're unique. They need to know what true love is and that they are capable of loving and being loved by another."

While listening to Mister Rogers, I pulled out the pen I brought with me (I forgot I had it) and started writing down his answer.

"That's the problem with our world. There's so much hate going around and it affects us all hard, especially our children. I hope when I'm done with this president stuff and after I die that people will see I left some positivity..." Mister Rogers paused during his answer. His eyes became watery. "And some love in this world. That's all we can hope to leave as people."

I finished writing the rest of his answer down on the paper. After finishing, I glanced up, smiled and said, "You have left the message of love and everyone already knows it."

After my questions, Mister Rogers asked for a hug and I obliged. Once we finished hugging, he thanked me again for coming by and asking him questions. Mister Rogers truly is a saint, and this was one of the best experiences of my life.

The private presidential jet that brought me into Washington, D.C., also took me home, back to New York City. Once back, I continued on with school, and spent a lot of time with my father. Oh, and with the inspiration from Mister Rogers, I started to volunteer at the library, reading books to children. And yes, this was the same library where during another timeline I discovered the internet.

My interview with Mister Rogers got me an A+, which made me feel great. In 2004, Mister Rogers ran for re-election and he won, becoming the first president in history to win all 538 electoral college votes. Yes, President Rogers (I still feel like I should refer to him as President Rogers when speaking of his politics) won all fifty states crushing the Democratic nominee, John Kerry.

At the second inauguration for President Rogers, John Lennon and *The Beatles* showed up and performed their hit song, *All You Need Is Love*. During his second term in office, President Rogers got what he wanted, free universal healthcare. This got a lot of criticism from his own party, the Republicans. Most Democrats actually liked the bill, and they controlled both the Senate and the House at that point.

So many poorer people who were dying from not being able to afford the proper care were able to live, thanks to President Fred *Mister* Rogers. Yes, a lot of good things have come in this new timeline, but not everything was perfect. Evil still resided in the world, but I suppose it always will. Like back on April 20, 1999, at the Columbine High School in Columbine, Colorado, a tragedy unfolded. Two students, whose names I won't mention, entered the school with samurai swords hidden in their trench coats. They ended up stabbing and killing three students. Then, as the police entered the school, they stabbed and killed themselves.

At least the gun laws were so tight that they couldn't get any guns. Damn, I can only imagine how much worse the situation could have been. Also, the Twin Towers were never hit by planes on September 11, 2001, which was a good thing. But on that same day, a terrorist stole a city bus and slammed it into the Empire State Building, killing everyone on board and killing two people in front of the building.

Even though I changed the timeline, killing the main source of evil, that evil still tried to show up on the days where it was worse, during the previous timeline. As you see, not everything was perfect. President Fred *Mister* Rogers passed away before finishing his term. February 27, 2007, he passed. The cause was stomach cancer. Even though it was sad, he left us all in good hands. His vice president took over, which felt weird seeing another President John F. Kennedy in office.

Once President Rogers' term ended, the new President John F. Kennedy Jr. decided against running for his own first term. His reasoning for not running was because he felt like Mister Rogers left such big shoes to fill and he didn't believe he could live up to it. Honorable, yet a little sad. President John F. Kennedy Jr. appeared to be doing a good job during the time he took over. So for the 2008 election, we had two new candidates facing off for the presidency. On the Republican side, we had a war hero and U.S. senator from Arizona, John McCain. On the Democratic side, we had the U.S. senator from Illinois, Barack Obama. Now what made Obama unique was the fact he was African American and no African American ever served as President of the United States. This would all change as Barack Obama defeated John McCain.

President Obama did a decent enough job, especially given the fight he had against the Republicans. This would change for the 2012 election. President Obama's vice president was the senator from

Delaware, Joe Biden. Now, in 2012, Biden stepped down as Vice President, due to a sickness he developed. In the spirit of President Rogers, President Obama asked a member of the opposite party to be his running mate. Believe it or not, he asked his former opponent, John McCain, and McCain said yes. With the Obama-McCain ticket, they won pretty easily securing a second term for the first African American president.

In 2016, an angry businessman who also appeared on television named Donald Trump ran for president. His entire campaign was to rile everybody up. This seemed to be working. The Republican party, though divided, appeared to be backing their new loud candidate. But a new candidate on the Democratic side emerged. This man also appeared in front of a camera, starring in some of the biggest movies. He decided that all this hate wouldn't be tolerated. And while all the candidates for the Democratic bid seemed to shy away from Trump, this Hollywood actor wouldn't. This new candidate was actor Tom Hanks.

Yes, the wonderful actor from many of your favorite films was the one who stood up to Donald Trump. There seemed to be a similar compassion in Hanks, as there was in Mister Rogers. America lucked out when Tom Hanks narrowly defeated Donald Trump. Of course, I was shocked it even ended up being close, but like I said before, there always will be some sort of evil in the world. So far, President Hanks is doing a pretty stellar job. He basically achieved something that not just

American presidents have tried, but people of the world have tried since the beginning of time, or so it seemed.

The turmoil in the middle east has always been in conflict. Everyone always said they wanted to bring peace to the middle east, yet it never came. Now, I'm not going to say it's perfect over in the middle east because it's not. But the deals President Tom Hanks pushed on the governments of the middle east have seemed to be doing a good job. Just as John Lennon himself once said, "All we are saying is give peace a chance."

So what did you think of my little history lesson? Now, you probably already know all of this. If you're from the timeline that I've helped to create, and if you're reading this book, then this should be the only timeline you know. None of this would be new to you. But if somehow my story would get out and transport back to the previous timeline, then this might be a shocker for you.

Now, if you read up to this point, I bet you are wondering, *did he ever go back to Red Lion and speak to Barry Frey?* I will dive into this part of my story now. Just like in the previous timeline, my father passed away from a heart attack on September 26, 2005. Some things don't truly change, no matter what timeline you live in. But there was a difference from the last time. This time around, I didn't get sucked away to the future, missing out on so many years. Plus, we got along a lot better. My father and I made so many wonderful memories throughout the remainder of the 1980s, then through the 1990s, up till his death in 2005. I'll never forget him, he made me the man I am today.

Even though my father lived and passed away in New York City, his body was taken back to Maxwell, Pennsylvania, our hometown. He put this in his will that he wanted to be buried in Maxwell, so we granted his wish. After the funeral and the burial service, I drove back home to New York City. On my way back, I passed a sign saying, *Red Lion this way. 5 miles.* This intrigued me, knowing my old time-traveling buddy lived there in the other timeline.

So naturally, I made a detour and headed to Red Lion, hoping to find him. Once in Red Lion, I drove straight to the Outer Space Conspiracy Society building. After parking, I walked up to the building and discovered something different. On the door, it stated the name of the building. *The Red Lion Planetarium.*

Well, shit, the name on the building is different, I thought, tracing my fingers over the name on the door. *Jeez, I wonder if Barry Frey even owns this building anymore.*

Inside the door, I walked. The front room looked to be the same as I remembered. Out from the back walked a young woman. "Hi, may I help you?"

"Sara Frey? It's you."

"Huh?" Sara replied, cocking her head to the side. "Do I know you?"

It then hit me that she wouldn't know me, not in this timeline. "Ah, I'm an old friend of your father. Say, is he around by any chance?"

"Sorry, no. He took the day off."

"Oh." I frowned and Sara noticed.

She stepped up to me and smiled. "Hey, I can give you the address of his house. Then, you can stop by to see him."

"Wow, thank you, Sara. That's so nice of you."

Sara smiled. "You're welcome. Say, let me get some paper and I'll write his address down."

She turned and walked to the back. While waiting, I picked up an astronomy book and flipped through it.

Sara returned a minute later and handed me a piece of paper. "Here's the address. He should be home right now. The baseball game is on."

"Oh, yeah, who's playing?" I asked while glancing at the address.

"The New York Yankees and the Baltimore Orioles are playing. It's in Baltimore too."

"Is your dad a fan of one of those teams?"

Sara laughed. "Yeah, he likes the Yankees. But at the same time, he really hates the Orioles. So if the Yankees win, he will be the happiest man alive."

He might be the happiest man alive, but will he remember me? After getting the address from Sara, I left. Now, I didn't have a GPS, so I had to focus on every street sign, trying to find the right street; Barry lived on High Street. *Maple Lane, no, that's not it. What's that street? Oh, that's West Gay Street. Nah, that's not it, either.*

I kept passing by different streets in Red Lion, hoping to find High Street. *What street is this? Oh, First*

Avenue. After passing First Avenue, I turned down on *Main Street* and after a short twenty-second drive, I saw the street sign for *High Street.* My fist slammed on the steering wheel as I let out a joyous scream, "Woo hoo!" *There it is, High Street.*

I turned right to go down the street. High Street was on a hill, I went down the hill, slowly, observing all the house numbers. I found the right number on the last house. After this home, the road disappeared into a wooded area. Next to the house was an alley, I pulled my car in the alley and parked along the grass, hoping he wouldn't be mad that I drove into his yard, slightly.

I stepped out of my car, glancing up at the house. It had a faded red roof and white siding. Inches above where I parked were cement steps that led up to the back of the house. Once I reached the top, I was going to walk around the side to the front of the house, but I noticed the backdoor was open. The screen door was shut, but not the main door. So I walked up and peeked inside. Some noise echoed inside the home; it sounded like a TV.

"Hey, Barry, are you inside?" I called out and knocked. The movement of a person soon entered into my vision, but it was dark and hard to see.

The figure walked closer to me. "Hey, who's there?" A familiar chuckle followed the question.

That's Barry Frey, for sure. I stepped back, away from the screen door. "Hey, Barry."

The screen door opened and Barry Frey now stood in front of me. "Hello? What do you want?" The chuckle again followed the question.

"Hi, Barry. You might not know me, but I know you. My name is Joe Miller. Does my name ring a bell at all to you?"

Before he could answer, another voice called out from inside the home. "Who is it, Barry? You're missing it, Judge just hit for an RBI double."

This voice I remembered hearing before. Glancing past Barry, I watched another figure walking toward me.

"Who is at the door, Barry?"

Barry turned around. "Well, Dad, it's a guy who says he knows me."

"Well then, why don't you invite him in, Barry?"

Barry glanced back at me. "Come on in, Joe."

I entered the home; it looked to be old-fashioned. Inside I passed through a pantry first, then a kitchen, then finally it led me into the living room. The walls of the home were painted blue and orange. Two blue chairs sat at each side of the living room, in the front. Barry went to the chair that sat on the right side of the room. He plummeted down on the chair. The other man went to the chair on the left side, sat down, and reclined in the chair. He placed a cane he used next to the chair.

A canary yellow couch sat in the far back of the living room. I walked past Barry and his father, as I heard him say that's who he is, and sat down on the couch. Then it hit me. *Wait, Barry's father?* I glanced at the other man's face. Damn, he sure looked like the motorcyclist I met at the gas station years ago in the other timeline. The only difference was his age, but that made sense.

"How do you know me?" Barry asked while rocking in his chair.

Before I could answer, his father, James Frey, spoke. "Say, haven't I met you before?"

This struck me as odd. *Wait, if Barry doesn't know me, how in the hell would his father remember me?*

"I haven't met you ever," Barry said, examining my face. "Sorry."

"Barry, you might not of, but I swear I have," James said. He donned a medium-sized white beard at this stage of his life, and he gently rubbed his fingers through it.

By now, I felt at a loss for words. I just sat in silence watching Barry and James try to figure me out. Oh, and I kept peeking at the baseball game.

James suddenly snapped his fingers. "Yeah, I know where I've seen you at before. It was at a gas station."

Shit, there's no way he remembers me from the previous timeline.

"Yeah, your dad was inside the gas station and we sparked up a little chat," James said, still rubbing his beard. "Come to think of it, I think you said you were on your way to a concert."

I gulped intensely. This was what I wanted to find out. If someone other than myself had memories of things from the previous timeline. I guess since James got sucked up into it like me, that he would have some memories. But how much does he remember?

"Am I right... did you say your name is Joe?" James asked.

"Ah, yes, my name is Joe. Also, you're correct about your memory."

"Now what concert were you going to see?" James plucked at his beard harder. "Was it, John... John..." He grabbed the bottom of his Santa Claus beard. "That's it! You were going to see John Lennon and *The Beatles*. Must of been for their reunion tour, right?"

I rubbed the back of my head. "Ah, yeah, that's right."

"I kind of remember you being a kid, but maybe my memory is off," James said.

It then hit me that I wasn't young, as I lived my life up to 2023 in this timeline like a normal person. He was right, I was a kid when we met, but now I am not. I was a man when the Beatles reunion occurred, so clearly, he must be mistaken about when he met me, but how does he remember at all?

Barry grunted as he watched an Orioles player smack a home run.

"When was that, a while ago, right?" James asked. "Maybe, 1999, or the year 2000?"

"Ah, yeah, one of those years, I believe," I said.

"Yeah, that's right. Well, it's good to see you again, Joe," James said. "But tell me, what brings you by?"

I stood up from the canary-colored couch. "Ah, nothing really. Just wanted to stop in and say hi."

"Oh," James said, glancing over at his son. Barry didn't see him as he kept his focus on the baseball game.

"See, I got your names confused. I met you, James, but mistaken you for Barry. This happened while looking for you online."

James repeated what he said a minute ago, "Oh."

Now walking, I glanced at both James and Barry, shooting them each a small wave. "Well, I suppose I should be going. Thank you for inviting me into your home."

"You sure? You can stay, right, Barry?" James asked.

I made it into the kitchen, glancing back once more to see Barry stand up.

"Yeah, well, I suppose. If you want to stay." Barry's sentence ended with his trademark little chuckle.

My legs kept moving, reaching the pantry. "No, that's okay. I have something I need to do."

Outside, I ran to my car and slammed the door shut. *James remembered me but got the date we met wrong. Does he remember the orange ball at all?*

Knocks at my car's window startled me. At my window was James. He stood, leaning on his cane; his arms looked shaky.

I wind the window down. "Yes, James?"

James smiled. "I want to thank you."

I looked confused. "For what?"

"Thank you for getting rid of the evil that plagued our world," James said.

James held his hand out to me. I shook it. "What evil?" I asked.

"What you did allowed me to come back to my family... to my son. Thank you, Joe."

"You're, ah, welcome," I said.

"Dad, you coming?" Barry called from behind us.

James looked back at Barry. "Coming, Son."

James looked back at me and winked. He turned and walked back to the steps.

I watched James, feeling confused yet relieved. *James remembers the orange ball of light. He remembers everything.*

An old car pulled up and parked in front of me. Out of the car stepped a familiar face. It was Ollie Oggy... an older Ollie Oggy.

I watched, stunned, as Ollie walked past me. As Ollie passed my car, he shot me a small glance, and he smiled in a way that made me feel as if he knew me... or knew what I had done.

I drove away and looked in my rearview mirror. There I saw James standing at the bottom of the stairs next to Ollie. They were both waving. I stuck my hand out of the window and waved before I sped away.

A moment here in the year 2023 has a similarity to something that happened in the previous 2023. This new timeline event was all my idea. The similar event from the previous timeline, on the other hand, was not.

What I'm speaking about was the stabbing I took in the prison yard. It cost me my kidney, but luckily I survived.

Now, fast forward to this new timeline. In what seemed like the right thing to do, I decided to donate my kidney. Yes, my mind kept replaying things and seeing their similarities. Plus, the interview I had with Mister Rogers inspired me to do more. To save another life would be wonderful. So I found the *Donate Life Foundation* and they linked me up to a woman who was in dire need of a kidney. The woman's name was Macey Andrews, and she was only twenty-one. Now, I didn't pick her to receive my kidney; the foundation did that. But I'm glad they did, she's a sweet woman who's been through a lot.

You want to know something? The donation happened about three weeks ago from this writing. As you can probably tell, since I'm writing, I didn't die. Macey Andrews also didn't die. In fact, my kidney, which is now inside of her, is performing perfectly. They released me from the hospital only three days after the donation.

The doctors took the same kidney that had been injured from the knife attack. Which a sign of the connection, for sure. Now, normally when someone donates their kidney, the doctors take the left kidney. Don't ask me why, but that's what the doctor who performed my surgery said. During my tests to see if I was capable of donating, the doctors found my right kidney had a small kidney stone. He told me it wasn't anything to worry about. The stone was so small I'd pass it in my urine without even noticing. Still, they wanted to keep the perfect one inside me. So as I said, they took my right kidney, the same one the doctors took before. Funny how that works, right?

My surgery was held in the same hospital that I found myself in when I first time-traveled. So a different hospital and a different doctor from my previous kidney surgery. But something similar would enter into my life...

Chapter 21

Let's *time travel* back to my surgery, if you don't mind. Outside of the operating room, I found myself on a bed with wheels. The anesthesiologist asked me to count backward, starting from ten. So that's what I tried to do. How far did I make it before blacking out? Nine. Yup, only one number down before the shit kicked in. When I woke up (which I found was a little over four hours later) a pretty face entered into my vision.

"Hello, Joe. How do you feel?"

"Ah, where am I?" At this moment, I definitely felt confused. But the soft voice of the pretty woman comforted me.

"You're in the hospital, Joe. You just had your kidney donation surgery and guess what?"

"Ugh," I moaned. I was completely out of it from the drugs and the pain.

"Your surgery was a success!"

My memories suddenly resurfaced. "Oh, yeah, that is great news."

Thick blankets covered my body. A squeezing sensation on my legs felt all too familiar.

The pretty woman smiled and asked another question. "How's your pain? Give me a number from one to ten. One being no pain and ten being unbearable pain."

At that moment, I recognized the pretty woman. "Alexis?"

She stepped back, a little startled. "How do you know my name? Have you been a patient here before?"

This confused me at first. Clearly, I remembered her, but *why doesn't she remember me?*

"Maybe I have been your nurse before. You have no idea how many patients I attend to in a given week," Alexis laughed.

Then it hit me. *Damn, I'm in a new timeline. Alexis doesn't know me.*

"Tell me, Joe, how is your pain?"

My hand gently touched the lower right side of my stomach. "Ah, it's a solid nine right about now."

Alexis giggled. "Here." She touched a button on a machine that sat next to my bed. "I'll give you a shot of morphine. It will take away the pain."

The morphine shot through my veins and a fuzzy sensation overtook me; my mind wondered. "Alexis," I said, grabbing her hand as she attempted to leave.

"Yeah, Joe?"

"Tell me why, Alexis?"

"Why what, Joe?"

My eyes focused on Alexis. By now I saw three of her standing in front of me. "Why did you turn me into the FBI?"

Alexis pulled her hand away from me. "Sir, I'm not sure what you're talking about." She turned and walked to the door, stopping and turning back to me. "If you need anything else, just ring your call bell... somebody will come."

As half of her body exited the room, I called out one last time. "Alexis, please, let me know one thing."

Her head poked back in. "Yeah, Joe. What is it?"

A question I thought about asking her in the old timeline entered my hazy mind. I planned on asking her the question that night, after the concert. Of course, I never got that opportunity. But now here I was, with her again. I needed to know.

"Alexis, if I were to ask you to be my girl, what would you say?"

She chuckled, tapping her fingers on the door. "Joe, I think you're a cute older man, really, I do."

Shit, that's right. I'm not no twenty-three-year-old man anymore. I'm fucking sixty-five years old. The morphine clouded my mind so much that I had forgotten which timeline I was in. Alexis was her beautiful twenty-five-year-old self, just as she was when I first met her. Of course, I wasn't. The hope of rekindling anything between us would have to stay a fantasy... maybe a *Double Fantasy.*

Alexis took one step back into the room, revealing her full, glorious body. "Joe, in another lifetime at a different age, I'd say yes." She smiled and left the room.

A huge smile grew on my face and I softly whispered, "How about in another timeline?"

On the third and final day of being stuck in the hospital, I sat in my chair next to the window. My stomach aches and so does my back. I returned to my room after my morning lap around the nurse's station (not my idea; they forced me to walk). Alexis wasn't assigned to me after that first day, but on my walks, I'd see her and wave. She'd smile and wave back and you know what? That was good enough for me.

Now, in my chair, eating my scrambled eggs and sausage breakfast, a TV special caught my interest. I was watching an old seventies sitcom but got bored with it and flicked around, seeing what else was on. There, I found the special. It was a show where a man interviewed a celebrity. Every week, a different celebrity would come on. One week it would be an actor, then next week an athlete. Sometimes the celebrity would be a musician, just like this week's guest. Can you guess who graced the TV on this fine morning? If you said John Lennon, give yourself a round of applause.

"Hello everyone out there watching. I'm your host, Gary Stewart. Today's guest is none other than *The Beatles* legend, John Lennon."

The camera panned to John Lennon. "Hello, Gary. It's great to be here."

He basically looked like himself, just older of course. His hair was long and a grayish color. He wore his trademark small, round dark glasses. Yes, in 2023, John Lennon was alive and well.

The camera switched back to the host. "Now, John, before I go on with the interview let me wish a happy birthday to you."

Shit, I thought. *It is the ninth of October.*

The camera panned over to John. "Why thank you, Gary. It's a trip getting old, you know?"

Now the camera switched to a long shot. Now you could see both John and Gary. Two comfy-looking chairs sat with a small table near the chair on the right. John sat on the chair opposite of the table.

"I mean, I remember being sixteen and starting my group, *The Quarrymen*," John said.

The camera panned to Gary; he chuckled. "That was before *The Beatles*, right?"

John laughed as the camera panned back over. "Sure, man. I was in school and named my skiffle band after my school." John grew a youthful smile on his face. "Yeah, I remember seeing Elvis, getting inspired by him. Watching him groove. He definitely showed me what rock-and-roll was about."

"Was Elvis Presley your biggest rock idol?" Gary asked off screen.

With the camera still on John, he rubbed his finger under his chin. "Well, no. I idolized Chuck Berry a little more."

The camera panned back to Gary, he now rubbed his chin. "Oh, really?"

Images of Elvis Presley popped up on the TV screen. John continued talking behind the images. "Yeah, man. Elvis was a performer, real good, man. But Chuck Berry was cut from a different cloth."

The images now changed from Elvis Presley to Chuck Berry. "Man, Chuck could do it all, that's what separated him from Elvis. Chuck wrote, performed, and recorded his own words and music."

The image now changed to the performance of John and Chuck on *The Mike Douglas Show*; this was in 1972.

Gary's voice shot over the image. "Yes, you're right about that. Now, our viewers are seeing pictures and now video of the time you performed with Chuck. How was that, John?"

Video of the performance with the sound, faintly playing took over the TV screen.

John's voice overtook the video clip. "This was great, man. To actually perform with Chuck was great. I mean, I've covered Chuck plenty of times. But to perform with him was just plain great. Chuck Berry was a good dude."

Gary's voice sounded off-camera. "Tell me more about your start in rock and roll, John."

"Well, Gary. Like I said, I was sixteen when I started *The Quarrymen*." John paused, his finger rubbed against his temple. "Well, I guess I was still fifteen, turning sixteen in a month or so. To think of that time, then to *The Beatles* and everything else is crazy." The camera panned to Gary, he sat nodding his head. Quickly, the camera panned back to John. "Now, like you said, it's my birthday and I turned eighty-three today, eighty-three, can you dig that?"

Off-camera, Gary responded with, "Yeah, I can. I'm seventy-three myself."

John laughed. "Yeah, getting older is a trip. But I'm thankful to even have this opportunity to see seventy-nine. Cause, things could have been much different." John took off his dark round glasses. His eyes were watery; he wiped them dry. "I'm grateful to of had this opportunity to live and spend time with not only my wife and kids but my friends as well..."

The camera panned to Gary, he continued to nod his head.

"For all you young kids out there," John started to say as the camera quickly jumped back over to him. John, with his glasses still off, leaned forward and stared directly into the camera. "Never give up, appreciate life, and make the most of it. Because in a blink of an eye, it could be taken all away."

"Wise words, John," Gary said off-camera.

John sat silent for a couple seconds, staring into the camera. He quickly placed his dark glasses back over his eyes. A smile formed on his face. He pointed to the camera. "Thank you, Joe Miller. Thank you for letting me live..."

John's words on that TV show touched me deeply. My mission was complete, and though the world wasn't perfect, it appeared to have a little less evil in it.

****

It's been six months since the hospital released me. I only had one checkup since my surgery, but the doctor told me I appeared to be doing good. I went back to work two months after my surgery. Do you wonder what job I have? Well, I work for *The New York Times* as a journalist. Now, I like my job, but my dream is still to become a novelist. What better story to lift my career than my life, my adventure?

Since my surgery, these past six months have been pretty good. I started to date a woman named Alexis about three months ago. She's really great and no, it's not the same Alexis. This Alexis is my age, and she's a top editor at the *New York Times*. To be honest, I've never been happier with another woman in my life. So that's definitely a good thing.

It's now April 2023, and I'm sitting in my room, finishing up this story, listening to *The Beatles* hit song, *We Can Work It Out*. Damn, John's lyrics sum it up best. *Life is very short, and there's no time, for fussing and fighting, my friend.* He's absolutely right, my friends. No matter what may be happening in your life right now. From a dispute with a family member or friend, to problems with your job, or maybe your car. Whatever may be going on in your life, remember, life is very short. Forgive and move on. Exhale during tough times, they will pass.

It truly is as simple as that folks. My life has been an adventure, so many ups and downs. You know what? I wouldn't change a thing. So you, reader of my story. I want to tell you to sit back and think about living the best life you can. Think about how much better life could be if you blocked out the negativity and the evil that surrounds us all.

Can you imagine?

The End

About the Author

Titan Frey is an author, screenwriter, editor, and journalist. He's the author of the *Literary Titan* Gold Award-Winning & the *Readers' Favorite* 5-Star winning novel - Reflection: The Paul Mann Story. He's also the author of the *Literary Titan* Silver Award-Winning & the *Readers' Favorite* 5-Star winning YA novel - A Player's Path: A story about life and football.

Titan has also written three short films, a video game, and is the head editor and journalist at a basketball news website. When Titan isn't writing he loves to spend time with his family.

About the Publisher

Kingston Publishing Company, founded by C. K. Green, is dedicated to providing authors an affordable way to turn their dream into a reality. We publish over 100+ titles annually in multiple formats including print and ebook across all major platforms.

We offer every service you will ever need to take an idea and publish a story. We are here to help authors make it in the industry. We want to provide a positive experience that will keep you coming back to us. Whether you want a traditional publisher who offers all the amenities a publishing company should or an author who prefers to self-publish, but needs additional help – we are here for you.

Now Accepting Manuscripts!
Please send query letter and manuscript to:
submissions@kingstonpublishing.com

Visit our website at www.kingstonpublishing.com